Dedication

To
Roz & Sandra Flower
and
Tom & Elizabeth Quayle
and their darling families . . .
cousins all.

By Beverly Lewis

ABRAM'S DAUGHTERS

The Covenant
The Betrayal
The Sacrifice
The Prodigal
The Revelation

❖ ❖ ❖

THE HERITAGE OF LANCASTER COUNTY

The Shunning
The Confession
The Reckoning

❖ ❖ ❖

ANNIE'S PEOPLE

The Preacher's Daughter
The Englisher
The Brethren

❖ ❖ ❖

The Postcard · *The Crossroad*

❖ ❖ ❖

The Redemption of Sarah Cain
October Song · *Sanctuary**
The Sunroom

❖ ❖ ❖

The Beverly Lewis Amish Heritage Cookbook

*with David Lewis

BEVERLY LEWIS, born in the heart of Pennsylvania Dutch country, fondly recalls her growing-up years. A keen interest in her mother's Plain family heritage has led Beverly to set many of her popular stories in Lancaster County.

A former schoolteacher and accomplished pianist, Beverly is a member of the National League of American Pen Women (the Pikes Peak branch). She is the 2003 recipient of the Distinguished Alumnus Award at Evangel University, Springfield, Missouri. Her blockbuster novels *The Shunning, The Confession, The Reckoning,* and *The Covenant* have each received the Gold Book Award. Her bestselling novel *October Song* won the Silver Seal in the Benjamin Franklin Awards, and *The Postcard* and *Sanctuary* (a collaboration with her husband, David) received Silver Angel Awards, as did her picture book for all ages, *Annika's Secret Wish.* Beverly and her husband make their home in the Colorado foothills.

The gravity of the hour fell heavily on the membership that Lord's Day long ago. One by one the men reached for a black songbook in the center of the table, for the drawing of the lot. In keeping with the sacred rite, only one man was to be found among the elect, Jehovah God's choice. The husband of one wife, of good reputation, hospitable, not given to wine, the father of obedient children, with the ability to teach sound doctrine, according to the Scriptures. A God-fearing man whose name, along with six others, had been whispered to the bishop on this most holy day of Communion.

Seven hymnals, each bound by a rubber band, lined the table, and deep within one, a single slip of paper inscribed with the proverb: "The lot is cast into the lap; but the whole disposing thereof is of the Lord." The candidates—selected from the church district by the "voice" of the People—each chose a book, wondering who would be struck by the lot.

The bishop examined each hymnal. Opening the one chosen by the final candidate, he found the lot and uttered the life-altering words: "The Lord God and heavenly Father has chosen our brother Daniel Hochstetler."

Prologue

If Isaac's mamma were still alive and knew her son's bones were being dredged up she would surely be weeping now. It was all *I* could do to choke back tears, walking past the People's cemetery this morning. Our sacred knoll was blocked off with yellow police ribbon, and *Englischers* were swarming about like so many ants on a hill.

This must be why Esther hasn't heard a peep from Zeke since he turned himself in a few days ago. Maybe he's not allowed to talk to anyone while he awaits the outcome of what appears to be a mighty serious investigation. But I sure won't be describing the commotion at the graveyard to Essie— I'll spare her that. I just hope the grapevine doesn't spread its tendrils out to little ears, because like their mother, six-year-old Laura and her younger brothers, Zach and

John, have been through too much already. It was bad enough when Zeke was causing havoc at home, but this? Seems to me he must've gone completely berserk to say he killed his four-year-old brother all those years ago. And why? It makes not a whit of sense that Zeke and Isaac should be another Cain and Abel, and the brethren must surely think the same.

The People are all a-buzz about Zeke's arrest, but I can't allow myself to stew, 'cause I need all my strength and courage to help dear Essie and her children, who are floundering so. Even though Essie is holding fast to her newfound faith, she also seems to be holding her breath about Zeke. We all are, really, because what one person may be found guilty of affects us all.

I am presently holding my breath, too, counting the days till my six-month promise ends. Then I can pick up where I left off with easel and paintbrush, even though my first responsibility is being a "mother's helper" to my dear friend. So, for now, I keep myself busy redding up for Essie, along with the filthy chore of slopping Zeke's hogs. It's survival of the fittest most days, with the biggest pigs lining up first around the trough, the smallest ones constantly blocked by the fattest ones. A lesson in the demise of the confident, for it is the fattest that get slaughtered first.

In addition to that, I manage to put in two days each week at my Ranck cousins', who have clearly upped their fervor for witnessing since Essie's shunning from the People, and since I left home to stay with her. Irvin and Julia see me as another lost soul ripe for the picking, as does Essie. No doubt about that.

As for Ben Martin, someone came along and snatched up the job at the harness shop, freeing Ben to leave for his home in Kentucky, according to Julia. She says her husband, Irvin, plans to keep in touch with him.

Despite Ben's departure, my life has not returned to normal. Truth be known, thoughts about Ben often keep me awake at night. Daydreams distract me, too. Images I tend to will into existence by my forbidden yearnings, intermixed as they are with my sadness at having sent Ben away. Still, I try to remember what the Good Book says, *Blessed are they that mourn: for they shall be comforted. . . .*

Who shall lay any thing to the charge of God's elect?
It is God that justifieth.
—ROMANS 8:33

Chapter 1

A meditative haze parted and soon began to dissipate as a May sunrise spilled onto dogwood blossoms—white, pale, and deep pinks. An early morning rain had dimpled the dirt on the shoulder of Frogtown Road, populated now with pecking wrens and robins.

At the reins in the Hochstetler buggy, Annie Zook breathed in the tranquility, aware of plentiful insects and thick green grass, fresh paint on fences and a new martin birdhouse at Lapps' dairy farm. Clicking her tongue to speed the pace, she leaned forward in the seat, grateful for Zeke's fast horse, as it was a good long walk between Essie's house and *Daed*'s.

Only four days had come and gone since she had impulsively packed up her belongings and gone to Esther Hochstetler's, so Annie was surprised to experience a sudden twinge as she made the turn toward her father's house. *Am I homesick already?*

She wondered if Yonie, her nineteen-year-old brother, would be at home when she arrived. *I miss the rascal,* she thought.

Taking in the vibrant springtime colors, she longed more than ever to immerse herself in art once again. *I want to paint my beau.* But Ben was no longer that, and their breakup was all her own doing. Hers . . . and Daed's.

I never should've written that good-bye letter, she thought. Yet she had done so to obey her father.

Her separation from Ben was cause for ongoing sorrow. Thankfully, Esther wasn't one to ask questions, even when tears sprang unexpectedly to Annie's eyes. She had come awful close to blurting out her beloved's name upon awakening one morning, only to grit her teeth, forcing down the aching lump in her throat. Speaking his name, even in the private space of her room away from home, would not have hurt a thing. But she never knew what little ones might be roaming the hallway, and she didn't trust herself to even breathe his name lest she be overtaken with grief. Or was it pure foolishness?

There had been plenty of times in the last few days when she had tried to think of some way to return to the lovely, secret world she and Ben had so happily shared— till Daed had caught her riding in Ben's car, wearing her hair down. Exactly which of those transgressions was worse, according to God and the brethren, she didn't know. She had almost asked Cousin Julia for Ben's mailing address on more than one occasion. And even more shameless, she had been tempted to get on a bus, show up at his doorstep, and beg his forgiveness.

I'd be out of my mind to do such a thing. . . .

Yet she was beside herself at the thought of living without him.

Annie saw a horse and buggy approaching, coming fast. She strained to see who it might be out so early. When she recognized Jesse Jr.'s wife—her eldest sister-in-law—she wondered how Sarah Mae might act toward her. Still, Annie was eager for any contact with family.

Surprisingly, Sarah Mae offered a warm smile and a wave. "Pull over and stop awhile!" she called out.

Annie was ever so pleased. She leaped from the buggy and tied Zeke's horse to a tree trunk before plump Sarah could even begin to get herself down from her carriage. Annie ran like a girl who had not seen hide nor hair of her kin in the longest time. "Ach, Sarah Mae, 'tis such a nice surprise to see you!"

"And you, too," Sarah Mae said, still holding the reins. "I've been meaning to stop by."

"Over at Essie's, ya mean?"

Sarah Mae was slow to nod. "Well, maybe so . . . but—"

"I know it's terribly awkward," Annie interrupted, "but do come sometime. I know Esther would enjoy the company, just as I would."

Sarah Mae bowed her head for a moment, then raised her pretty blue eyes. "Jesse Jr. could scarcely believe it," she confided, telling how the People had been talking up a storm about Annie's winning the first place award for her covered bridge painting. "Downright surprising, 'tis."

"Jah, I 'spect so." Annie didn't know quite how she felt about this, folks discussing amongst themselves her secret sin. Well, secret till now, anyhow. *Sarah Mae must think I'm brazen . . . and I guess I was.*

Had Jesse and Sarah Mae seen her painting featured on the cover of the *Farm and Home Journal* or merely heard about it through the grapevine? She didn't ask, wouldn't seek out praise or criticism. She had known it was only a matter of time till word got around. So now there were two names floating about—Zeke's *and* Annie's. One a confessed murderer and the other an artist born into the wrong church district— or into the wrong family. . . .

Sarah Mae's expression was questioning, though she spoke not the words Annie might have expected. "I hope you won't be gone from home for too much longer," she said softly.

"Mamm misses me, no doubt." There was that lump in her throat again.

"Not only Mamm . . ." Sarah Mae didn't need to say more.

Annie knew. She, too, disliked the discord between her father and herself. But could she make amends? He was more than put out with her, and no wonder. She had been too hasty in leaving, thinking only of herself. Yet being with Essie and the children was a blessing in disguise, a way to escape her father's rigid expectations.

"I think it best that I stay put for the time bein'," she said, leaning into the carriage. "Especially since Essie needs me."

Sarah Mae sighed heavily, her bosom rising and falling as if she were having difficulty catching her breath. "I'm sure you've heard all 'bout Zeke, then?"

"Some, but Essie doesn't know much yet. What does Daed say?"

Sarah Mae hesitated. "Only that they're holding Zeke until they can figure out if the bones are really Isaac's. Though how on earth they'd do that, I'll never know."

Little Isaac's dead. . . . The hard, sad knowledge slapped at Annie's brain every time she heard it.

"Daed's talkin' of sending a letter to Zeke's father . . . to let him know officially of Isaac's death." There was a little catch in Sarah Mae's voice, and she placed her hand over her mouth.

"I feel sorry for Daed," Annie said, "havin' to break such sorrowful news."

Sarah Mae shook her head. "I can't imagine it. But Daed already got his address up in Canada from their cousin Nate, I guess."

Annie shivered. "I daresay Daed should wait till Zeke's father gets over the death of his wife. Seems only right . . ."

"But who's to know if that will ever be."

"I s'pose," Annie said. "Honestly, can a man be expected to suffer his wife's death and his son's all in the space of a few weeks? Ain't like Daed to jump ahead like this."

"Oh, your father's not the one insisting on gettin' in touch with Isaac's father. This comes down from higher up . . . if you understand my meaning."

Annie's gaze caught Sarah Mae's. "This is the bishop's word, then?"

Sarah Mae's hand trembled. "I would not want my husband or any man I know to be in Daniel Hochstetler's shoes. But the brethren know best."

"I 'spect you're right."

"No, Annie, you *know* I'm right."

Annie stepped back, her anger rising suddenly at the mention of the brethren. "Actually, I *don't* know and that's the honest truth. Some days I can't decide whether to cling to what I was always taught or to reach for something altogether new." She paused, recalling recent talks with Esther. "Something that makes wonderful-good sense but stirs up ever so much trouble. Ever think thataway?"

A slow frown passed over Sarah Mae's face. "Can't say I ever have, nee—no."

Annie felt an urgent need to step back, and she did just that, waving good-bye.

"Aw, don't go away mad."

"Oh, I'm long past that," Annie said over her shoulder, returning to Essie's horse and buggy . . . sorry she'd ever opened her mouth.

When Annie arrived at her parents' house she knew, even before detecting the pleading look in her mother's eyes, that she was upset. Mamm had pressed her hand against her cheek upon first seeing Annie at the back door, although Annie hadn't bothered to knock. She'd gone right in, like she always had when living here.

The two of them sat at the table, drinking freshly squeezed orange juice. Mamm's soft blue eyes were somber, even intense. "Ach, Annie, 'tis gut seein' you again."

"Oh, you, too, Mamm." Annie mentioned having seen Sarah Mae out on the road on her way over.

"Jah, she stopped by on her way to market," Mamm replied, staring at Annie still.

"Seems she's mighty worried 'bout Zeke. Which is why I'm here. I just felt I might burst if I didn't talk to you."

"Such a shame for all the People," Mamm said. "Right startling, too, I daresay."

"Yet how can such a thing be true?" Annie paused, wishing now she could right her own wrongs—leaving home so impulsively for one.

"Just why would Zeke lie 'bout something so awful?" Mamm said. "It makes not a bit of sense that he would tell such a story—one that's near impossible to believe. Unless he's . . . not quite right . . . in his mind."

"Even so, if he says he killed Isaac, then who are we to say he didn't?"

Mamm nodded slowly. "Jah, 'tis best not to judge."

Annie turned in her chair, wishing to lessen the distress in her mother's gaze. "For the longest time, I assumed Isaac was alive somewhere. Didn't you?" She looked at Mamm, whose eyes were now downcast.

"It's the most difficult thing, to think of your child as gone forever." Mamm blinked back tears. "In a way Mary Hochstetler's recent passing was a godsend. She went to her grave unaware of the fact of Isaac's death, though thinking him kidnapped must've eaten her up inside."

"And she must have supposed, even known deep within, that her little Isaac had passed over, jah?" Seeing such grief imprinted on dear Mamm's face, Annie swallowed back her own tears, not wanting to add to her mother's sorrow.

"It is one thing, though, to lose a child that way . . . and quite another to lose one to her own stubborn will." The words cut Annie to the quick.

"Oh, Mamm. I never left here out of spite. Surely you know that."

Her mother's reply was slow and soft. "Even so . . ."

Annie rose and went to stand at the window overlooking the backyard and the two-story barn's lower entrance. "I 'spect you want me to talk to Daed 'bout it?"

"Well, *shouldn't* you?"

Something winged up within, like a bird about to soar. *I have no desire to say one word to him.* "I've done too much damage already."

"You're his daughter, for goodness' sake! Why not speak kindly to him . . . see what can be done?"

Annie turned slowly. "I don't know if I can."

"Oh, Annie. . . . We miss you something awful."

Annie shook her head. "I can't talk 'bout this now, Mamm." With that, she hurried out the back door, hoping to find Yonie, the one brother who had always understood her.

Chapter 2

In his parents' home in Kentucky, Ben Martin awoke early with an unnamed dread. In spite of it, he was determined to make a fresh start. Since returning home, he had not been able to shake his frustration at the way things had ended with Annie. He missed seeing her, talking to her, and spending time with her. He thought of her nearly constantly.

He also thought of her bridge painting, the one he'd stumbled upon in the Rancks' attic prior to his leaving. As close as they had been, why had Annie kept her artistry a secret from him?

Getting out of bed, he reached for his robe and stepped to the window, staring out. Since discovering Annie's painting, he often found himself imagining her at work . . . how she might look as she pressed colored pencils or brush to paper or canvas. Did she stand at her easel or sit on a stool? Where did she work—at home or some secret location? And when would she ever have the time? Considering the great planning that would have gone into the painting of the covered bridge, he was baffled. With all the clamps put on Amish women, he was surprised such self-expression was permitted—or was it? Had she attempted to keep her work hidden from view, just as she had hidden *him* away, slipping out of her father's house and going to their private rendezvous place?

He recalled her eagerness whenever she walked out to meet him at his car. His heart had always pounded at the sight of her, as well. Smiling at the fond memory, he pictured a studio, unknown to her father and the People, where Annie happily hummed while drawing and painting. A cottage in the woods, perhaps? Julia's attic, where he'd seen the marvelous painting? And did she whisper to herself in Pennsylvania Dutch as she worked? There was much he wished to know about Annie—even more so now that he was here and she, there.

He stared down at the street, glad for the stillness before the neighborhood grew noisy. There was no question in his mind that Paradise, Pennsylvania, was as peaceful as any place he had ever been. One of his dreams from the previous night floated into his conscious memory: he had dreamed he was again walking through the covered bridge over Pequea Creek. How long would it be until his subconscious comprehended he was no longer in Pennsylvania?

Ben shuffled to the bathroom. Picking up his electric shaver, he wondered, *How would I look with a full beard?* He stared at his reflection, noticing the unusual dullness of his eyes. Absentmindedly he began to shave, pondering the fact that he'd never known how to go about courting Annie Zook. At first, he figured he'd just wing it, hoping all would go well. And it certainly had, but only for a time.

Then, right when things between them had begun to pick up speed and he was beginning to think she might be falling for him, she'd cut him loose. Even now his curiosity over what might have happened if her father had not caught them together was driving him a little crazy.

If we hadn't taken the long way back that evening . . . if we hadn't run into Preacher Zook, I might still be seeing her. But her father had laid down the law and she had chosen to obey him, denying her own heart.

Ben wondered how he ever could have convinced Annie to leave her world for his. In short, that was the kicker. Nothing he imagined, either in the hush of midnight or in the reality of early waking hours, would ever change the cruel fact that they simply were not meant to be together. After all, it had been a no-no from the very beginning for Annie to acknowledge his attention, let alone his affection. Why couldn't he just accept that Paradise was not his home and never would be?

Later, after his two youngest sisters, Sherri and Diana, had rushed off to school in Dad's old beater, Ben washed breakfast dishes and contemplated his plan of action. It was time to get on with real life and stop fantasizing about what might have been. He had always wanted to extend himself to people in need, and he liked the idea of doing something useful with his hands. So building houses in a Third World country seemed like a good way to go. If nothing else, it would distract him and help get the preacher's daughter out of his system.

He plodded across his mom's kitchen to the coffee maker, poured another cup, then settled at the table while his mother dried the dishes. "I've been thinking about making a big change in my life," he said.

"Getting married?" She turned from the sink to wink at him.

"No, the Peace Corps."

Her grin faded but he rushed on. "I started researching this possibility more than a year ago. I think now might be a good time to apply." *Since I can't have Annie.*

Mom froze in place at the sink, dish towel in hand. "Oh, Ben," she said, shaking her head. "Please . . . you can't mean it."

"I'm entirely serious. I meet all the requirements. They prefer people who speak more than one language, but . . ."

"Well, you *did*," Mom murmured, almost to herself. "Not that it would help you any."

"What?" he asked, not understanding.

"Benjamin . . ." she said, as if she had only enough breath to form a single word.

She walked to the table and stood behind a chair across from him, no doubt formulating her next attempt to talk him out of it. "This doesn't make sense. First you rush off to Pennsylvania for no apparent reason, and now you're home for only a few days and you want to volunteer overseas?" She stared down at her hands, fingers tense as she gripped the back of the chair. "Ben, please forget this idea."

"Mom . . ."

"I can't think of you leaving again. I can't—"

"Mom, relax. It won't be forever." But even as he spoke, he was aware of the quiver of her lip, the pallor of her face. *Why such a dramatic reaction?*

With a loud sigh, she pulled out the chair and sat down. "I know your father will be glad when he hears what I'm going to tell you. You see, it's been a long time coming. Perhaps even too long."

He hoped whatever she was about to say was not as alarming as her somber face seemed to forecast.

"Oh, honey, I don't know how to start. . . . This is so difficult." She blinked fast, as if she might cry.

"Mom? What is it?"

She inhaled deeply. "Ben, hear me out. Please . . . try to understand."

He nodded and reached over to cover her hand with his own. "Did someone die?"

"No . . . son. What I have to tell you has nothing to do with death. On the contrary, it's about life. *Your* life."

Chapter 3

Determined to find Yonie, Annie first peeked in the barn but saw only Luke, another younger brother, shoveling manure. *My least favorite barn chore of all!*

Going to the buggy shed, she saw Daed checking the steel bands on the buggy wheels. Quickly, so as not to be seen, Annie crept away. She hurried past the woodshed, then out behind the barn toward the manure pit.

Eventually she spied Yonie plowing with their youngest brother, Omar, behind a team of eight mules, preparing to plant sweet corn in this big field. She would happily wait till they paused for a break, whenever that might be. And if Omar went inside to get some of Mamm's sweet lemonade, which he sometimes did, then she and Yonie would talk. Omar was pretty understanding that way, aware of her closeness with Yonie.

She perched herself on an old tree stump at the far edge of the empty field, glad for these warmer days of spring. The distant hill sloped in shadowy patterns beneath midmorning's light, and she gazed in all directions. This was her whole world, as far as her eyes could see, right out to the horizon—with the sky hanging like a sheer veil over it all.

She thought of Ben, wondering what captured his attention when he sat outdoors in Kentucky. What intrigued him about nature? She recalled he had been quite taken with the variety of trees here in Paradise and smiled at the memory. She realized they hadn't spoken much about his home surroundings, although he had mentioned his family—his parents and four sisters—quite often. Annie had written down the girls' names, hiding the paper in her box of letters from Louisa. Evie, Patrice, Sherri, and Diana. Ben had enjoyed speaking of his sisters, but he'd asked many more questions about *her* life.

Her eye caught sunlight bouncing off an airplane high in the sky, brilliant like a beacon. Then, just as quickly, the light disappeared, and she was struck by its fleetingness. "Life passes too quickly," she whispered, thinking now of her friend in faraway Colorado. Annie wished she had access to one of those fancy smart phone gadgets Lou had used so often to keep in touch with her outside world. Annie was not at all bashful about voicing how much she missed Louisa. She'd said so to Essie, and to the Hochstetler children, too. Just now, though, she told it to the bumblebee lazily buzzing nearby. "What I wouldn't give to see Lou again." Truly she had enjoyed the companionship of her fine and fancy friend, the sound of Louisa's voice . . . and their near-nightly talks about Ben and Sam.

Will she be surprised that Ben and I are no longer together? That I'm staying with Essie? She could only imagine the shock on Lou's face when she read the letter Annie had recently sent. *Lou will ask how I like "hanging with Essie."* Annie laughed at the thought of one of Lou's favorite expressions.

She looked up and saw Yonie walking toward her. Omar had stayed behind with the team, but he waved to her nonetheless.

"Hullo, Schweschder!" Yonie called, all smiles.

She rose quickly and strode through a furrowed row to meet him.

Yonie stopped and removed his straw hat, then wiped his forehead with the back of his arm. "What brings you home?"

She saw the mischievous twinkle in his grayish-blue eyes. "You mean I can't drop by for a visit?"

"Not according to Daed, no."

Her breath caught in her throat. "You can't mean it."

"He's mighty put out with you, Annie. I 'spect he'd like you to stay far away . . . till you come to your senses."

"Just 'cause Essie's under the shun and I'm stayin' with her?"

His blond hair shone beneath the sun. "Why's that any surprise? You should know how he'd take it—you rushin' off like you did. Choosing Esther, of all people."

She squared her shoulders. "Well, *you* can't say a word 'bout it."

He slapped his hat back onto his head. "I can if I want to."

She eyed him curiously. "You've got yourself a mouth on ya, brother. Next thing, you'll be getting hitched to Dory."

Yonie stepped back. "Just never you mind."

"Ah, so you might be, is that it?"

"What I do ain't for you to say."

She wrinkled her face. "How is it Daed keeps lookin' the other way? Are you ever goin' to quit your running round and join church?"

He chuckled. "Lookee who's talkin'."

She thought defiantly of her boxes of art supplies, the many sketchbooks waiting to be filled. And fill them she would, with pages and pages of drawings. She would begin the minute the day dawned marking the end of her six-month promise. She must answer her heart's cry, and she could scarcely wait.

Yonie looked at her, obviously amused. "So, why'd you come over?"

She smiled. "Guess you must think I'm here to pick on you."

"Well, aren't you?"

She shook her head.

"You miss fussin' with me, is that it?"

"I guess I do."

He laughed heartily. "Dummkopp, why'd you go and leave home only to come back so quick-like?"

"I'm here for a visit, that's all," she said with a sigh.

" 'Tween you and me, I say you're better off." He squatted on the ground next to her, his face serious. "Even with Zeke makin' all kinds of trouble . . . even with Esther under the Bann, 'tis best you're over there."

"And why is that?"

He kept silent, as though deliberating whether to say what was on his mind. Then, when she figured he wasn't going to continue, he cocked his head back before saying, "Daed made you break it off with your English beau, ain't that right?"

If she had ever suspected he might blurt this out, she would've prepared herself, would've managed to keep inside the gasp that sucked air straight into her mouth. "Ach, it's true, but you shouldn't be surprised, jah?"

"I feel awful sorry for ya, is all." He looked away quickly.

"Truth be told, I feel sorry for myself. Ben and I never had a chance . . . not like you and Dory."

He nodded sadly. "Well, it ain't so easy courtin' a fancy girl, neither."

"Jah, I s'pose."

"That's all I'd better say."

Her heart went out to her brother, and she felt compelled to change the subject right quick. Mamm's admonition to talk with Daed continued to echo in her head, and although she didn't know what to say, Annie wandered toward the barn.

Jesse Zook pulled the letter from his pocket and slid it into his mailbox, wishing

Bishop Andy might've asked Old Preacher Moses to write and send such grim tidings to Ichabod. Although Jesse *did* agree the time had come to get word to the man.

Rubbing his thumb on a coin in his trousers pocket, he turned and strode toward the house. The place had stood there for more than a hundred years, sheltering one family of Zooks after another. Not a single one of them with a rebellious daughter—at least not that he'd ever heard of. And now with Annie staying over at Esther's place, well, he could hardly let his mind think too long on that, not as defiant as Zeke's wife continued to be.

Stopping momentarily, he looked back at the mailbox and noticed he'd forgotten to raise the red metal flag. He quickly walked back to do so, swinging his arms to hasten his pace.

That done, Jesse changed his mind about heading to the house and decided to cross the road to the barn instead. He craned his neck upward. *The sky's mighty big today,* he thought, taking in the heavens above.

He found his thoughts returning to the brief letter he had been asked to pen, hoping his former friend, Daniel Hochstetler, might in some small way be comforted in knowing the remains of his lost son, Isaac, had been found. *A father's in need of such information.*

Heading into the barn, he wondered how Daniel would react to the news. Had he and his now-deceased wife, Mary, made new connections in another Plain community, clear up there in Canada? "Most likely not," he whispered, shaking his head. Truth was, the man was a troublemaker, just as his son Zeke was.

Prior to Daniel's refusal of the divine lot, his ill temper and touchy ways had often stood in the way of the People's unity, which was required in order to perform their sacred rites, the spring and fall communion and foot washing. It had been surprising to Jesse to learn, years later, that *three* undoubtedly disgruntled members had whispered Daniel's name to the bishop on that long ago ordination day to make it possible for the contentious man to be among the nominees. Even their bishop had never understood it.

To think Zeke wants me to represent him in court. He thought suddenly of yesterday's visit to the jail, curling his toes in his work boots. *If it should come to that.*

Jesse made his way up the ladder to the haymow and began rummaging around in the corner till he located the old rope swing in its long-standing hiding place. It was the one young Isaac and many other children had enjoyed swinging on for many happy hours . . . even his own daughter had done so. His sons, too. The grove of black locust trees had been something of a play area back then, and he had been the one to hang the swing there, high on the sturdiest branch of the largest tree. Daniel had helped him.

Pulling the swing now from the secure spot, he hoped the confirmed news of Isaac's passing would not bring further animosity toward the man referred to as Ichabod, meaning *the spirit of God hath departed.* The brethren, including himself, had agreed upon the name, and the pronouncement had stuck, even in Daniel's absence.

Jesse breathed in the sweet hay fragrance of the loft and savored the stillness. Silence was his friend, out here alone with the animals and the dwindling hay bales. The quietude had the power to heal him, he knew. He couldn't help but think of Ichabod again, wondering if the man had managed to find the least amount of solace over the years. Did he ever allow the silence of morning to wash over him?

Jesse sat down on an old three-legged

stool, one his father had hewn out of left-over wood. He pondered the seeming curse the Lord God had slapped on Ichabod for his refusal of the divine lot. Did such a blight follow a man to his death? Was there no way out?

He wasn't about to delve into Scripture the way his cousin Irvin Ranck delighted in doing. *Even boasts about it.* And Irvin's wife, Julia, had gone and spread her opinions to Esther, causing confusion amongst the People, he knew. To think his own Annie was living with a shunned woman. Unthinkable! *And what of my embarrassment over Annie's art boldly printed on a magazine?*

There were shuffling sounds, and he turned to see his daughter standing not but a few feet from him. "Annie," he said.

Face solemn, she stared at the long rope in his hands, the wooden seat hanging limply near the floor. "Where'd that come from?"

He looked at her, this young woman who continued to defy him.

"It's our swing—mine and Isaac's—isn't it?" she asked.

He nodded. "I've kept it, safe . . . all these years." He wouldn't admit to wanting to give it to Zeke years ago. He was too struck by the pout of her lip, the distrust on her face.

She moved near and touched the swing with tears in her eyes. She whispered hoarsely, "Why, Daed?"

Stunned by his daughter's reaction, he handed the whole thing over to her. "Here, keep it. It's yours now." With that, he left her standing there, clutching the rope to her chest with trembling hands.

Chapter 4

As she watched her students at their easels, Louisa Stratford understood again why she had not been able to deny her love for teaching for very long. Four students, including Cybil Peters, a girl with exceptional talent, worked to the strains of Secret Garden's *White Stones,* one of Louisa's favorite CDs for creating an atmosphere of repose. To her musical taste, there was something inspirational about the ethereal blend of violin, oboe, and guitar.

Louisa demonstrated light values, linear perspective, and vanishing points at her own canvas, where she was creating a pastoral scene complete with mules grazing in the foreground and a windmill in the distance.

"Remember," she said, "in one-point perspective, the height as well as the width of the object is parallel to the painting's level surface."

She moved to Cybil's painting of two white swans, pointing out the imaginary extension lines and vanishing points.

Roman, the only male student, asked for assistance with his painting of a tall southwestern-style vase with sunlight pouring down on it from an open window.

"How's the shading?" he asked.

She kept her voice low, so as not to disrupt the concentration of the others, but someone opened the studio door and walked in before she could respond. She wasn't sure at what point she became consciously aware of him, but when she turned to look, she was surprised to see Michael Berkeley, her former fiancé, standing there.

He looked more handsome than she remembered, maybe because an easy smile lit his face in place of the disdain he'd worn during their dismal farewell. He was also more casually dressed, in khakis and a blue oxford shirt. This was new, as Michael was typically "money walking," in fine tailored suits over crisp white shirts and designer ties. She couldn't quite resist the urge to glance at the clock. Wasn't this considered business hours? Had he taken the day off? Or had he really given up the partnership at her father's prestigious law firm, as Courtney had suggested?

Louisa braced herself for his direct approach, remembering all Courtney had said about how Michael wanted her back, wanted a second chance, wanted . . . her. But although his smile was warm and friendly, he didn't walk over. Instead, he paused at Cybil's easel, greeting her and nodding his head appreciatively as she explained the piece she was working on. He laughed at something the young woman said, and Louisa remembered that Michael had met quite a few of her students during the years they had dated.

Trying to concentrate on Roman's question, Louisa offered a suggestion but knew she was only half focused on her work. What was Michael doing here? After a few more minutes, he wrapped up his conversation with Cybil and casually made his way over to where Louisa stood.

"Hi, Louisa."

"Michael."

His eyes met hers, and then he looked away. "I'll bet it feels good to get back here."

She shrugged, her defenses rising.

But before she could reply he continued, "In this studio, I mean. You always were a fantastic instructor."

She smiled briefly at the compliment but felt instantly skeptical of his sincerity and motives.

"Your students missed you," he said.

"And I missed them."

"Though I'm sure you're fond of your friends in Pennsylvania, too."

She shrugged. She wouldn't admit to missing Pennsylvania. She wasn't interested in opening the door to friendship—at least not to the kind of intimacy they had once shared.

Michael said, "Courtney mentioned you created quite a new life for yourself there."

"Did she?"

"I was surprised to hear you'd come back."

It was on the tip of Louisa's tongue to say flippantly, *Really? Even though you sent her to haul me home?* But she resisted. He was being very polite, and she had her students to think of.

"I missed my parents." She swallowed hard. What exactly had Courtney told him? Would he ask her about Sam?

But he only said, "It's really great to see you again, Louisa."

She couldn't say the same. In all truth, she wasn't sure how she felt about seeing Michael again. So instead she asked, "How do you like the way I set up my studio?"

He looked around. "You rearranged everything."

"Yes. Someone once told me—I forget who—that if you don't get to travel as much as you'd like to, move the furniture around a lot." She laughed softly, and Michael joined in. His laughter put her at ease, and she suddenly felt as if they were long-time friends, picking up where they'd left off months before.

Michael straightened. "Well, I'm on my lunch break. I'd better head back."

"It's only ten o'clock. . . ."

He shrugged easily. "My only free hour. I'll be tied up with client meetings the rest of the day. You remember how much I *love* meetings."

She laughed again. She wanted to ask about the firm, but she hesitated. Had Courtney already confessed to him that she'd let the cat out of the bag about his job change? She didn't want to reveal that Courtney had betrayed his confidence, so she simply nodded. She was curious, though. She was surprised, in fact, given this opportunity, that he didn't tell her about leaving the firm himself. Surprised, too, that he made no reference to their past, nor to the possibility of seeing her again.

Instead he looked around the room once more. "Well. I just thought I'd stop by . . . and welcome you home." He met her eyes again. "Take care, Louisa."

She nodded. "Bye."

With one last grin, he turned and left the room, with only a brief wave in response to Cybil's farewell.

Louisa was stumped at Michael's appearance and his even faster exit. Had Courtney exaggerated his determination to resume their relationship? If not, then why hadn't he asked her out? She strolled over to help the next student, feeling relieved that Michael hadn't pursued her, yet there was another emotion present, as well. Was it some misguided sense of wounded vanity . . . or was she truly disappointed?

Esther's body trembled and she felt her legs might not hold her as she crept away from the window to the chair. Sighing, willing back tears, she slowed her breathing. *I can do this. . . . I must be all that my children need . . . with your help, Lord Jesus.*

Esther refused to look out the window yet again, to stare at the spot where the police car had come rushing into the drive a week before. They had asked for Zeke and she had quickly led them to the barn. There, she and the police had slid open the big door and found Zeke pacing, the same way she'd seen him do in their bedroom. Before she'd scurried back to the house to look after the children—and to escape the nightmarish scene—she'd heard him mutter something about knowing where Isaac's bones were buried.

Will my life ever be right again? She knew she must pull herself together before Essie Ann awakened, which would be soon. Laura would be home from school any minute, too. "What's he done, dear Lord in heaven? What has my Zeke gone and done?"

Leaning her head back, she thought of all the years, the tears, the ongoing conflict in this house. She breathed in the present peace of the room, attempting to count her blessings. *Oh, I must think on the good things. The great goodness of my Lord and Savior. Place your hand of compassion and mercy on my family,* she prayed. *Especially on Zeke.*

She thought of Annie, who had readily taken on the role of guardian—more like a she-wolf than a young woman, railing under her breath that morning about Zeke's abusive streak. *"Maybe he'll try slapping around one person too many down at the jail,"* Annie had said, as if she wished it so.

Esther wrapped her arms around her middle as uncontrollable tears sprang to her eyes. Was this how it felt to mingle the light with the darkness? She wondered about that particular Scripture. Zeke had repeatedly taunted her, demanding that she abandon her "ridiculous" beliefs and come back to the Amish church. *"You'll be happier back here. Return to my side."*

But how could she ever go back? Tears clouded her vision; maybe they were tears of relief. She didn't rightly know, because she felt awful sad, too. And each day that passed, she felt trapped in one horrid pressure cooker, as if she might blow up if she didn't cry. So she let the dam break, sobbing into her hands.

As Louisa's first class of students was leaving, her mother stopped by the studio unannounced, as she often did lately. Louisa was eager to show what she was working on and the many photos of Amish farms she had taken over the months in Paradise. What she didn't tell her mom was that she'd just missed Michael—the son-in-law of her dreams—by about fifteen minutes, a thought that made Louisa bite back a smile.

"Here are some of Annie's peacocks." She pointed out one in the photo with a prominent fanned-out tail. "I did a painting of this one. I need to contact the gallery owner in case more of my work has sold."

Mother nodded. "I'd like to hear more about your Amish friend Annie."

She smiled, remembering her friend's contagious laughter, the way Annie's eyes lit up, especially when whispering about Ben Martin, whom she was no longer dating, according to Annie's last letter. What a shocker that was.

"I'm not sure where to begin." She thought of asking why her mom hadn't shown much interest before this, but she had no intention of spoiling this pleasant moment. "When Annie and I first began exchanging letters, she would draw little flowers and animals on each letter to me. It's funny, because she insists now that I was the first to notice her talent."

Mother listened as Louisa recalled that Annie had never drawn stick figures like some kids did. Her sketches, usually in the margins of the letters she wrote, most often depicted the birds, newborn animals, or flowers of spring, Annie's favorite season.

Springtime in Paradise. . . . Louisa shrugged off the memory, willing it away.

This was home now. Here, where her true roots were deep, where she had chafed under the ongoing prospect of becoming materialistic, like her parents. She had run from here for dear life and now, surprisingly, was back and making a bumbling attempt to reconnect.

How can I possibly fit in here? I know too much about life. And about love. . . .

Sighing, she heard her mother making superficial comments about Pennsylvania Amish traditions, admitting she had "conducted some research" while Louisa was there. Mother sat stiffly on one of the stools, appearing out of place. "You rarely showed me any of Annie's letters when you were growing up. I know I should have asked about her long before this. I *was* always curious, though. I never knew why you felt so close to her."

This surprised Louisa, but how could she explain that hers and Annie's correspondence had been a special world of their own making? "Annie was someone who understood me right off the bat. Funny, isn't it? A Plain girl with no sense of social decorum . . . who seemed to just *get* me. Even from our earliest pen pal days."

"But you left her world behind," her

mother stated. "You came back to your real home."

Louisa cringed. She hated hearing that, but she looked into her mother's face and saw the absence of barbed insinuation. No, Mother wasn't being the prickly pear she could certainly be. Not today, not here in Louisa's small, cheerful studio.

"I came back for lots of reasons," she said. "If anything, I think I found my way— my good senses, you might say. I found everything I've ever longed for in Amish country. Especially peace."

"Since I have no idea what that means, I'll just say how nice it is that you found yourself with your Amish friend, though that *is* hard for me to understand. All your education, your wonderful upbringing . . . doesn't that amount to anything?"

My upbringing wasn't so great.

"Your father and I—"

"Please, let's not bring Dad into this." She felt beyond weary at the thought of her father's financial aspirations for her future. *What's done is done, as Annie's Mamm says.* She excused herself and rose quickly.

"Louisa, what is it?"

She fully understood where her mother was coming from, so she tried again. "Have you ever had your senses thoroughly awakened? Have you ever experienced the incredible feeling of community—neighbor caring for neighbor?" She sighed, fighting back the frustration. "And that's only part of what I experienced so fully with the Amish, Mother."

"But Amish people are behind the times. Certainly you know that."

The pronouncement stung. "We'll talk later." Louisa rose and went to get her purse.

Her mother rushed toward her, desperation on her face. "I want to hear more, Louisa. Believe me."

She turned around, forcing a smile. "I can't now, Mother. Really . . ." She headed for the studio door, determined not to lash out in anger.

"Wait. Before I forget, Courtney called. She wants to see you but says you aren't returning her calls."

"I'll catch up with her."

Mother frowned, touching Louisa's sleeve. "Well, please, give her a call soon."

Exhaling, Louisa lifted her chin. "I'm not opposed to seeing Courtney, and if you must know, she is one of the main reasons I came home when I did."

"Really? I had no idea."

Louisa opened the studio door. "I'm

sorry, but I need to get going." She hurried out of the strip mall and to her waiting car. A half hour remained before her next students would arrive, and Louisa was in need of some coffee and some air.

Chapter 5

Preacher Jesse watched his daughter prance shamelessly up the back steps and into the house, carrying the rope swing he'd just given her. *She struts about like a peacock.* "And does as she pleases," he added aloud, spitting out the words. Such a time he'd had lately, folk fussing from all directions, since near everyone in Paradise, or so it seemed, had now heard of Annie's painting on that there magazine cover. "Downright bigheaded she is," he muttered to himself, lifting the harness over Betsy's small ears. "Comin' back here to my house . . . ach, without so much as an apology yet."

He was still mumbling and fretting when a police car turned into the lane. He'd heard from the smithy and others that oodles of Englischers were in the neighborhood, going from farm to farm, asking questions.

His neck hairs prickled as the police officer opened the door and climbed out of his vehicle. "Not on this property," Jesse whispered to himself, making a beeline toward the officer. *I don't want Barbara to have an encounter with him.*

"What can I do for you?" he called, recognizing the tall blond man as the same one he'd spoken to the day Zeke had been taken away.

"I believe you're the preacher I met last week. Preacher Zook, isn't it?" The man smiled. "Lots of folk with that name around here." He pulled out his ID and showed it quickly. "I'm Officer Kipling . . . and thanks for your time today, sir."

Jesse was once again intrigued by the gold badge on the navy blue uniform shirt and could scarcely stop staring at it. "What brings ya over here?"

"I'd like to ask you and your wife a few questions regarding Ezekiel Hochstetler."

"Well, now, things will work better if you put your questions to me and leave my good wife out of it."

The policeman frowned, blinked his eyes, then continued, "How many children eighteen or older live in your house, Mr. Zook?"

This man must be deaf! "As I said, no need to be talkin' to anyone but me, Mr. Kipling."

The younger man seemed taken aback, but he pulled out a small pad and pen from his shirt pocket. "Thanks for your cooperation, Mr. Zook. I appreciate it."

Jesse squared his shoulders, inwardly preparing for what lay ahead. "Glad to be of help."

Annie and her mother peered out the kitchen window. "Ach, what's this?" Annie whispered, her heart in her throat. She'd heard more than she cared to from Essie about *her* frightening day with the police, though on that day, Zeke had been the one to call them. Not a soul had invited this intrusion today, as far as Annie knew.

"Oh, what do you think they want?" Mamm said softly. "I've never seen the likes of this."

She wouldn't frighten Mamm unduly by describing the alarming scene at the cemetery. "Come, let's head over to the Dawdi Haus and stay put with Dawdi and Mammi Zook lest they become frightened, too."

"Jah, gut."

They headed to the front room and opened the connecting door. Annie wondered, all the while, if Essie might be sending a prayer toward heaven were she here witnessing all this.

Thank goodness she's not! Annie thought. Esther had been through enough trauma for a lifetime.

"What're ya doin' with that swing I saw ya bring in?" Dawdi Zook asked, lifting his chin toward the adjoining door.

"It's the one Isaac and I used to play on at the locust grove," Annie explained. "I want to have it put up again. It's been down too long."

Mammi smiled, as did Mamm. "You and Isaac were quite the youngsters," Mammi said.

To this, Dawdi agreed with a nod. "Never saw anything like it the way the two of yous took to each other. You'd-a thought you were twins or some such thing."

Annie hadn't heard that before. "Isaac's surely in heaven, jah? Little ones go there, even before judgment day?"

"That's up to the Good Lord," Dawdi was quick to say.

Annie sighed. *Everything's up to Him,* she thought.

The birds suddenly quieted when the police car pulled into the lane. Esther ran from the barn into the house, closing the back door securely behind her.

In the kitchen, she found Laura standing on a chair at the sink, wiping the counter clean. "Bless your heart." Esther hurried to her daughter's side. "You're the best little helper, ain't?"

Laura nodded. When her lower lip trembled, Esther gathered her near.

"I miss Dat." Laura buried her face in Esther's neck.

"Well, sure you do."

"When will we see him again?"

"Soon . . . soon," Esther said, shushing her. She had no knowledge of when Zeke might return, but she had every hope that it would be right quick. "'God is our refuge and strength, a very present help in trouble,'" she said, quoting the Psalms. She must not let fear overtake her—must keep her heart wide open to the Lord Jesus. She knew all too well the lack of joy that came from shielding her heart.

When loud knocking shook the front door, she breathed in sharply. She wondered what might happen if she simply ignored it. Most of all, she must not let on her worry, not in front of the children.

"Why is someone at the *front* door, Mamma?" Laura asked, her eyes wide.

"I'll go 'n' see. You stay here with your brothers and baby sister." She kissed the top of Laura's head and turned to go, heading through the small sitting room between the kitchen and the long front room. Her heart pounded so hard she could scarcely breathe.

Timidly she opened the door. There stood two police officers, a man and a woman, both dressed in navy suits with trousers, and bright gold badges on their shirts. *Like the policemen who came for Zeke.*

"Mrs. Hochstetler?" the woman said. "Mrs. *Esther* Hochstetler?"

She wondered how on earth they knew her name. "Jah."

Both of them held out thin wallets with their pictures in leather frames. "Officers Keller and Landis," said the dark-eyed woman with long black eyelashes, which were surely painted on. "May we come in and ask you some questions?"

Esther faltered, hand on her throat. *What would Zeke say to do?* Her husband was not here, and neither was Annie. It was just the children and herself, so she must decide how to answer on her own. "What's this about?" she asked softly.

"This shouldn't take much time, if you cooperate with us," the woman named Officer Keller said. "Your husband is Ezekiel Hochstetler, is he not?"

"Jah, goes by Zeke . . ."

"We've been assigned to ask those in the neighborhood to attest to his character," Officer Landis continued.

"Well, I've known him a gut long time." Esther assumed they knew as much, but she felt terribly uneasy and hesitated to let them in.

"We'll be brief," said Officer Keller, smiling through pink lips. "You just tell us what you know. It's as easy as that."

Esther's palms were sweating and she felt queasy. Her experience with Englischers was ever so limited.

Officer Keller frowned and pushed back her hair. "There's nothing to be afraid of, Mrs. Hochstetler. This won't take but a minute."

One minute? She was feeling ever so put upon. Was she required under God to speak with them?

"What you know may help your husband," Officer Landis said.

"If that's so, then I . . . s'pose." She opened the door a bit wider.

"Thank you," the two said in unison

and stepped into the house.

Esther offered them a place on the settee in the front room, then excused herself to hurry to the kitchen. "Laura, dear, are you all right? Mamma's goin' to be busy for a short while. Keep your eye on your sister and brothers, won't you?"

Her daughter's eyes glistened as her focus darted toward the front room and back. "Oh, Mamma, what's goin' to happen? Why are those Englischers here?"

She realized that Laura was worried the police people might be here to take all of them away, just as they had Zeke—even she herself wasn't so sure they wouldn't. "You call if you need me, ya hear?" she told Laura.

"I will, Mamma."

Poor thing. First her father's gone, and now this. Esther couldn't help but pray as she headed back to the waiting officers. *I trust you for wisdom, O dear Lord.*

Zeke Hochstetler recalled holding his drinking glass up to the gas lamp at home some weeks back to peer through it curiously. Esther had muttered something about it looking as if he were searching for some answer in the glass, and he'd mocked her but good. What was it about that woman, thinking she could flap her lip whenever she dared? He could hold a glass up to the light and stare through it if he wanted to.

Frustrated, he stopped his mental rambling. He was torn in two. One part liked telling Esther what to cook him for supper or demanding how many logs to throw into the belly of the stove to warm the house. The other part of him knew he'd been terribly harsh, even brutal, with her. Sure, he could make her do his bidding—during the daylight hours, and after dark, too. Wasn't he the head of his household under God? Yet requiring his family to be at his beck and call, allowing no lip from any of them, had gotten him hardly any respect.

Stiffly he paced in this strange English place, though it was no longer as foreign to him as the day he'd arrived. *The police detectives must be done digging up Isaac's bones,* he thought, recalling how he'd given them directions to the burial spot. He was surprised the brethren had not reprimanded him for doing so.

Continuing to pace back and forth in his cell—his cage—he suddenly wondered what it would be like to wear the heavy fur coat of a lion or a tiger—the nap and wool of a powerful animal's skin connected to his own body. Yet he grew weaker with each step.

What'll they do to me when they see I was telling the truth all along?

He'd had the oddest feeling not a soul believed what he'd said about killing Isaac. At least one of the detectives had looked askance at him. Only when he'd insisted he could direct them to the bones—the proof they needed—did he get their attention at last.

Isaac . . . my brother! You didn't deserve to die. Still, I spared you a life of dread. I kept you from becoming a man. I cut you off before you could become like our father . . . and like me.

He sighed heavily, feebly stroking his beard. He let his thoughts slip away further, back through the blurry curtain of years.

They'd gone north on Belmont Road, he and little Isaac, both disobedient as all get out that night. No, it had been *he* and not his innocent brother who had ignored their stern father. *"Tomorrow's plenty soon,"* Dat had said. *"Put the dead pup out behind the barn till morning, and then we'll bury it."*

Nonetheless, Zeke had crossed his father, driven by the desire to do things his own way, just as his father's cruel and defiant nature ruled him.

Zeke couldn't help but notice the light at the Progressive Shoe Store as they made their way along the deserted road. Like a distant star the yard light beaconed to them, its message pulsating through the blackness: *Turn back, return home. Beware!*

The small wooden coffin became heavy after all that walking, but never once did Zeke ask Isaac to carry his own dead puppy dog. It was Isaac who'd suggested the grove near Pequea Creek for the grave—a place where they often played while Dat and Mamma visited nearby neighbors—where the now stabbed-to-death puppy had romped and yipped at their heels and splashed in the creek. It had been Zeke's idea to count the steps to the tree and then turn toward the creek. Eight steps and four, for the years of their lives . . . his own and Isaac's.

There was such unspeakable sorrow between them. The silence was thick, except for Isaac's constant sniffling and weeping, which became annoying. Isaac had loved this puppy more than any boy ought to love a pet.

And when the time came, Ezekiel began to dig the hole with the big, hard shovel.

Angry, vicious strokes . . .

Chapter 6

Ben leaned hard on the kitchen table and buried his face in his hands.

Adopted?

Completely stunned by the news, he shook his head. "I wasn't born to you and Dad?"

Mom sighed, her face clouded with sudden grief. "We should have told you long ago. Your father wanted to, but the longer it went, the more reluctant I became." She stopped to brush away tears. "I'm so very sorry."

He stared across the table at the woman whom he had always believed to be his mother. "How could you keep this from me?"

Her chin quivered. "It was my idea to spare you further hurt, though I wanted so much to tell you right after your adoption was finalized."

"You don't struggle over whether to tell a baby these things. How old was I, anyway?" He felt overwhelmed with the knowledge of this betrayal.

"You were only four when all the legal work was finished. Well, we assumed you were still that age, although in the end we had to decide on a birth date for you." She stopped to catch her breath. "And every year that slipped by, your father and I worried we should be telling you the truth."

He glared at her. "Why didn't you?"

"We should have. I see that now all the more . . . how restless you are, as if you're searching for something. First going off to work in Amish country and now wanting to go overseas . . ." She covered her eyes with her hands, whimpering. "I'm sorry, Ben. I'm just so sorry."

He rose. "I don't get it. What possible reason could you have for keeping this from me? And what does my move to Lancaster County have to do with anything?" He didn't wait for her answer, though. He felt as if his chest might cave in and suffocate him. Rushing through the living room, he made his way toward the front door, where he yanked his jacket off the coat tree and left the house.

———————

Annie was becoming anxious now, still staring out at her father and the policeman from the kitchen window in the Dawdi Haus. "How much longer will he stay?" she asked.

Mammi Zook came and led her away. "Ach, not to worry, dear one. The Lord God has us all safe in the palm of His hand."

"Honest, Mammi?"

"Oh, jah. I'm ever so sure." Her grandmother's eyes glistened, but not from tears. She'd always had shining eyes. "We'll have us some chamomile tea with honey, Miss Annie," Mammi said, readying the teapot and setting a cup at the place next to hers at the table.

Annie forced a smile and sat beside her father's mother. Dawdi had gone upstairs to rest, and Mamm had returned to the main house to prepare lunch. Annie wasn't so much thankful to have a cup of Mammi's well-brewed tea as she was having this opportunity to simply spend time with her diminutive Mammi Zook. Living with Essie was all right, but Annie missed her family and knew there was little she could really do to help her friend, flustered as she was about her husband. No one seemed to know much about Zeke's crime. Now, it seemed, Daed was getting things straight from the horse's mouth.

She resisted the urge to turn and peer out the window again, trying to be calm about the unexpected police visit. "S'pose they have a job to do," she said softly.

"Jah, according to their ways," Mammi remarked. "We know not the way of the fancy. We live in the world but are not of it."

Annie had heard that said enough times, but as Mammi spoke, it reminded her of the great big world out there, far from Lancaster County. Far away, where Ben Martin lived, on the other side of that seeming vastness that separated them so.

"How does the Lord God keep track of everyone?" Annie had asked the same thing of Julia on occasion. More recently, she'd put the same question to Essie. "Does He look down from on high? Does He care what's happenin' with each of us?"

"Oh, I don't know *how*, but He cares, all right. I know this in my knower," Mammi said, pointing to her head. "I believe it in here, too." She patted her heart, sighing. "Your fancy friend, Louisa, used to ask me things like this, too, Annie."

"She did?"

"Oh my, quite often. A nice girl, Lou was. Too bad she upped and ran off so awful quick."

"She had her reasons."

Mammi nodded her head, the strings on her *Kapp* falling forward. "I thought she might've found herself true love here."

Annie scarcely knew what to say. She wasn't going to admit it by revealing Lou's secret meetings with Sam Glick.

Mammi had a peculiar look in her eye as she poured the hot tea. "I have the feelin' Lou might be a good one for getting her pies in early enough to head outside to watch the robins skitter about the birdbath of a mornin'."

Annie laughed. *Mammi must think Lou would make a good Plain woman.* She blew on her tea gently before taking a sip. The taste was so appealing, it made her feel nearly homesick. Yet she was right here, sitting and enjoying such good fellowship this minute. "I honestly don't expect to ever see Louisa Stratford again," she declared.

Drawing a breath, Mammi blinked her eyes several times before saying, "Ah, well, I s'pose we'll just have to wait 'n' see on that, won't we?"

Annie couldn't begin to imagine it. Truth be known, Lou was not exactly a predictable person. She was a woman of many interests, and Annie was just as sure as could be that Lou had returned to the life she'd missed.

Jesse strolled along with Officer Kipling out to his car. His head was pounding at the thought of what the policeman had said to him a few minutes before—that the authorities felt sure they had something big to go on with Zeke, what with him leading them to Isaac's bones and all. Jesse had been mighty careful what he said. He certainly didn't want it known that he'd been the one who had originally found and buried Isaac's remains.

"When all's said and done, how can you punish Zeke for a crime he committed as a child?" Jesse asked, still baffled at the possibility that Zeke had actually killed Isaac as a boy.

"First things first," the man said. Jesse had found out quickly that the officer was not one for offering simple, straightforward answers. "Forensics will determine what it can regarding the remains—the gender and age of the bones."

They have to be Isaac's . . . no doubt on

that, Jesse thought. But he didn't say as much. The brethren had long ago decided not to divulge the news of the boy's disappearance, and they still wanted to keep their hands clean of any connection. God's ways were misunderstood by outsiders, for sure and for certain—God's ways and the Old Ways.

Jesse was still mighty surprised that Zeke had not implicated either the bishop or himself, as he was so sure he would. Because, after all, it was not Zeke who had discovered and then buried those bones.

And it was right then that Jesse stopped in his tracks. *Was it a crime not to report a missing child? If Isaac was ever truly that . . .*

When the policeman finally left, Annie returned to the field to talk with Yonie, who had just finished plowing that section of land. "You've still got yourself a car, ain't?" she asked as they walked toward the house together.

He looked at her. "Why do you ask?"

"I want you to take me over to the Pequea Creek covered bridge sometime soon. How 'bout tomorrow?" She explained that she wanted him to put the old rope swing back up on the tree, where it belonged.

"What the world for?" he asked, eyes wide.

"Don't ask questions. Just help me get it up there again."

He argued with her a bit more but finally agreed to take along a ladder—tied to the top of his car—because she warned there was no other way to reach the branch due to the thorns. "If I'm to put the swing up, I'll have to smuggle the ladder out of the barn."

"Do whatever you have to. Stop by for me tomorrow, maybe?"

Surprisingly, he agreed. "That might just work." He said he'd heard Daed talking about possibly meeting with the brethren at noon tomorrow. "Jah, that's fine. Be ready, though, so I don't have to wait."

She scrunched up her face. "I'll be ready." Then to herself she added, *Been ready for years.*

"Your bishop, Andrew Stoltzfus, has granted us permission to ask you a few questions," dark-haired Officer Landis said to Esther, folding his hands as he leaned forward on Esther's settee. He glanced at the policewoman next to him. "And Officer Keller, here, will get things started."

The woman had a peculiar habit of

squinting her eyes and fixing her gaze on something far away. Just what, Esther didn't rightly know, but it was clear the woman was not at all comfortable with the task at hand. "Is your full name Esther Hochstetler?" she asked.

She nodded.

"How long have you lived here in Paradise?"

"My whole life."

"And how long is that?"

"I am twenty-three years old, as of last September."

"How long have you known your husband, Ezekiel Hochstetler?"

"Since my first singing, seven years ago."

"How long have you known his family?"

"Never much knew them."

The policewoman stared down at her notebook, pen poised on the page. "How many years?"

"Same as I've known Zeke . . . seven."

"How many children do you have?"

"Four."

"Please give their names and ages."

Esther felt her hands go clammy. "Is this ever so necessary?"

The woman offered a quick smile. "It is

public record, of course. We just need you to verify."

She breathed in slowly. "Laura, our eldest, is six. Zach is three, John is two, and the baby, Essie Ann, is fifteen weeks old."

The woman flipped her notebook page and scribbled something at the top. Then, looking up again, she continued. "Have you ever known your husband, Ezekiel Hochstetler, to threaten anyone with bodily harm with the intent to murder?"

"No."

"Has your husband, in the past or presently, ever abused you or any of your children?"

She paused. She didn't know quite what that meant. "I'm not sure."

"Has your husband ever punished you or your children unduly?" The policewoman's chest rose and fell, and Esther could see that she seemed to struggle.

Is this a trick? She began to whisper a prayer in her first language. "O Lord God be ever near. . . ."

"Esther, please answer the question to the best of your ability."

She wanted to help and not hinder her Zeke, so she considered what she best be saying.

"Explain what you mean by punish?"

She managed to eke out the question to the strangers as they looked at her as if *she* had done something wrong. These Englischers had nerve to come here. Then she remembered they'd said Bishop Andy was all for the questioning. What on earth did that mean? Did he know the sort of things being asked of her this day? And wasn't her own experience as Zeke's wife . . . wasn't that how most women were treated by their husbands? *But Annie says Preacher Jesse is gentle and kind to his wife,* she recalled.

"Has your husband ever physically abused you or your children?" the policewoman repeated.

Sure he has . . . when any of us disobey, Esther thought.

"I'd rather not say," she said so softly she scarcely heard herself.

Officer Keller gave a fleeting look to her partner. The man frowned briefly then glanced about the room, as if looking for clues. What did he hope to see—holes in the wall? Broken dishes?

"I really need to get back to my little ones," Esther said, getting up from her chair.

Surprisingly, the officers rose when she did and followed her to the door. She could scarcely breathe as they said their goodbyes and left the sanctity of her house. "O my Lord and Savior," she prayed, folding her trembling hands tightly to her breast.

Ben drove to one of his favorite hiking trails, ten miles from the house. His chest ached every time he recalled his mother's shocking revelation.

Adopted? The startling knowledge was like a ton of bricks smashing into his psyche.

"Twenty-one and just now finding out?" He parked his car, got out, and slammed the door.

He hurried toward the trailhead, moving swiftly up the dirt path. He was aware of boulders on one side and a shallow ravine on the other. Farther up he noticed some deer—a doe and two young fawns—looking at him momentarily before scampering into a grove of white oaks.

"If I'm not really Ben Martin, who am I?" He asked it of the trees, the sky, and a blue jay nearby as he made his way up the gradual incline.

He had the urge to shout but suppressed his emotions. It was bad enough that his father was scarcely ever at home and his two best buddies were away at out-of-state colleges. The idea of joining the Peace Corps appealed to him even more. For a flicker of a second, he'd actually thought his mother crazy, but knowing her as he did, that notion quickly melted into disbelief. Now, though, he carried anger and a real sense of betrayal with him as he made furious strides up the trail.

He considered his family . . . all the framed pictures of his sisters, parents, cousins, aunts, uncles, and grandparents on both sides. The extended family he'd always known. Not a single person with his blood in their veins? No one he resembled? Why hadn't this fact hit him before?

"They are not my real family . . . not related to me at all," he spit out. "My sisters aren't my sisters." He could not begin to fathom it and suddenly felt more alone than ever before in his life. Lonely and lost, he realized anew how very much he missed Annie.

Chapter 7

Louisa was already awake the following morning when she heard banging coming from the other side of the wall, from the apartment next door. It sounded like pots and pans tumbling out of a cupboard. At first she wondered if she had been dreaming, but how could that be when she had been looking at the clock off and on for the past full hour? Annie's mother had been such a quiet cook, even graceful at times, adeptly juggling baking many loaves of bread each morning and pies, too, along with many other homemade goodies.

The thought of Annie's mom creating her homespun culinary delights pulled Louisa quickly back to Paradise. But it was not the Zooks' house nor their kitchen that held her captive. She couldn't get Sam Glick out of her mind, in spite of Michael's visit to the studio yesterday. There was something unique about Sam, something she hadn't encountered in any other man. She was still trying to decipher the quality . . . and decide whether she could walk away from it for good.

Fer gut.

She smiled. Quaint Dutch words and phrases kept popping into her mind, nudging her back to Amish country, where, she was afraid to openly acknowledge, so much of her heart still resided.

She wondered how Sam was doing. Had he managed to move on without her? Her departure had been too swift even for courtesy's sake, although she had taken a few minutes to write him a good-bye letter. Too often, even now, she had the urge to write him again or to call him at his barn phone . . . just to hear his voice.

Getting out of bed, she hurried to the shower, attempting to push away thoughts of her mad dash from Pennsylvania. It seemed mad dashes were getting to be almost a habit for her. Last year, she had been rather insane to take off so impulsively from Colorado, leaving her parents holding the financial "bag" for Michael's and her planned lavish wedding. And part of her had been equally crazy to leave Sam behind, no doubt wondering what kind of flighty girl she really was, and maybe even thinking *good riddance.*

Reaching for her towel, Louisa determined that today she must discard all thoughts of Sam and set him free in her own mind. "Once and for all," she whispered to her cat, Muffin. "*This* is where I belong, ain't so?" She groaned as yet another Amish saying rolled from her tongue.

Over the noon hour, following the main meal, Jesse huddled with Bishop Andy and Moses in the bishop's barn. "This thing with Zeke could get out of control in a big hurry," Jesse began. "There's no tellin' what could happen."

Andy nodded, slow and long, pulling on his beard. His face looked mighty pale. "I daresay we keep our peace and stay out of the public eye as much as possible."

Old Moses shook his head, eyes solemn, head bowed. He drew in a deep breath; then his eyes rose and met Jesse's, holding his gaze for a time. "Here's what I think, and Bishop, you tell me if I'm wrong on this." Moses leaned forward, as if to be heard better, though it was he who suffered the hearing loss. "The Lord God knows what's what, and none of us is guilty of any wrong-doing here."

Jesse thought on that. "Well, in your thinkin', did we do wrong not to report Isaac's disappearance back when?" He looked right at Bishop Andy.

The bishop was slow to respond. When he did so, there was fire in his eyes and his voice was high-pitched in agitation. "Jesse Zook, you as a minister of almighty God know better than to question the appointed shepherd over this flock . . . of which you have been entrusted with the care, as well."

Jesse groped for the right words and wished he'd kept his mouth shut, even though he felt this was something the three of them must discuss. They did not have their ducks in a row, so to speak, and they were all vulnerable to attack from the outside world. And, what with Zeke wanting representation from Jesse . . . well, he wished they'd been honest from the outset. "I know it was your word we followed, back in the beginning," he admitted, knowing that the rule of thumb was clearly on the side of trusting what the man of God decreed. In this case, it had been Bishop Andy's words that had guided all of them, all these years.

"If we'd been forthright with the police,"

Old Moses spoke up, "we'd have had an even bigger mess on our hands, I daresay."

The bishop turned suddenly. "We daresn't question the Almighty."

Jesse was reminded once again what his father and father's father had always believed, what the ministry, the brethren, said was always right. "There is little room for budging on this," he stated, hoping to drive home the point that they, each of them, were in a real pickle with Zeke in jail saying who knew what. "We must help the police if need be, but only as much as necessary."

"Jah, we hold steady . . . stay the course," Andy said. "No reason to doubt when God has spoken through His servant."

Jesse had always believed that the bishop was to be honored and obeyed. There had never been any question on that till now. Now he struggled, day in and day out, and not one thing Andy or Old Moses said today, tomorrow, or next week could convince him otherwise. Honesty was always the best way, his father had taught him. Honesty must prevail under the Lord God. Sadly, in this case, covering up the truth had led them down a path of thorns, and Zeke's telling the police where to find Isaac's bones might be only the beginning.

Days of sorrow, he thought, greatly fearing what was bound to come. Bishop's decree or no.

Annie was ever so glad Yonie kept his word and came for her at Esther's, although his car looked awful funny with the ladder tied to the top. She called her farewells to Esther and the children and went out to her brother's car with the swing in her arms.

During the ride over to Belmont Road, she was restless and excited both, until she spied a cash box on the floor of the car. "What on earth is that for?"

Yonie's ears blushed red. "Don't be askin'," he said. "I forgot it was even there."

"You're driving the People around for pay, aren't you? Takin' them to work, to the doctor, and whatnot all?"

He nodded sheepishly. "Got the idea here lately, and honestly it's helpin' me pay off my car loan."

"Well, isn't that a fine howdy-do?" She was truly shocked.

"When Daed got wind of it, he told me never to bring my car onto his property till I got my wits 'bout me again."

"And just when do you expect *that* to ever happen?"

He shrugged, pulling out a cell phone

from his pants pocket. "See this? I'm a taxi service amongst my own folk. They call me, day or night, and I drive to their houses and take them wherever they want to go."

She held her breath. "I hope you're kidding."

"Nope. I'm tellin' you the for-sure truth."

Sighing, she looked out the window, watching the fields blur as she stared, not sure why tears threatened to fall. "I guess you're not planning to join church anytime soon."

"You guessed right."

She couldn't say anything to him, really. Her own procrastination had been and continued to be a thorn in their father's flesh—for both their parents, truth be known, and for the brethren as a whole. This she knew, though she simply couldn't change anything about that now. *Maybe never.*

When they arrived at the familiar covered bridge, Yonie untied the ladder and hoisted it over his shoulder, and Annie led the way down the bank, toward the grove of trees. In a matter of minutes, Yonie had the ladder in place and the rope swing swaying from his efforts.

Annie stared at it, taking in the beauty of springtime in every direction—the flowering trees, the verdant slope, and the gurgling creek below. For a moment, she was a little girl again, and she and Isaac were swinging together, their laughter on the breeze.

"Hullo? Annie! Quit your daydreamin' and steady the ladder." Yonie's voice jerked her back to reality, and she was sad to return.

────────

The next day, Louisa was pleased when her father called the studio in the midafternoon. "Your mother baked a lemon sponge pie," he said with a chuckle. "Imagine that."

"What's the occasion?"

"I've offered to grill salmon in hopes you'd join us for dinner this evening."

She smiled. Her father was like a puppy dog when he was desperate. "Sure. When's dinner?"

"Come over when you're finished at the studio."

"Okay. I'll bring a salad."

"Sounds great. Your mother will be happy about this," Dad added. "Good-bye, Louisa."

"See you tonight," she said. "And thanks!"

She clicked off her Palm and began the

cleanup between classes. When that was done, she hurried to her own easel, anxious to get in some work on her painting of an old barn. *Jesse Zook's barn,* she thought, wishing she'd taken even more pictures of it than she had in her possession.

She often thought of simply going back to visit Annie, over a long weekend perhaps, if for no other reason than to surprise her. Annie occupied such a huge portion of her thoughts. Their letter-writing days had already resumed, yet she still longed to call Annie, to hear her voice. But she knew the nearest phone was the neighbor's barn phone up the road from Esther's. There was always the option of simply writing to Annie and alerting her to what day and time she might call. Of course, Annie wouldn't want to break the *Ordnung*—as decreed by the bishop—and use the telephone for personal communication. Though what was one more broken rule?

And Sam? No point in stirring up anything she couldn't follow through with, even though she missed him terribly. He was somewhat more progressive, as some Amish referred to themselves, so it wasn't out of the question that she might contact him by phone.

Someday.

There's not a lot of wisdom in growing older, Louisa decided as she sat on a fine upholstered chair at her mother's lovely long table in their spacious, candlelit dining room. Wisdom came in appreciating the true but simple things in life. Things more important than the topics her parents seemed to delight in discussing this evening, like bridge partners and golf scores.

"Did you watch that special on the Triple Crown last night?" her father asked.

"No. I . . . um, got rid of my TV."

He furrowed his brow. "Why would you do that?"

She shrugged. "Never watch it. Mm . . . this salmon is so delicious." Her mouth watered as she cut the tender salmon fillet with the side of her sterling silver fork. Her father had outdone himself with the basil butter. Her tossed salad and the steamed veggies were delicious, and Mother's lemon pie rivaled Barbara Zook's.

Louisa refused to let the aroma of great cooking send her thoughts whirling back to Annie and her people this time. No, this was home, and here she was destined to stay. She had grown up in this luxurious place nestled in Castle Pines, just south of Denver. Sure, it was her parents' exquisite abode now, but it was hers, too. She was, after all, her parents' daughter, Louisa Victoria Stratford. A modern high-tech girl with a yearning for the simple life. And no longer did she wonder how she could possibly fit into this world with its opulence and elitist mentality; she knew how—by being her new self. She would dress the part when necessary, but she would live with an eye for the significant. She would live, if not a less complicated life, then a tranquil one filled with true purpose. For she had tasted and embraced a peaceful, meaningful life, and it had changed her from the inside out.

Following dessert, Dad asked her to join him in his private study. The secluded room was lined with custom cherry wood built-ins on nearly every wall. Louisa sat in her father's favorite wingback chair, a maroon, hunter green, and tan plaid. It was the only piece, along with a coordinating area rug, that had been chosen by her mother for the decor of Dad's home office.

Louisa settled into the comfortable chair, propping her feet up on the matching ottoman. She enjoyed the fire in the gas fireplace and was amused by her father's ritual of selecting a cigar from his cigar box, lighting up, then leaning back in his leather desk chair, his eyes closing for a moment, his chiseled face breaking into a familiar smile. "Well, daughter dear, not only did I miss out on a son-in-law, but I lost a promising young law partner, also," he remarked. Then for effect, or so Louisa thought, he blew the smoke into defined grayish-white rings.

By his tone, she knew he was not angry, only interested in talking about her plans for the future. No doubt he hoped she might say she was resuming her engagement with Michael. "Oh, Daddy, surely you know Michael and I will never be more than friends now."

His smile turned solemn. "Is there no hope for the dashing Mr. Berkeley?"

"I don't see how." *After Sam, I can't begin to imagine it. . . .*

He puffed on his cigar. "It's difficult to understand what went wrong between the two of you."

"I'd rather not go into it."

"You're upset," he said, narrowing his gaze.

She wouldn't reveal the reasons—too late for that. "The Amish have an apropos saying: 'What's done is done.'"

He nodded. "Fair enough." He studied her, then studied his cigar. "You might not know it, but Michael left my firm to become a public defender in a low-rent district." He scratched his head, grimacing. "I tried to talk him out of it, but he was so eloquent. And adamant."

"Really?" she said. "Then a partnership with Michael is evidently not in the cards for either of us."

"He's already getting established in his new area of interest." Dad shook his head again. "Any idea why he would make such a monumental career change?" The twinkle in his eye suggested she ought to know the answer, or *was* the answer.

Trying to get my attention, maybe? That's presumptuous.

Reaching for the cigar box, she opened the lid and selected a cigar. "Don't worry, I have no intention of smoking this." She took a long whiff, sliding it beneath her nose, breathing in the rich scent. "Honestly, I don't know what I want where men are concerned. I wish Michael hadn't been so impulsive, leaving you in the lurch, Daddy."

He raised his eyebrows. "Look who's talking."

Mother was calling from the hallway, carrying coffee on one of her sterling silver trays, Louisa assumed. She rose to her feet, thinking, *Saved by café au lait.*

Later that evening, Louisa and Courtney sat on Louisa's funky black-speckled sofa, flipping through fashion and entertainment magazines. After quoting an article about a celebrity wedding, Courtney declared she was absolutely sure Michael was going to call Louisa for a lunch date. "I'd bet money on it."

"Better watch your gambling habit," Louisa joked, but she couldn't disagree more. "You didn't see him playing it cool at my art studio."

"Oh, I've got it all figured out, girl." Courtney's pretty green eyes shone with knowing.

Louisa laughed and reached for her can of pop.

Courtney was insistent, turning a page and swishing her thick shoulder-length brown hair away from her face. "You'll see I'm right."

Wanting to change the subject, Louisa asked, "Ever hear of this?" She looked down at the magazine she'd been reading. "This says that washing your hair with very hot water gets the blood circulating."

"So?"

"It's supposed to really get the creative juices flowing."

Courtney leaned back, pulled her hair in a bunch, then let it go free. "And why does someone as wildly creative as you are need a crutch?"

"I think we all need a boost on low days."

"You have down days? No way."

"You haven't been around when I'm staring at the foreground of a canvas, trying to pull my thoughts into one cohesive idea." Louisa shook her head. "It's not the easiest thing in the world to create day in, day out."

"Okay, so you boil your head," Courtney said. "How's that supposed to help?"

"It gets the blood flowing to the brain."

Courtney hooted. "And this is a *good* thing?"

"Wunderbaar-gut, as the Amish say." Louisa reached down for Muffin, lugging him up onto her lap. "I'll have to tell Annie about it, won't I, boy?"

Courtney's expression became serious. "You ever going to get all that Plain nonsense out of your system?"

"Maybe. Haven't decided yet."

"Well, whatever you do, make sure you say yes when Michael calls."

"We're back to this?"

"Full circle, baby. That's why I'm here, you know. I'm your guardian angel, English style."

To that, Louisa laughed. "You're a dreamer."

"What, and you aren't?"

Louisa stroked her pretty kitty, whispering in his ear, "Tell Court to go soak her head."

Chapter 8

At breakfast on Friday, Annie helped little John by cutting his sausage into small bites. Then she poured some more fresh milk for Zach. Both boys were exceptionally quiet this morning, and she wondered if they'd heard something of their father's plight.

Esther talked about having seen Julia again. "Your cousin's inviting us to attend prayer meeting sometime."

The brethren weren't so much opposed to prayer gatherings as they were to Bible studies, Annie knew. She had never understood why the Amish ministers were outspokenly opposed to the study of Scripture. "I could baby-sit while you go," Annie said.

Essie looked at her. "You're not much interested, then?"

"Oh, I don't know, really."

"I do wish you'd go with me." There

was pleading in Essie's voice. "I wish . . ." She stopped abruptly.

"You wish I'd accept your faith?" Annie finished for her.

Essie smiled, nodding her head. "You know me well, and jah, I surely do."

"Ach, I'm already beginning to feel a bit cut off from the People," Annie confessed. She lowered her voice so as not to involve the children, "Livin' here . . . since you're under the shun and all."

"I wondered if that was goin' to be a struggle."

Annie reached over and clasped her friend's hand. "You know I'd do most anything for ya, don't you, Essie?"

Essie smiled. "It must be hard, you stayin' here . . . being the preacher's daughter, too. That can't help things. Folk expect more from you."

Annie couldn't disagree with that. "I see changes in you, Essie. When you speak of you-know-who, well, I don't notice as much bitterness anymore." She was careful not to spell it out too directly in case Laura and Zach should understand she was speaking of their Dat.

"God is giving me the ability to endure this hard trial day by day." Essie paused to drink her coffee, then slowly she began again. "Without His love, I could not be so calm . . . or forgiving."

Annie shook her head. "You mean you honestly forgive him?"

"Yes. Forgiveness is proof of love."

Annie was stunned. Zeke had treated Essie and the children horribly and now claimed to be a murderer. Could Essie simply overlook that? "Well, your God must be different than mine." *At least, the Jehovah God I grew up knowing.*

"He's filled me up with His loving-kindness," Essie said. "And that's all I can tell you."

Never before had she seen the likes of Essie's attitude. She supposed that if Zeke ever got out of jail, his wife would take him back with open arms. The thought made her worry all the more.

"Oh, you would not believe the changes happening in the Amish world," Louisa told Michael by cell phone. She was driving to the studio, having left the house a bit early, as she wanted to work on her own project before her students arrived. Michael had caught her as she was making the turn into the little strip mall where her studio was located. Now she sat in her car, wondering why he had really contacted her again. Was Courtney right, after all?

"I read somewhere that Amish women are using cell phones, recharging them at their craft shops in town." Michael laughed softly. "Is that true?"

"Yes. Some of the less traditional bishops are allowing them, but only for work-related business." Saying this, she almost felt as if she were betraying a confidence. "They aren't to use their phones for personal reasons." Even so, she had heard some of the women talking fast in Dutch and laughing on occasion. Of course, she hadn't ever questioned Annie on the subject, though she'd wondered. "Why do you ask?" Louisa was curious as to why he would bring this up.

"Ever since you moved to Pennsylvania, I've been noticing articles coming out about the Amish in Lancaster County and in Holmes County, Ohio."

"I'm impressed! One's the original Anabaptist settlement and the other is the largest community of Amish in the entire world." She smiled to herself and added in her best announcer voice, "For two tall lattes, can you tell me which is which?"

Michael paused. "Uh . . . no."

"Wrong answer. Pennsylvania's Plain

community came first, in the early 1700s."

He chuckled, then asked, "Why Pennsylvania?"

Is he really interested? she wondered. Still, she answered seriously, "William Penn offered land to people who wanted sanctuary from persecution, such as Quakers, Amish, and Mennonites. Some of the original Amish communities migrated to Ohio many years later from one of the original Pennsylvania settlements in Somerset County. I've read up a lot on Annie's people, as you can tell." She waited for his response and was somewhat surprised when he said he'd like to continue their discussion over lunch.

So this was where he had been leading her. "I'm busy with students all day today," she said, which was true.

"I can wait till you're free," he said quickly. "You pick the day."

She flinched. "Michael . . . we really don't want to do this, do we?"

"Do what? Have a harmless lunch for old time's sake?"

Harmless, my eye.

"C'mon, Louisa, what can it hurt?"

She didn't know how to answer. His changing career paths did have her curious, though. It was hard to believe he had walked away from the lucrative position offered him by her father.

"We can put a cap on it, if that would make you feel better," he offered.

"Like what?"

"A one-hour lunch. No longer. How's that?"

She paused, then agreed. "All right. I'll meet you for lunch next week. How's Wednesday?"

She felt his exuberance through the phone. "Wednesday it is."

But after his call, she realized he hadn't specified the place. *Which will give him another excuse to phone again,* she thought.

Walking up the sidewalk to her studio, she was reminded once again how shrewd her former fiancé had often been. *Why am I agreeing to see him, anyway?*

———————

Annie quickly finished up mending some odds and ends of clothing for Essie before midmorning. After folding and putting away the children's items, she had a hankering to write to Lou. She had begun to miss her desk back home, wishing at times like this she'd had Yonie haul it over here. Instead she made do with a book in her lap and her stationery placed on top, as she had before.

Happily, she began to write to her beloved fancy pen pal.

Dear Lou,

I hope you don't mind me using the nickname Yonie and I picked for you. It might seem peculiar seeing Lou written at the top of my letter now that you're back teaching your art students again, back in your modern world. Tell me if it bothers you, all right? Also, tell me if you'd rather I didn't bring up your connection to Sam, which must cause you many different feelings nowadays. (If you're anything like me, you're terribly lonesome for him, just as I am for Ben, though no one knows it but you.)

Well, enough about that. You haven't said much about Michael in your letters, so I guess I'm wondering how he fits into your life now that you're a fancy girl again, if he does at all. Oh, this is so hard trying to share with you on paper, when we became so close face to face!

I miss our talks and all the laughter. It seems like months since you were here. How's Muffin? Is he settled back into his cozy place in your apartment? I wonder if he misses being here.

Annie paused, looking out the window.

"I'm rambling," she whispered. Never before had she experienced difficulty in expressing herself while writing a letter. Never to Louisa, anyway.

She tried to picture the pretty apartment where Lou lived and the studio where she instructed her eager students.

Sighing, Annie resumed her writing.

> *I've begun marking off the days on the calendar, and I'm sure you can guess why. On July 17 my promise to Daed will be up, and I have plans to start painting again. Are you surprised? I'm sure my father would be . . . and furious with me besides. There are rumors that the preacher's daughter is causing a stir amongst the People, what with my art published on that magazine cover AND my staying here with shunned Esther. And now the preacher's son is driving a car, too! Add to this Zeke saying he killed his brother, and all of Paradise seems to be in an uproar.*
>
> *I went to see Mamm a few days ago and it felt odd to be a visitor in my old home. I haven't gone to Preaching since moving here to Essie's, but if I were to go, I can only imagine the stern looks on the faces of the brethren and others. Truth be known, I almost prefer avoiding the stress and simply going with Essie and the chil-*

dren to Julia's church.

There's more to that. You see, I've been listening right quiet-like when Essie talks about her "Lord Jesus." I'm not saying that I agree with anything thus far, but something is happening inside of me. My heart—Essie calls it my spirit— is growing ever so soft to all her spiritual talk. And I've found myself whispering prayers at night instead of thinking the rote ones in my head.

I'm anxious to know what you think. Tell me if it's the strangest thing you've heard from me yet. All right?

I look forward to getting your next letter. And I send you a dear hug over the miles.

Love from your Amish friend,
Annie Zook

She placed a stamp on the addressed envelope before hurrying downstairs to help Esther with the noon meal preparations, dicing cooked potatoes for a big batch of potato salad she and Essie planned to take to the family of a sick neighbor that afternoon. "I can only imagine how this gesture of kindness will be received," Annie said.

To this, Essie nodded. "We can keep giving even if the gift is refused."

"You just amaze me," Annie said, chopping away.

"Ain't me." Essie's eyes glistened. "It's God's spirit in me."

Annie was beginning to believe her, for there seemed no way Essie's devotion to helpfulness—despite continual rejection—could be from anything other than a heavenly source.

Chapter 9

Zeke peered through the glass separating him from his visitor at the county prison. He leaned back in his chair and looked across at Jesse Zook, wearing his for-good clothes. "Hullo, Preacher. What's the weather like out today?"

"Mighty nice, I daresay." Jesse paused, a brief smile appearing. "A gut day to be in the clear, Ezekiel."

"What's that ya say?"

"You're free to leave here. The court is releasing you to my custody."

I'm in the clear? "How can that be?"

The preacher began to explain what the police had told him—how the initial report on the bones had come back from forensics. "They aren't at all what we thought. It's downright surprising, but the bones are the remains of a six-year-old *girl*! They matched

right up with a cold case, connecting a confessed serial killer to the dead girl."

Zeke felt dizzy-headed. Was he dreaming? How could it be . . . Isaac's bones were
someone else's?

Mighty strange if true, he thought, looking at his arm where they'd taken blood
samples. They had taken snippets of hair,
too. Gotten permission from the judge, he'd
been told, although he hadn't been needed
at the courthouse on that particular day.
Something called a search warrant had been
granted, ordered by the court and coordi-
nated by the police.

"So, you've helped solve a long-ago
crime," Jesse told him.

Zeke stared at his feet. They felt awful
cold, right through his shoes—through his
socks, too. So were his hands, now that he
thought on it. In all truth, he had been shiv-
ering endlessly for the past few days.

He knew he ought to raise his head and
pay attention, so at last he did. "I'm all be-
fuddled." Zeke knocked on his chest with
his fist.

"You'll be returning to the People today.
I'm here to take you back."

Zeke shook his head. "There's no place
for me now. . . . I tell you, everywhere I
look, I see blackness, Preacher."

"You aren't to blame for any killing, Zeke. Don't you see, this is not your doing?"

"The voice says so. You just don't know."

Jesse frowned. "What's that you say?"

"In my brain. I hear it, Preacher. Each and every day . . . an accusing voice."

"This will all pass in due time—once you understand you're free. You had nothing to do with your brother's death. That is, if he's even dead. We don't know one way or the other."

"No . . . no, I *am* at fault."

"You're lying to yourself, Zeke. Listen . . . you did not kill your brother as you supposed. The bones are not Isaac's."

Saying he'd meet him out front, Jessie excused himself, but Zeke continued to sit there until the guard came to remove his handcuffs. *I'm goin' home.* And with the realization, he shuddered.

Annie was walking back to Essie's after delivering the potato salad to the neighbor when she saw Yonie driving his car, with Daed and Zeke riding in the back seat, of all things! She stopped walking and watched as her brother made the turn into her family's driveway. *Well, what the world?*

Then she understood. "Zeke is out of jail!" She ran toward the house, not thinking what she was doing. Even so, she couldn't understand why Daed was bringing Zeke back here of all places . . . and why Daed had allowed Yonie to drive them. *Ach, nothin' round here makes sense anymore.*

By the time she reached the yard, the three of them were making their way inside through the back door. Pausing to catch her breath, her brain began to spin through the possibilities. *Did Daed help Zeke out of his pickle? What could've happened?*

Last she'd heard, Zeke had admitted to killing Isaac, which had never made sense to her. But someone's bones were part of all this. What of those?

Annie slowly walked toward the back door and slipped inside. Not wanting to eavesdrop because that sin was equal to most any other in the Good Book, according to her father, anyway, she made some noise in the outer porch, taking time to remove her sweater. Even with that amount of rustling, the men continued to talk in the kitchen, seemingly unaware of her. Since she couldn't be seen, she wondered what to do next. Cough? Shut the door again? Or were they so caught up in whatever they were doing they truly did not care if they were overheard?

What came out of Daed's mouth just then shocked her no end. "You must cease your talk of being guilty, Zeke. Those bones aren't Isaac's. You are mighty troubled, is all. I'll look after you here . . . till you're better able to return to your family."

Annie was glad no mention had been made of her staying with Essie. She was ever so sure Zeke wouldn't take too kindly to that.

Zeke was saying something now, although she couldn't quite make it out. Something to do with wanting Yonie to drive him somewhere.

No, no . . . not home to Essie!

Annie cringed as she listened, hoping Daed would put the nix on that.

"Listen to me," Daed said. "It's high time you got some rest and had a nice hot meal. You'll stay upstairs in the Dawdi Haus for a few days. We'll see how you're doin' after that."

Zeke replied, "I wish I could see my wife . . . even just a glimpse of her."

Annie cringed, felt the roots of her hair tingle on her scalp. *Ach, say no, Daed! Essie isn't ready to handle Zeke yet.*

"We'll see what the brethren have to say

on that," Daed told him.

"Jah. Always what the brethren want, ain't?" Zeke's speech sounded slurred, like he'd been drinking alcohol, though Annie couldn't imagine how that could be. His words were biting, too. Wasn't this man grateful to be out where the sun could shine on his ruddy face, send a ray of hope to his hardened heart? She couldn't understand why Zeke had always been something of an oozing wound. He'd taken the loss of Isaac much too far, and now he was "mighty troubled," according to Daed. What did it mean for her father to bring him home here to dear Mamm . . . and Dawdi and Mammi Zook, too? Where was the wisdom in this?

Feeling horrid about listening in and not wishing to hear more, she reached for her sweater and let herself silently out the door.

I must hurry and tell Esther! Oh, poor, dear Essie.

———————

Everything would have been going according to plan by now. Ben would have applied to the Peace Corps and been making plans to leave home for overseas somewhere. *Anywhere I can make a difference.*

Instead he kept busy around the house for a few days, helping Mom with spring cleaning—sweeping out the rain gutters, hauling large boxes of sorted clothing and other odds and ends downtown to the Goodwill, flipping mattresses, moving furniture, and taking down window drapes to be professionally cleaned. He did all this to pull his own weight, not wanting to leech off his parents while home. Well, while *here*.

Curious as he was, Mom had asked him to wait until Dad returned from a business trip before they delved further into his past. Ben had sensed there was more to the adoption story. Much more.

The evening Dad returned, following supper, Ben sat brooding while Dad reclined in his favorite chair rustling with the paper. Ben reached over to the stack of books and magazines on the end table and idly pulled a few onto his lap. The top one, he noticed, was a Bible. He opened a sports magazine instead. Mom wandered over to sit with him on the sofa. "You're a lost soul these days." She touched his shoulder. "Is it so difficult to discover I'm not your first mother?"

He felt his pulse pound. It was not so much *that* as it was the secret withheld. His life. His right to know. "I'm reading," he mumbled.

She eyed his magazine, then Dad. "I

think you'd rather talk, son."

He winced, not even attempting to keep the scowl from his face. This woman had been a party to deceit, as he saw it. He said nothing for a time, trying to find some memory from his distant childhood, wondering why it was easy to remember things that had happened when he was a few years older, like moving out of his childhood bedroom to make room for one of his sisters. But why couldn't he remember anything from his earlier years—not even an important event like a birthday?

Suddenly a strange memory scurried across his mind before disappearing again. This woman, his mom, handing him some new bright white shoes. He remembered looking at them in surprise, the shoes seeming so strange, so oddly foreign to him. Why had he thought of that now? Why could he not recall the day of his adoption? Why could he not make heads or tails of any of this alarming news?

Mom spoke up, interrupting his thoughts. "We'll tell you everything we know, Ben, though it isn't much. I'm sorry we didn't tell you sooner."

"We both are, son," Dad said, getting up and coming over to sit near Ben.

"Why was it necessary to keep my

adoption from me?" He clenched his fists, looking at both parents.

Dad leaned forward, staring at his hands. "One thing led to another, Ben. That's the only way to describe what happened."

Mom shook her head and looked like she was trying not to cry. "Your father's right. Nothing about your entrance into our lives was the way we'd planned."

"Planned" . . . *not "hoped,"* but he decided the latter was precisely what she'd meant. They had most likely hoped for something, someone far different. Had they simply settled for him?

Dad inhaled slowly. "We were foster parents," he said with some degree of pride. "Had just become eligible to care for children."

Ben listened, furious with them, yet he yearned to know everything they knew and more. He longed to know why his mother— his first mother or real mother or whatever it was you called the woman who birthed you—hadn't kept him.

"I see it in your eyes, Ben. You despise the truth, but you do want to know," Mom added.

He bit his lip. Why was this difficult? Why was he struggling so?

"We can't let you simply imagine the rest," Mom said.

He had to hear the story—how it happened that he'd come to be adopted by the Martins. "All right, tell me. Tell me everything."

"You officially became Benjamin David Martin," his dad started, "six months to the day after your arrival on a stranger's front porch in downtown Marion, Kentucky."

Listening, Ben guarded his soul.

According to the Department of Social Services report, the wide-eyed boy was approximately four years old on the day he was discovered lost. He was too traumatized to speak, and for months they understood him to be mute, but not deaf. When he did finally talk, after the adoption was final— and after months of therapy—his language was considered a folk rendering of the Pennsylvania German dialect, or so said the linguist who had been hired to translate the boy's terror-filled babbling. This meant he was from Pennsylvania or any of the other numerous states where the Pennsylvania Amish had migrated to find fertile land.

When asked his name, the boy answered in halting English only after much coaxing. "I . . . Zach," he whispered. Short for

Zachary, the linguist concluded.

Vague on his hometown and his parents' names, the boy eventually hinted at having been taken against his will by a big *Mann* who frightened him. The boy knew little more, or at least was too disturbed to say.

The Martins received Zachary into their home while officials searched for his family. But his description had never shown up on any missing persons report.

"So we kept you and cared for you," Mom explained, "and your dad and I loved you so much we secretly hoped you might become our son. Then in a surprisingly short time, you were eligible to be adopted."

Ben considered these puzzle pieces of his life, so foreign to him. How did they fit together with what he *thought* he knew? "I didn't know where I lived?" he asked.

"No," his father spoke up. "And even after extensive searching by the authorities, we never found out where you were from."

"My parents never reported me missing?" *How bizarre is that?*

"We always wondered about that, as well. Made no sense . . . you were the most darling boy." Mom looked at him fondly. "We thought perhaps you'd been orphaned. We had so little to go on. You wore ordinary clothes—though they were very big on you, I remember. You had no identifying marks, no medical bracelet, no backpack of belongings that might have indicated your origins."

Ben fiddled with the magazine in his lap, growing more and more frustrated.

"You carried nothing, Ben, except for an old peach stone in your pocket. You clung to it as if it were a prized treasure," Dad said.

Staring at them now, Ben suddenly felt strangely disconnected from these people. Had he always been so completely unaware they were not related to him, or had he known on some subconscious level? "You still have no idea who my parents were?"

"Sadly, no."

He was beginning to think he must have been dropped off by the side of the road . . . dumped like some unwanted stray.

He leaned forward, staring at the floor. He recalled a nagging memory from the past—a mischievous cousin's visit, and Sherri and Patrice jumping all over the joke about him being adopted.

Aware of the silence, he asked, "Did my sisters ever suspect I wasn't their biological brother?"

"Not that I know of," Mom offered.

"Why did you change my name from Zach to Ben?"

Mom sighed. "I suppose that was selfishness on our part. Your Dad had always hoped . . . always planned . . . to name his son after *his* father, Benjamin David. When we adopted you, we had all but given up hope of having a son of our own. But you became our son. Our only son. You have to understand that we loved you as our own from the beginning, Ben. Still do. We became so attached to you, loved you so much, that we, or at least I, feared someone might try to take you away from us. You may think that paranoid, but I've talked to enough adoptive parents to know it's a common fear. We wanted to give you a new identity as our son and, yes, to protect you."

"Protect yourselves, you mean," he whispered. He was moved by her words but fought the compassion that swelled within him, burying it under his pain, his feeling of betrayal.

"I don't know how we kept it quiet for so long," Mom went on. "Your dad's work associates knew, as did a few of my girlfriends. It was an enormous risk we took . . . and now I see it was so unnecessary."

"A little late for that." Wanting suddenly to be alone, Ben rose and hurried from the room, the books and magazine still in his hand. He tromped downstairs to his bedroom off the family room, where they'd moved him on his twelfth birthday, when he was old enough to want his own space. *A boy needs his privacy,* the man of the house had said. And they had all agreed their only son should move downstairs to the basement. *More up than down,* Mom had said. Funny he should remember that. In effect, she'd wanted him to know he was gaining ground, getting a much larger room—his own bath, things like that. But with more space came more responsibility, he had been told.

Ben paced a while, did fifty fast sit-ups, then lay on his bed, staring at the window. Another memory fluttered through his brain, so short and insignificant he scarcely believed it was a memory at all. Green shades on windows in a long front room of a farmhouse. *Was it Zeke and Esther's house?*

Restless, he picked up the Bible he'd inadvertently brought downstairs with him. He thumbed through it and his eyes fell on a Scripture he'd heard somewhere before. *"And we know that all things work together for good to them that love God, to them who are the called according to his purpose."*

"All things?" he muttered, reading the

verse again. "How can that possibly be?"

Feeling the need to get out of the house, he grabbed his keys and headed back upstairs and out to his car. In some illogical way, driving over the winding country roads seemed to be a good idea right now. He was eager for the serene sight of thriving stands of trees and horses grazing on lush grassland.

"All the beautiful, simple things," Annie had often said with a big smile on her sweet face. How he missed her!

What if he simply wrote her a short letter? Would that be so bad?

No, he reminded himself, *I don't want to cause her any more trouble.*

Yet at this moment she seemed more closely related to him than anyone on the face of the earth.

Chapter 10

With the news of Zeke's release, Annie's emotions were a jumbled mire of relief, then worry, and back again. When she arrived at Hochstetlers', Annie sat Essie down and told her in hushed tones everything she'd overheard about Zeke. "Your husband's free. . . . The bones weren't Isaac's after all."

Esther looked both numb and sad.

"I thought you'd be happy to hear this," Annie said, intently looking at her. "Zeke's innocent."

Tears welled up and Essie turned away.

"What is it?"

Essie shook her head. "I can't believe this. He's out of jail, ya say? Comin' home?"

"Well, no, not just yet he's not."

"Why not?"

"He needs some lookin' after, according

to Daed." She explained that her father was handling things. That in due time, Zeke would return home again.

"So then, something's still the matter?"

"Zeke's a little mixed up, I guess. Still thinks he's guilty. Might be best for my Daed to oversee him for a time, especially with young children in the house here . . . and the baby."

Essie burst out sobbing again. "And . . . ach, Annie, another . . . on the way, too."

Shocked that Essie should cry over such a thing, Annie didn't know what to say.

"You daresn't breathe a word . . .'cause you don't know what the Bann requires of marrieds, Annie." A frown on her face, Essie glanced toward the doorway. "And I'm not goin' to say fully." Essie nodded her head, hands shaking as she fumbled in her pocket for a hankie. "Zeke's sin will be found out, is all. He'll be shunned, too."

Annie didn't comprehend at first, but slowly she began to put it together, feeling terribly embarrassed as the light dawned. "I'm awful sorry for you both. Not 'cause of a new life coming, not that at all." She patted Essie's arm softly. "Are you sure you're expecting another wee one?"

"Jah. Now I am."

Annie kissed Esther's cheek and wiped

away her tears. "Well, this is a good time to be puttin' your newfound faith to work, ain't so, dear one?"

That brought the sweetest smile to Essie's face, and Annie took heart, hoping she hadn't spoken out of turn.

———

At noon the day after his release, Zeke sat stiffly in the small front room of the Zooks' Dawdi Haus. Preacher Jesse's parents had vacated the room a quarter hour before, making their way feebly over to the main house. Zeke had watched them without offering to assist, not because he didn't want to but because he felt too weak to move. By now they were surely preparing to sit down for dinner. Zeke, however, had no desire to eat, having refused all offers of food and drink since coming here. He was not at all inclined to change his mind on that point.

Talking to himself about having to stay here at the preacher's place, he was somewhat irked when he looked up and saw Jesse standing in the doorway with Irvin Ranck right behind him. "Look's like you've got yourself some company," Jesse said. "Since you ain't hungry, maybe some talk will give you an appetite."

Nodding awkwardly to Zeke, Irvin looked sober-faced at first. "Hello again, Zeke. I drove right here when Jesse told me of your release. Certainly hope you don't mind me barging in."

"Not to worry," Jesse offered, slipping back through the connecting door and leaving the two men alone.

"Take a load off, Irvin." Zeke motioned toward the vacant chair. "I know you've got something to say, jah?" Zeke hung his head, then jerked up. "I'm out of jail, but what good's it doin' me?"

Irvin sat across from him, unbuttoning his windbreaker. "I'd say, time to rejoice."

"No joy in it for me."

Irvin leaned forward, face beaming. "Well, there can be."

Zeke breathed in mighty deep. "I guess then you've never had to put up with such a heavy cloud. Guilt, I tell ya. Thick enough to slice through. Nee—no, solid enough to chop through with a hatchet."

"You're not a murderer, Zeke."

He shook his head. "But I was responsible for Isaac. I know it."

"But you didn't kill him, don't you see?"

"Oh, sure I did. In every way important, I did."

"Look, Zeke . . . you're not thinking clearly."

He huffed at that. What gave this man, this outsider, really, the right to come over here and talk like this?

Irvin wrinkled his brow. "You got your life back. A second chance, so to speak."

That caught Zeke's attention. But even so, he didn't see how this changed anything. He was still as guilty as before this recent news that the bones were those of a missing little girl. Just because the bones weren't Isaac's didn't mean he hadn't caused his brother's death. Why was this so hard for everyone to accept?

Irvin pulled out a small New Testament from his shirt pocket. "This may sound peculiar to you, but I want you to imagine the Lord Jesus nailed to a crossbeam. For you He died, Zeke. For the blame of sin you feel so strongly."

Zeke sighed, pulling on his beard. *Same old salvation talk.* He was starting to feel nauseated. From not eating, he guessed.

Irvin kept yapping. "No matter what you've done . . . or think you've done, God's Son can and will forgive you."

Zeke wanted to stop up his ears. Feeling strangely dizzy, he closed his eyes, then blinked them open, only to find Irvin still sitting there, his hair parted on the side, combed like it always was, eyes bright, face clean-shaven.

"We can trust the Savior even when we can't trust ourselves."

Zeke ran his hands through his hair, wishing he could sort out all the chaos—the unrelenting noise—in his head. His leg twitched and he felt pressure behind his eyes. "You're goin' to get me shunned if you keep talkin' this way." He glanced toward the preacher's side of the house. "Himmel, you sound like my Esther, you know that?"

Irvin nodded, smiling. "Better to be shunned on earth than for God to turn His back on you on that day of days."

Irvin's words jolted Zeke.

"Miracles still happen," Irvin continued.

"Maybe for other folk . . . not for me."

"God's love outshines all, even when we think we're unworthy."

Zeke sneered. "The Lord God has left me. Ain't that easy to see?"

Just then, Preacher Zook's dismayed face appeared in the doorway. He had heard, probably, Irvin's salvation talk and wanted to put the nix on it. "Why don't you join us for a nice hot meal?" Jesse was including both men in his invitation.

"I'll accept if Zeke here will." Irvin rose and waited.

But Zeke stayed put. He could feel his neck muscles tense. "Count me out," he uttered.

Ben stared out the window, watching a bird preen on the sill. *Love conceals itself deep in the gaps of longing, between finding and losing . . . and finding again.* He didn't know where he'd heard this, or if perhaps he had read it somewhere. Either way, it was true of him. "All too true," he whispered, glad for the privacy of the empty family room.

Torn between loneliness and concern for Annie's family situation, Ben decided to take a risk. *At the very least, she and I can be friends,* he told himself. *And I could use a friend.*

Writing the date, *Saturday, May 6,* he began to put his thoughts on paper.

> *Dear Annie,*
> *I wish we could have said a proper good-bye before I left so suddenly. I've wanted to let you know that I'm back in Kentucky again and doing well. It's good to be home.*

He lifted his pen and shook his head.

What he'd written so far wasn't even re-
motely indicative of his true feelings, but he
didn't wish to worry her.

*My sisters were glad to see me again,
but you know how it is with siblings. I
still wish I might have had the opportunity to introduce you to my family.*

*I just wanted to say again that I en-
joyed getting to know you. I won't forget
you, Annie, nor can I simply dismiss my
time in Amish country, short as it was.*

*I hope you'll be very happy—what-
ever you decide to do.*

He cringed. Is this what he really wanted to say? No. He wanted to tell her how
disconnected he felt. How much he missed
their conversations. How much he missed
her.

But what good could possibly come of
it? He took a deep breath and finished his
letter.

*I'd love to hear from you, just to be
assured that things are all right. But
please don't feel any pressure, as I understand your situation. (I'm sending this in
care of Irvin Ranck in hopes that it might
find its way to you.) The last thing I
want to do is to trouble either you or your
family, as I have in the past.*

Your friend,
Ben Martin

Rereading his letter, Ben was tempted to crumple it up and throw it away. *How can I be so selfish? Surely she's glad to be rid of me.*

In the end, desperation won out and he mailed it.

————

Late in the afternoon, Annie had just returned from her usual Tuesday cleaning job at the Rancks' when Julia Ranck came driving up the lane. *Maybe I left something there,* Annie thought.

All aglow, her cousin came rushing into the house through the back door. Dressed in one of her floral-print dresses, Julia called to her, standing in the middle of the kitchen, smiling to beat the band. "Annie . . . Annie!"

"I'm right here, for goodness' sake." Annie set the baby down in her playpen and hurried to greet her. "Did I forget something?"

Julia held out an envelope. "It arrived in the mail right after you left."

Annie's heart leaped at the sight of Ben Martin's name on the return address. *Why's he writing to me? Oh, I hope he's all right.* She studied his firm hand and saw her name written beneath Irvin's, where Ben had sent this in order to avoid her father's scrutiny, she guessed.

"For goodness' sake," Annie whispered, moving toward the sitting room, away from the kitchen. "Do you mind?" She wished to read the letter in private, so she slipped away, leaving Julia alone with the baby in the kitchen. She knew Essie was upstairs getting the boys up from their naps, and Laura was playing outside.

Annie sat near the window for the best natural light and held the envelope next to her heart. "Dare I read it?" she whispered into the quietude. "Dare I *not?*" She opened the envelope, unable to draw a full breath, she was so elated.

When she'd finished reading Ben's words, she couldn't stop smiling. *I won't forget you, Annie. . . .*

She folded the letter feeling giddy, and then at once she felt sad, too, missing him.

With a sigh, she slipped the letter into her dress pocket. Her first free minute she would write a reply, as there was nothing and no one to hold her back now that she was not living at home.

"Oh, Ben, I have so much to tell you," she whispered, brushing a tear away. To think he'd contacted her again. He surely knew how fond she was of him . . . how she'd dreaded sending him away.

She inhaled deeply, straightened her apron, and headed back to the kitchen and Cousin Julia.

Chapter 11

Wednesday at noon, Louisa met Michael in the lobby of Maggiano's Little Italy on the Sixteenth Street Mall in downtown Denver. When he had called back to suggest this restaurant, she hadn't been surprised. It was one of her favorites.

"Hey," he said, smiling when he saw her. She noticed his eagerness and returned the smile.

They were shown to their reserved table, with a red-and-white-checkered table-cloth, surrounded by Old World ambiance—fake bread in baskets and bottles of wine on the wall. After they were seated, Michael asked how her day was going.

"Really well. How about yours?" she said, turning the question back on him.

"Interesting. I'm in the middle of helping with legwork on a much-publicized murder trial. It's time-consuming but challenging."

"Sounds like it," she said. "Are you enjoying your new line of work?"

"Yes, very much. Though it's a whole different world than all those prenups and divorces I used to handle."

"I don't know . . . divorce and murder both sound pretty violent to me."

He chuckled.

Then she asked more seriously, "Have you been successful in dodging the media?"

"So far." He handed her one of the menus. "And since I really can't talk about the case . . . let's see what you'd like to eat."

She opened the menu and scanned the choices. "I don't see any apple butter on here," she joked. "Or shoofly pie."

He glanced over his menu at her. "I've heard of that pie. Sickeningly rich, right?"

"The mother of all rich desserts. The best is the wet bottom kind, unique to Lancaster County."

He closed his menu. "Louisa, look, I'm not here to discuss Amish desserts, as I'm sure you know."

"Neither am I." She looked over at him. "So why *are* we here, Michael?"

He was staring at her. "I'd like to see if there's anything left of us," he said, his voice noticeably ringing with expectation. "Is that so surprising?" He continued talking, re-hashing their past—all the things that had led Louisa to cancel their wedding last fall—then voicing his frustration and anguish at her sudden leaving.

She let him talk, listening and wanting very much not to hurt him further. Even so, she was hesitant to let him think this lunch-eon date heralded the continuation of their former relationship. Although the way she felt when he smiled at her almost made her wish he'd never revealed her father's match-making scheme.

"You must try 'n' eat," Barbara Zook coaxed him.

Zeke shook his head in short jerks. He had been sitting in the same chair all day—for more than a full day, he realized. He'd sat here to sleep, to read, to stare, and now he was sitting here telling the preacher's wife to leave him be, in so many words.

"You'll feel better if you have some-thing, Zeke," she said, standing in the door-way that led to the large front room of the main house.

She smiled. "You're welcome to have your pick of pies. I've got apple, and there's chocolate silk. Oh, and a few slices of banana cream from yesterday. Which would you like?"

He knew she was hoping he'd bite. And the banana cream did sound mighty tasty, but it reminded him of Esther, and that put him right back under the mist in his mind. The haze of tormented thoughts and his grief over the news of his mother's death— all of it—overwhelmed him. Even though he saw that Barbara's mouth was still moving, he heard not a word.

Some time later, Preacher Jesse came over to see him, bringing a tall glass of water. "Here, best be drinkin' this. . . . Small swallows to start." He was telling Zeke what to do, and Zeke didn't like it— not one bit. "You'll dry out on us and we can't have that."

"Might land me in a hospital somewhere," Zeke whispered.

"Which might not be such a bad idea, really."

Zeke didn't know what Jesse meant. "What's that ya say?"

"Been over to see the folk at Philhaven, in Mount Gretna, today. They've got a room waitin' for you if you'd like to go and get to feeling some better."

They can't get me to eat here, that's why.

"I'm fine here. Don't need no doctor." He'd heard all about that place for mental folk. There'd been a call for Amish house parents some time back, if he remembered correctly.

"Come on, Zeke. What do you say?" asked Jesse.

Zeke bowed his head, the lump in his throat threatening to turn into a tear in his eye. "I'm not myself. Ain't been for quite a while." A sudden fire ignited in him. "But I have no interest in goin' anywhere 'cept home. So leave me be!"

Jesse sat across from him. "You're to be in my custody, Zeke. Don't think it was easy getting the police to do it that way. They wanted to release you to an English institution first, but I spoke up. It's 'cause of me you're not there already. They believe you to be a detriment to your family . . . from your own mouth. Remember what you told them that day the police came and picked you up?"

Zeke wished he had earplugs or something to push into his ears. He sure didn't want to be reminded of what he'd said or what he didn't say . . . or what he should've said. Truth was, he was here now, in this chair, and he didn't much feel like budging.

Jesse reached over and put a hand on his

shoulder. "I'll see to gettin' you there, if you'd like to get better."

"If you need to be getting back to your routine here . . . you and your missus, then just say so." He knew he was glaring, because he felt the burning behind his eyes.

"You're no bother a'tall," he heard Jesse say, but he saw the frustration in the way the preacher's eyes squinted, his mouth all pinched up.

I'm in the way. He recalled having the same feeling as a boy, of being rejected by those who supposedly loved him most. His father, for one. "I know when my welcome's wore out." Reluctantly he rose. He refused to be underfoot the way he surely was here.

Passing through the kitchen, Zeke tuned out the chatter from both Jesse's wife and his elderly mamma, then scuffed his way outside toward Yonie's car.

The entire ride was a blur in his brain, and when they arrived in Mount Gretna at the sprawling place called Philhaven, he was startled by Jesse's strong hand helping him from the car and up the walkway.

"You'll have plenty of folk visitin' you while you're here," Jesse told him, guiding him toward the entrance.

"Esther too?"

"Jah, soon, Zeke. Soon."

He didn't know whether to believe the man of God or not, though he wished he could. The flat tone of Jesse's voice made him wonder if he would ever lay eyes on his sweet wife again. "They won't hurt me, will they, Preacher?" He shuddered.

"Ach, no. They're here to help. You'll see that soon enough. You'll meet with doctors twice a day."

"Not sure if I ever remember bein' well. It's been a long, long time, if at all." It felt good to admit this, though the confession was all wrapped up in the fires of guilt that burned in his soul night and day.

When Zeke asked more about where he'd be sleeping, Jesse kindly explained. "You'll have your own bed, that's certain. You'll feel right at home here. The whole place is Plain just like you're used to—no carpet on the floors, no TVs, computers, or radios. You'll like the peace of this place, Zeke. I promise you that."

He didn't reply, allowing Jesse to lead him to the door of the complex, trying hard to push away the notion that he was being led like a lamb to the slaughter.

"I'll stop by your house tomorrow and pick up several changes of clothes for you," Jesse said as they made their way inside.

"So you'll visit again?"

Jesse nodded, removing his hat. "You can count on that, Zeke. Jah, I'll see you tomorrow."

And if he wasn't mistaken, Zeke thought he heard a catch in the preacher's throat and wondered why.

Chapter 12

On the Lord's Day, Annie went with Essie and the children to the Rancks' church yet again. But after they'd all come home and eaten together, she'd felt the need to get outside and drive the horse and buggy.

Allowing Zeke's horse to plod along at his own pace, Annie pondered some of the things the minister had said from his fine wooden pulpit. She wondered if she dared crack open a Bible and begin reading the Gospel of John, which the Mennonite pastor had preached on today.

But then, in the midst of all her brooding, she spied Sam Glick walking toward her along the road. "Hullo!" she called to him, pulling on the reins.

"Annie . . . it's good to see ya." He nodded cheerfully, but his eyes turned sad when he asked about Louisa. "Is she doin' all right, do you know?"

Annie climbed out of her buggy to talk, keeping the reins in her hand. She told him Lou was living back in her own apartment and had started to teach art again.

Sam quickly changed the subject to Zeke. "I hear he's at Philhaven now."

Annie didn't let on she'd seen him with her father and brother on the day they'd brought Zeke home. "Jah. I hope he'll be all right, in time."

Sam pursed his lips, frowning. "Do you think it's true, then? That he might be a bit mental like they're sayin'?"

Annie figured Zeke must be awful bad off, otherwise her father would have kept him at home and looked after him there. "Well, I guess you'd *have* to be to think you'd killed your brother when you were only eight, jah?"

Sam nodded. "Seems like a long time ago to be just now comin' forth with something like that. Never made much sense to me when I heard it."

"Sixteen years of despair, thinking you're the one responsible for your little brother's death. I'd say a body could get awful hazy in the head thinking that way, don't you?"

"And now, what with the bones not bein' Isaac's, it seems like maybe there might be some hope in all this." Sam leaned down and picked up a twig off the ground, snapped it, and tossed the pieces toward the roadside ditch.

"Hope that Isaac could still be alive?"

Sam shrugged. "Wouldn't surprise me. Would it you?"

"Hard to believe, but I guess maybe it could be true—Isaac out there somewhere in the modern world, livin' with Englischers." She wasn't about to admit she'd fostered that hope for years. It was one of the reasons she'd painted the locust grove by the covered bridge.

Sam talked of the weather and then, surprisingly enough, he asked Annie what she thought of his writing a long letter to Louisa.

"Why are you askin'? I say write it and send it off. Let Louisa know how you feel."

He grinned at that. "Jah, I've thought as much, but . . ."

Annie took note of his hedging. "You oughtn't be worried that she won't write back. Are you?"

He shook his head. "There are worse things."

Jah, that's the truth.

"So what're you waitin' for? Write your letter and see what she says."

"Ain't what you may think, Annie. I'm not writin' to tell Louisa that I love her."

The sun felt unexpectedly too warm now. "You don't care for her after all?"

Sam pushed his hands into his trouser pockets. "That's just it," he said softly. "I do love her. And I'd do most anything to make her understand how much."

Eager to know what on earth was holding him back, she said equally quietly, "You want me to pave the way for your letter, is that it?"

He came to life. "No, no . . . don't you dare, Annie!"

"Well, what, then?" She studied his face, which was now as bright as a ripe red McIntosh apple, unsure what he meant to say.

"I'm makin' ready to do something big. And if you say a word of this to anyone, I'll . . . You just better keep mum!"

She laughed. "Oh, I'm shakin', Sam . . . look at me."

"Don't, Annie. I'm serious. I'm on the fence, ready to jump."

"Ach, I should've known." She sighed, pondering his statement. "Every fall, when baptism rolls around and you don't join church, I wonder why not."

"That's what I'm putting in my letter to Louisa. I want her to hear it from me first. Maybe she can give me some pointers about the English world."

"Oh, Sam, are you sure about this?"

"For sure and for certain."

This was good news for Louisa . . . and bad for the community. Annie could only imagine how hurt Sam's family would be, not to mention the brethren. Yet another strapping young man lost to the People.

———————

A letter with the name Samuel R. Glick in the corner of the envelope was waiting for Louisa in her mailbox when she arrived home on Wednesday afternoon, along with several pieces of junk mail and a colorful postcard of London's National Gallery in Trafalgar Square. *Louisa, please reconsider?—Trey* was scrawled across the back in a slant. More pressure, and she had no interest in this lame attempt by her former boyfriend. Her reaction had nothing to do with her lunch with Michael. There was simply no future for her and Trey. As for Michael, she really didn't know how things might go between them. He had taken her out for one nice meal and offered sensible, serious reasons why she should think about dating him again. And she had been tempted. But opening Sam's letter now, thoughts of Michael flew from her mind.

Hello, Louisa!

I've waited longer than I wanted to, really, to sit down and write. You see, I'm making every attempt to go fancy, as we Amish say. It is a tedious process, but one that has been a long time coming. You may have guessed as much, but even I didn't know how much I wanted to start a new life on the other side of the fence till a few weeks ago.

I wanted you to be one of the first to know, not that I'm presuming it will have any bearing on our friendship.

There are a good many things I've learned already since coming out from under the authority and covering of my father. I am living with a former Amish couple who are in the business of helping folk like me make a new start. I will pay them room and board for the time being, with the understanding that I'll establish myself in a house of my own (I just may build one) in the next year or so.

So, odd as it may seem, I'm working at a home improvement store. Thanks to my college degree, I am already in training for assistant manager. Imagine that! Honestly, what I'm learning ferhoodles me at times, trying to understand how these English think. (Don't take that wrong! I didn't seem to have much trouble understanding you, now, did I?!)

I've purchased a cell phone. If you wouldn't mind, I would enjoy calling you sometime . . . to see how you're getting along there.

Always your friend,
Sam

"Wow." Louisa set the letter on the coffee table, imagining the stir Sam's leaving the Amish would cause.

Looking at the letter again, she noted the way he'd signed off. Hadn't he vowed to love her always before she had so impulsively flown home? His words had burned in her memory for days, even weeks, afterward. So why the platonic-sounding sign-off? And why did it bother her?

Louisa sighed. What did she want? Was it Trey? Definitely not. Was it to renew her relationship with Michael, her former fiancé? She considered Sam Glick's confidence in pulling away from his staunch roots for a completely new life in the so-called modern world. That took real courage, and even though she was completely stunned at the timing of it, she wanted to let him know how pleased she was—without leading him on, of course. The fact was, Sam was comfortable with himself, and his leaving the Amish life behind was one more indication of that. But did that make him the man for her?

The more she contemplated her trio of male admirers, the more she realized there had been a reason for her meeting Sam when she did. "Annie would say to get myself back there before he gets away," she told her unconscious pet, watching as Muffin napped near the window. "What does his leaving mean for me? Or should I even be thinking that way?"

Louisa leaned her head back, reliving her arrival in Paradise, Pennsylvania, with Muffin in his pet carrier. She smiled, remembering how wound up she'd felt, yet anxious to meet Annie and her family and friends.

One of the best things I've ever done for myself.

Chapter 13

Sometimes feelings must be expressed, Annie thought. That was certainly true today. She hurried to gather her pale yellow stationery and best pen, then made a conscious effort to slow down as she shaped the words. *Don't hurry. This is too important.*

Stopping, she collected her thoughts. *If I were ever to see Ben again, what would I say? That I often dream I am forever trying to find my way back to him . . . always lost?*

She began to pour out her loneliness, even heartsickness, during the days without him, going so far as to admit second-guessing her resolve to obey her father's command. She wrote of living with Esther now, of feeling torn between staying with an outcast woman and returning home even while she embraced the unparalleled freedom and complete responsibility for making her own decisions.

Then, stopping the flow of too-honest expression, she looked down at the things she'd written, reading them carefully. Her letter seemed more like a personal journal entry than the kind of sentiments she ought to be sharing with an Englischer like Ben.

I shouldn't send this. It's too forward.

She decided it might be best to wait a while before responding to Ben's letter. Folding the stationery, she placed it in her drawer.

And wait she did. For several days, she tried to distract herself, keeping busy and trying to enjoy spring's blossoming blizzard of color. But the brilliant shades of loveliness all around only reminded her of her other love—and made her want to paint all the more. She wondered how she would explain her snug little art studio to innocent young Laura, Zach, and John once she got things unboxed and set up at Essie's. Oh, how she itched for the day her promise to her father concluded. *The end to the absence of my art, my life.*

Daily, and at night as she lay awake waiting for sleep, she contemplated the intense heart tug toward her great passion. She even considered having Cousin Julia take her to the gallery where Louisa had found such success in placing her paintings, to see what might be possible for *her* work. With Julia, she would not have to put any effort into explaining, for her cousin fully understood and appreciated her talent. After all, it was partly due to Julia's submitting the painting of the covered bridge and the locust grove—with the wonderful-good swing at the center—that she was in the pickle she was in now. Of course, being caught with her hair down—Ben at her side—had been the last straw.

Nearly shunned, I am. Just like Essie.

She contemplated their similar situations: Essie's heart captivated by something—*someone*, as she put it—forbidden by the Amish church. Annie's affection directed toward her art, also prohibited. "We're related in our sin," she said right out into the air, feeling frustrated and terribly bold.

———

A full week after she'd received Ben's letter, Annie was still undecided about sending hers to him. Pausing as she dusted the woodwork in her bedroom, she stared at the dresser drawer where she'd hidden the letter.

Dare I mail it?

Instead, she rose and left the room, heading downstairs to help with the children while Essie prepared supper. But when she found Essie peeling potatoes, she noticed streaks on her pretty face. "Ach, you've been crying," she whispered, leaning her head against Essie's.

Nodding, her friend placed a hand over her eyes momentarily. "Happy tears, I should say."

"Oh?"

Essie eyed the children and motioned for Annie to follow her into the sitting room. "I received a letter from Zeke. He says he's had several visitors and is getting some good help for his . . . uh, problems."

Annie had heard from Julia that Zeke was settled in and growing accustomed to his new home away from home.

"His handwriting . . ." Essie said softly. "Ach, I can actually read his writing. Oh, Annie, could this place—this Philhaven—be the thing that brings Zeke back to his senses? Might we be reunited?" Then, as suddenly as her optimism had emerged, her countenance shifted and the confident smile faded. "Ach, no. I'm shunned. And nothing's ever going to change that."

Annie's heart sank, but there were no hopeful words in either her heart or her mouth. The way she saw it, there would be no happy ending for the couple. Not as long as Essie held on to her assurance of salvation.

With that, Annie traipsed upstairs, retrieved her letter to Ben, stamped it, and slipped it into the outside mailbox.

One morning, nearly two weeks after he'd sent off his letter to Annie, Ben's mother called up the stairwell.

"Mail call!"

Eagerly, Ben opened the envelope she handed him, barely able to contain his excitement and surprise. *Annie actually wrote back!*

As he pored over the letter, he lost himself in her world again. He felt a lump in his throat as he read her admission of how much she missed him. He read and reread her letter, comforted by the unexpected honesty of her words.

This is just what I needed.

But then he began to read between the lines. Annie was as good as shunned. She'd changed her mind about baptismal instruction, and she seemed rather angry with her father.

My fault. He folded the letter and placed

it back in the envelope. Sitting at his desk, he pulled out a piece of paper and began composing a reply.

> *Dear Annie,*
> *So good to hear from you. Thank you for your wonderfully honest letter—and for trusting me with your feelings.*
> *I was sorry to hear about the problems between you and your father. I can't help wondering if I'm partially to blame.*

Ben stopped writing. This wasn't good enough. He needed to talk to her in person, find some way to correct the problems he and he alone had instigated.

Who am I kidding? he thought, chuckling at his own rationalization. *I can't stay away from this girl.*

Against his better judgment, he picked up his phone and called Irvin Ranck, guessing his former boss would be at work this time of day. After offering a greeting, he said, "I'd like to come back and talk with you, face to face . . . even though it may seem as though I just left. There are some . . . family issues I want to discuss with you. If it's all right."

"Why, sure, Ben. I'd be glad to visit with you," Irvin said. "And you should plan on staying with us."

"I wouldn't want you or Julia to go to any trouble."

"No trouble, Ben. I know Julia will be happy to have you."

"I can easily sleep in your attic room," he offered, recalling Annie's framed painting stored up there.

"Well, that's fine, if you wish."

Ben wanted to make things easy for the Rancks, and he didn't want to cause extra work for Julia or anyone. He was thinking now of Annie, as well, knowing she cleaned for the Rancks and helped with their children.

"When will you plan to arrive?" Irvin asked.

"Is tomorrow too soon?"

"Not at all."

"Then I'll probably drive straight through—takes about twelve hours if I don't stop much. If I get away early, as I hope to do, I should be there before dark." He despised motels, so he could avoid staying in one if he stepped on it.

"In time for supper?"

"I doubt it, but I'll let you know when I'm on the road."

"Sounds good, Ben. We'll look forward to seeing you."

They said good-bye and hung up.

Wanting to let his mom know about his sudden plans, Ben went in search of her. He found her outside working in her patio garden.

"I'm going back to Pennsylvania," he said. "Tomorrow."

She turned. "Why?"

"I still have so many questions. And after what you told me about my first language, Lancaster might be the place to get some answers."

Mom squeezed his arm. "I think I understand, honey." She attempted a brave smile. "This wouldn't have anything to do with that letter I gave you . . . the one with a girl's return address on it?"

He smiled back. "Well, maybe just a *little*."

While packing for his trip, Ben wondered if Annie had any idea he might show up. He could even visit her, now that she was staying at Esther's. But Irvin and Julia's home was close to Jesse Zook's, and the preacher would no doubt hear of his return. Ben wondered how to connect with Annie without creating even more problems for her.

———

Annie rinsed out a washcloth in warm

water and some liquid soap, handing it first to five-year-old James, then to Molly, almost three, waiting as they washed up before sitting at the table for lunch.

Minutes later, when Annie was helping carry the platter of roast beef sandwiches to the table, Julia whispered to her, "Ben Martin's arriving tomorrow night for a visit. I thought you might like to know."

Astonished, Annie almost said, *Are you sure?* But she knew better than to question her dear cousin and friend. "Why's he comin' back, I wonder."

Julia seemed unable to conceal her cheery smile. "Must be a good reason, I would think."

Annie couldn't believe her ears. *Ben's going to be here . . . in this house?* She cringed, recalling her too-forward response to his kind letter. Is that why he was coming?

"He just called Irvin at work. Wants to talk about 'family issues,' he said."

"Family? Whose?"

"His own, I suppose. But to tell you the truth, I'm not sure." Julia turned her attention to putting the finishing touches on their lunch, ceasing her talk of the unexpected visitor arriving tomorrow!

Annie could scarcely eat, let alone

concentrate on her chores at hand. What was so urgent to bring Ben all the way back from Kentucky?

After the children were tucked in for afternoon naps, while Julia went out to run a few errands, Annie carried the dry mop and other cleaning items upstairs to her former art studio.

Upon opening the small door, an onslaught of memories invaded her thoughts; she missed this cozy, inspiring place where she'd spent many happy hours drawing and, ultimately, painting.

But her feelings were mixed, because Esther and the children had also occupied this room not so long ago. *And now Ben will stay here, too.*

It wasn't that the room had to belong only to her, for that was impossible. This was not her house. It was the home of her father's cousins and she had been merely blessed to have the room offered her. *Blessed?* She pondered that, realizing yet again how influenced she was becoming by living at Esther's. Truly she was more than curious about Essie's devout faith.

Sighing, she set about working from the top down, the way all the womenfolk had been taught as young girls to clean house, beginning by wiping down the window frames, then cleaning and shining windowpanes. Next were the sills below and going over the walls with a damp rag. She dusted the bureau and carefully went over the legs and spindles of a lonely chair, getting in all the crevices, before washing down the woodwork. At last she dry mopped the floor.

When those tasks were completed, she put clean sheets on the guest bed brought up originally for Esther's use. It felt an oddly intimate gesture, making the bed where Ben would sleep. Smoothing the top sheet, she remembered the warm feel of her hand in his.

Looking around, she believed the room to be ready. She knew it was a downright silly thing to stay up here for as long as she could, feigning to clean, when she was all finished. Pining for the past, for what was, had nothing to offer her, yet she was somehow tied to this place, this room. And to think of Ben staying here, where she'd painted and allowed her heart to open wide to her love of art . . . well, it seemed peculiar.

Ben's coming to talk about family, Julia says. What could that possibly mean? Isn't he coming to see me?

She was afraid she might wear out the floor where Ben was concerned, pacing the small room as she was. It wasn't at all like her. Stopping, Annie sat on the chair, wondering why it was so hard to say good-bye to a place, let alone a person.

Sighing, she thought back to the first time she had ever met Ben—over yonder in the harness shop. As she did, she happened to notice her large framed painting, wedged in between the bureau and the wall. She knew another box of her paintings lay hidden in the storage cabinet, as well.

She rose and went to pick up the painting, noticing the slightest tear in the brown paper, something she'd not seen before. Quickly she dismissed it as the result of its being propped up here in this room, where young children had stayed and played and slept with their distraught mamma.

Pressing on the tape that held the wrapping together, she ran her fingers across the top of the frame, feeling the sturdiness through the paper, vacillating over whether to open it up and see it again for herself.

The painting . . . no, it was the setting that held a curious appeal for her. But with the startling news of the day—Ben's return—she felt strangely hesitant. A perplexing sense of having shared a tragic event fell over her just then, as if she had been in a buggy accident and managed to survive. She became a survivor of sorts whenever she looked at her own painting, though she had no idea why she felt that way now. So many long years had passed since they had lost Isaac.

Annie set the painting down lightly without opening the packaging.

She began to pace again, unable to bring herself to head downstairs, feeling stuck here.

Being up here has stirred me up but good.

She stopped long enough to stand in one of the dormer windows overlooking the vast fields and grazing land below. Her mind was a jumble of emotions. *Why do I still feel so close to Isaac—closer than a friend, or even a sister?* She supposed it was some form of "Absence makes the heart grow fonder." Surely she and Isaac wouldn't still be as close had he grown up in Paradise like any other boy from their church district.

And now another boy has been taken from me. She was thinking of Ben, and her father's hard stance—his insistence that she break it off. He had every right as a minister ordained of the Lord God to do so, yet he had not demanded the same of Yonie.

She felt angry, nail-spitting mad, for

having sent Ben away. Reliving her father's waiting for her in the darkness on the night she'd tiptoed back into the Dawdi Haus—hoping to hurry to her bedroom unnoticed—it was all she could do to keep from clumping her feet across the floor now, but she forced herself to be sensible. She turned to pick up the chair and carried it back to the window. Sitting there quietly, she let the sun shine on her face and shoulders.

Terribly weary, she recalled having gotten up late last night, in the wee hours, and feeling as if she hadn't fallen asleep at all, even though she knew she had. At some point she had wandered downstairs to look for some of her own newly baked cookies. She'd taken only one and poured a small glass of milk before padding back up to her room in her bare feet, mindful of the sleeping children. She had stared out the window then, too, wondering how you went about talking to almighty God the way Essie did, so personally and so effortlessly. She longed to do so herself, but did you have to break the Ordnung before you could pray that way?

She guessed so, but she didn't rightly know. She was afraid to ponder it too much now, lest she think herself right into Essie's way of believing . . . and that was not what she was being paid to do at the moment.

Rising and returning the chair to its original spot, she allowed herself one more fond look around the room. *I hope you enjoy your time here, Ben. . . .*

Chapter 14

Sitting near her wide studio window, Louisa drank her coffee, intermittently looking at her nails. *How did I ever manage without a professional manicure all those months?* She laughed softly and reached for her purse, pulling out a fingernail clipper. She knew precisely how: she had filed her nails herself. No biggee. *Mother must have thought I'd lost it for sure.*

She trimmed off a piece of unruly cuticle skin, then dropped the clippers into the small zippered pocket of her purse. She turned her attention back to the window, looking at the colorful flowers in the window box outside. The owner of the building had pushed red, yellow, and white silk flowers into the hardened earth along the walks, as well as the window boxes. An illusion of springtime. This being Colorado, the month of May often came with heavy snows and blowing winds. The "Albuquerque low" could easily close down the treacherous Monument Hill to the south and the I-25 corridor as a whole. As a result it was generally pointless to set out geraniums or other flowering plants until after the Memorial Day weekend in this unpredictable region. Still, the silk flowers were lively and pleasant if you didn't stop to look too closely—much like her own life had been, she realized, before her sojourn in Paradise.

Thinking about the short growing season here, she let her mind wander to Lancaster County, to the Zooks' farm there. She recalled the outhouse, the Saturday night baths, and washing her face each morning using the basin and pitcher Annie brought to the bedroom where she had first stayed. Later she and Annie had moved over to the cozy bedroom in the Dawdi Haus.

"Dawdi Haus." She spoke the Pennsylvania Dutch words that described the addition built onto the main house, remembering how Mammi Zook had taught her to pronounce the vowels. Now, without thinking, she began to put her hair up "by heart," as Annie often said, without the aid of a mirror, holding the thick bun she'd made of her own tresses, missing the community created by the Amish women in particular and the Plain life in general. *Have I learned enough about peace?* she wondered. *Did I stay in Paradise long enough?*

The sudden loud chirp of her phone startled her out of her musing, and she quickly let her hair fall, reaching to answer her cell. Checking the screen, she grimaced but answered, "Hey," knowing it was Michael Berkeley.

"Louisa . . . hi. I was hoping I'd catch you before you left your studio."

"Yep, I'm still here."

"I'm dying for an espresso. How does Starbucks sound? I could meet you there, or pick you up. Whatever you say."

She found this bordering on funny. "Well, you'll never guess what I'm sipping at the moment—coffee with just the right amount of chocolate. So you'll have to count me out." She paused. "But thanks."

"We could do pie instead." He was coaxing.

"Thanks anyway, Michael," she said, hard as it was to be semi-rude.

"All right. How about I come over and . . . we could talk?"

"What about?"

"Stuff . . . you know. Your day. Mine."

This wasn't the sophisticated and cool attorney she'd known. He was dying here and she was making him grovel. "Maybe some other time."

"Sure. See ya." He hung up.

She clicked off the power, not wanting to endure a repeat performance. Most girls would be thrilled to spend time with a guy like Michael. She'd seen the way other women eyed him, discreetly, of course, back when the two of them were dating. Michael was the most handsome guy she knew.

"Let's see . . . he's also bright, articulate, and rich, and he knows how to woo a lady." She sighed, reaching for her coffee mug and breathing in the delicious aroma before taking another sip. *So what's wrong with me? Why aren't I ready to take up where we left off?*

Finishing her coffee, she could hardly wait to get back to her apartment to change into her powder-pink sweats and cushy socks. She wanted to curl up with Muffin and peruse her new issue of *The Artist's Magazine*, but first she had to clean up her studio. As she picked up the last of the brushes to wash, she fondly recalled how hard she and Annie had worked to clean up after themselves in the little attic studio at

Julia's, especially without sink or access to water.

But that was the way of creativity; if there wasn't a mess to show for hours of inspiration, there probably wasn't much art to show for it, either.

Louisa went to the sink and rinsed out the brushes and her coffee mug, letting the water run longer than necessary. Staring into the sink, she decided to make a phone call. She felt nearly compelled to talk to Annie's Mennonite cousin Julia Ranck, having thought so often of their talks together.

If Julia lived nearby, I'd be hanging with her a lot these days.

Louisa turned her phone back on and called Julia. She was delighted to hear Julia's voice and such a cheerful greeting.

"It's wonderful to hear from you!" Julia said. "I was just sitting here enjoying a cup of tea."

Glad to have this opportunity to reconnect, Louisa asked if it was a good time to chat.

"Why, sure. What's on your mind?"

She couldn't just dive in and say she wanted to hear more about Julia's God, could she? She meandered a bit, groping for the right words, and as was typical of Julia, she eased things along until Louisa found herself close to tears, hungering for all this woman had to say about the Lord.

Later, after thanking Julia for her time, she hung up, then set to work scouring the paint from the sink. The smell of the non-abrasive cleanser made her nauseated, reminding her of car trips her family had taken when she was a young girl. Her mother would take along plastic bags in case of carsickness. Louisa hummed, thinking, *I'm redding up but good,* and laughed softly.

Washing her hands, she eyed the CD player and realized that the music had stopped. She dried her hands, and as she went to select a new CD, the door squeaked opened across the room.

Glancing over her shoulder, she was surprised to see Michael, sporting a vase of red roses. "Yikes," she muttered, wondering why he had decided to show up when she'd tried to put him off.

Michael looked at the flowers. "Something wrong with the color?"

"It's not that. . . ."

"You sounded down on the phone."

Maybe because I am. Remembering her manners, she took the vase from him and carried it to the sink. She filled it with warm water and set the bouquet on the counter, near her easel. "They're really beautiful," she said, turning to smile at Michael. "Thanks."

He shrugged, and it was apparent he wasn't sure what to say next.

"It's weird," she said idly. "I was just thinking back to my childhood, when Daddy took us for long drives in the mountains—up to Aspen for the summer music festival or to Breckenridge to ski, and I'd always get carsick."

He was polite, listening, making eye contact, even though he'd heard this tidbit back when they were dating. She had even taken several evenings to introduce him to her family via a bunch of scrapbooks.

She glimpsed the roses again. Fact was, Michael knew too much about her. More than any man she'd ever dated. More, at least, about the specific little things that unfold over time when two people are planning a life together, though not as much about the dreams of her heart as Sam. *And he knows nothing about my craving for spiritual things.*

"I'd like to take you out for dinner." He moved toward her. "Next weekend?"

I shouldn't.

His eyes shone with sincerity.

She hadn't forgotten their good times. But she found it impossible to overlook how they had gotten together in the first place. *Maybe someday I'll be able to forgive his part in Daddy's scheme. And maybe by then I won't still be hung up on Sam.*

Yet all that was in the past, wasn't it? His recent persistence had nothing to do with a corporate merger. Even so, was it fair to allow him to think he had a second chance with her now? She had no clue how to forge ahead with a friendship, let alone a bona fide relationship that could possibly lead them back to the wedding altar. *Full circle . . .*

"I want to get to know you again," Michael said.

She almost ached to look at him, seeing a hint of the pain he must have endured when she'd abandoned him.

"How's next Friday night?" he asked. "Or is Saturday better?"

Oh, what to do? Her feelings kept vacillating back and forth. She turned away, staring at the roses. The Amish didn't do the cut flower thing. Thoughts of Sam poked at her. She still needed to answer his letter, but what would she say? Was Sam the reason she hesitated?

"We need some time together," Michael said, trying again.

He deserves another chance . . . on his own

terms, without Daddy's interference, Louisa thought. *Doesn't he?*

Sighing, she moved back to face him. "Sure, Friday's fine. Thanks."

His eyes gleamed. "Perfect. I'll pick you up at your place."

"I have a class . . . so why don't I meet you?"

He mentioned Ruth's Chris Steak House down on Market Street.

She knew the place well—one of their former haunts. Very uptown: white table linens, attentive wait staff. "Sounds lovely." She wanted to mean it but felt stuck in limbo. She thanked him again for the roses and the dinner invitation, and watched him head for the door, an obvious spring in his step.

I must be out of my mind.

Chapter 15

Essie shuddered, a bundle of emotions—fear, hope, dread—as she approached the front desk at Philhaven. She breathed a shaky sigh, sending up a pleading prayer for something good to come of this visit.

Zeke greeted her with a big smile and gave her a peck on the cheek. He suggested they sit on the porch and she agreed, relieved not to be meeting him behind closed doors this first time. He led the way and she was comforted to see several staff people about the place. They offered kind smiles, and Essie felt reassured. Zeke could not hurt her here.

She settled into a chair on the veranda, overlooking a cheerful flower garden already blooming with daylilies, lavender, and annuals. Zeke sat a few feet from her, seemingly enjoying the sunshine, as he talked about his doctors and of attending his small-group session.

Small talk was something Zeke had never cared to do—except for his occasional comments about the weather. He inquired about the children, and it was pleasing to know that Laura, Zach, John, and the baby were keenly on his mind. Esther was quite happy to tell him how their Essie Ann was growing so fast, in a real growth spurt lately. And she described how Laura kept busy helping with weeding the flower beds and planting the family vegetable garden out back.

When their back and forth chatter slowed some, she spoke up. "I've come to tell you some important news." She was glad they were alone.

"What's that?"

"Ain't such good news, really." She quickly amended that. "Well, I mean, it *is* but also a bit . . . troubling where you're concerned."

He shook his head, appearing to become quarrelsome. "So, spit it out."

She kept her voice low and leaned near. "I'm with child again."

He moaned and shook all over, as if he had an uncontrollable chill. "I hope you're joking."

"No." She sat still, her hands folded in her lap. "I'm ever so sure now."

He cursed under his breath. "The brethren will have my hide."

Essie felt more sympathy for her husband than she would have thought possible. *Poor man.*

"I'll catch it but good," Zeke said. "I'll be under the shun as soon as you start showin'." He rose and went to stand at the edge of the porch. Hands deep in his pants pockets, he stared out at the grounds, muttering to himself. "This compounds my problems, jah?"

A trace of the old bitterness rose up within her. *He should've thought of this earlier.*

Silently asking God to help her show Christ's mercy, she said, "I'm afraid so. But we'll get through this somehow, you and me."

When he didn't respond for several minutes but only stood there morosely, Essie rose to her feet. "Well, I'd best be goin', then."

Zeke spun around. "No, now, you just wait! You mustn't be tellin' anyone this, hear?" His eyes squinted fire.

"I already have." She moved away from him, heading for the porch stairs.

"I'm not done with you, Esther! Come right back here."

She couldn't bear to be treated like this. "It's time I returned to the children. Annie's home alone with them."

He squared his shoulders. "You must've told *her*, then. Right?"

She nodded. "That I did."

He kicked the chair, his arms flailing.

"Good-bye, Zeke." She left the porch quickly, feeling sad over his response to a new little life but pleased that she'd not allowed him to crush her spirit this time.

———

Jesse washed his hands at the kitchen sink, watching as Barbara peeled potatoes—creating long brown spirals with her paring knife. *What a terrific cook.* He dried his hands and inched over to kiss the back of her neck, then went to sit at the head of the table, knowing full well supper was more than an hour away.

He'd brought in the mail a little bit ago, glad for Luke's and Yonie's willingness to finish planting the sweet corn. Weary from the day, he found a letter from Daniel Hochstetler addressed to him.

Grimacing, he opened it and silently began to read.

Hello, Jesse Zook, and greetings from Ontario, Canada!

I received your letter and have been thinking what to write back. First, let me say it was a big shock to hear of your discovery. Yet, I was somehow comforted to know Isaac has been found after so many years.

With Mary's recent passing, I had been considering making a trip down there to Lancaster County sometime. Then when you wrote of Isaac's remains, I felt nearly compelled to return. I'd like to see his grave.

For all the harsh words between us, Preacher, I would hope you and I might be able to talk some whenever I can come. Meanwhile I have a great yearning to see Zeke again and to lay eyes on his children—my only grandchildren.

I remain your old friend,
Daniel Hochstetler

Jesse was downright surprised at Daniel's response to his letter and his interest in returning to visit. And to think the bones weren't Isaac's after all and there was no grave for the man to see. He'd best be writing back to tell him so. Jesse sighed. Just now he would not say anything to Barbara, but he did need to get word to Esther that her father-in-law might be coming unannounced.

Ach, and what of Annie? No, it would not do for Ichabod to stay in their midst. Not with Zeke away and the preacher's daughter and one shunned woman running the house over yonder. But there was more to it. The brethren would have a problem with Ichabod's arrival without a confession first.

"Anything interesting in the mail?" Barbara asked.

"Nothin' to speak of." He didn't want to worry her, especially if he could put a stop to Ichabod's plans to return.

Stuffing the letter back into its envelope, he thought of something else that had been flitting around in his mind for weeks now. Esther was no longer attending Preaching service and was taking her children to hear who knows what at the Rancks' meeting-house of a Sunday morning—Annie was likely going with her. So he'd pay them a visit soon and kill two birds with one stone.

He had an hour till supper. Enough time to write back to Ichabod, informing him of the mistake; that there was no reason for him to come after all. He just hoped his second letter would arrive in time.

Fatigued from driving for more than

eight hours straight, Ben began to read bill-boards to pass the time. One popped out at him: the Hopalong Cassidy Museum. *William Boyd was a native of Cambridge, Ohio,* the large sign with bright lights touted. Ben was glad for any interesting sight, even though he was almost too tired to keep going. He had promised Irvin he would make it there in a single day, though not in time for supper, and he'd called to say as much around three-thirty, to give Julia plenty of notice.

Another billboard caught his eye: the Pennyroyal Opera House, featuring blue-grass music. Intrigued, and noting his gas supply was dwindling quickly, he took the exit ramp, hoping to find a gas station.

But he got distracted listening to a radio talk show and found himself on a back road, entering a small town. Up ahead, he saw a closed general store and a barn-style build-ing bearing the marquee of the Pennyroyal Opera House.

Flickers of a memory, or was it some-thing else, burst into his head. Why did the opera house seem vaguely familiar? Had he driven this way on his first trip to Pennsyl-vania? No, he'd taken a different route. Be-sides, the memory felt more distant. Had he and his family visited here once? But who comes to such a location on vacation?

He was really tired—this was exhaustion talking. And this was nuts, pushing it so hard. For what purpose? Just to avoid a hotel and arrive before Irvin and Julia retired for the night?

Reaching the end of the "blink and miss" town, he made a U-turn. Heading back, he noticed the sign: Fairview, Ohio. The town, he noted, had not a single gas station.

Just great.

He switched off the radio . . . and experienced another vision. A memory? Someone quite large had sat up in the driver's seat while he sat in the back. Someone with a smashed nose and an obscured face.

No . . . no, he must be remembering something he'd seen on TV or a movie when he was a kid. Sure, that's all it was.

But the memory kept coming at him. He was smaller . . . much smaller, sitting in the back seat. He remembered the pinching squeeze of being buckled in much too tightly. All he could see was the back of the large man sitting up front, behind the steering wheel. Not his father—a stranger.

Ben shook his head; his mind was playing tricks. He needed more caffeine . . . something to eat.

Getting back on the highway, he took another exit and found a small gas station. As he pulled in to refuel, he had another burst of sickening memory: he recalled crying out at such a gas station—similar to this one. He had shouted loudly that night, at the top of his voice, as if his very life depended on the volume of it . . . but there had been no tears. No, little brothers did not cry. They held it in, he had been told. They were brave . . . very brave. They sat quietly in the back while the big man got out of the car and purchased gas and some candy and hot coffee. That's what they did.

And if they weren't quiet or obedient, they were pushed into the trunk and there they stayed for hours and hours, till they were so cold they couldn't get warm, even though they shivered and shook and their little teeth rattled in their heads. And even though they dreamed they could kick and bite and run fast and get away, they could not. At least not at that moment.

And this little brother was left in that trunk long enough to think he would surely never get out again . . . until he believed that if ever he was found, people would look sadly at him all coiled up in a frozen ball and say, *Der Biebche is am Schtarewe*—the little boy is dying.

Ben shivered and shook his head again. *I've been driving too long,* he thought. *I'm imagining things.*

On Sunday, Annie fretted while redding up the kitchen after the noon meal for Esther, who was busy nursing Essie Ann upstairs.

Even though Annie was not thinking of breaking her six-month promise to Daed, she had begun to envision all the wonderful things about Ben in anticipation of the time she could draw them in a collage. She already could visualize how she wanted to set up the composition on the canvas and felt sure it would not be long after the sketching phase that she could bring it to life with the vibrancy of paint. Sometimes she even crept away to the barnyard and pushed a stick around, sketching out her layout on the ground. Surely that was not prohibited.

Oh, I can scarcely wait for that day.

To think of Ben staying over at Cousin Julia's right then seemed terribly strange . . . even awkward. *Will he come see me?*

Finishing up, she checked the time. *Plenty of time before I have to feed the hogs again and help Essie with supper.* She had a sudden eagerness to take a long walk, so she scribbled a note to Esther.

I'll be back soon, she wrote, leaving it propped on the table against the paper napkin holder.

Delighted to be in the locust grove along Pequea Creek, Annie sat on the old rope swing, at first testing it with her weight. *Seems nice and straight* . . . She leaned back, stretching her legs forward, allowing the swing to lift her higher and higher, shooting toward the milky blue sky, her dress tucked in carefully on either side. The generous length of the rope made it possible to experience a real thrill like when she was little, she realized, smiling. Whyever had Daed taken it down in the first place? Had he wanted to discourage children from playing at the site of a presumed kidnapping? Or had he not liked seeing the swing . . . and the memories it stirred? Annie continued to lean back and push forward, overjoyed to be here despite the past, reveling in the sunshine and this pretty, peaceful spot.

Before I sent Ben away, I was ever so happy.

She leaned into the sway of the swing— hers and Isaac's—thinking back to the many hours spent here, seeing who could swing the highest. And there was the risky jumping, too—jumping off and landing on two feet without falling forward. All childish games, but tantalizingly fun.

All this was a part of me before I started my art. Still, my love for it must have been there all along, she thought, having always been intensely aware of the Lord God's colorful palette of nature. She looked at the sky, pondering, as she often did, what heaven was like. Was Isaac there? What was he doing now?

Rising, she turned to look around, wondering exactly where it was that Isaac and Zeke had made a grave for Isaac's special pet.

Wandering down to the creek, she stared at the rushing water, watching it sweep leaves and other pieces of God's creation into a fluid yet textured portrait until she was drawn back to the swing. She sat and pushed herself back with her bare feet, glad for the smile of springtime on the lovely grass, the flowering blossoms in the trees overhead. This place was so private, yet resplendent with color and aroma. "Surely a glimpse into what heaven must be like," she told herself. After all, the heavenly Father was the supreme creator-artist. She closed her eyes, eager for the little tickle of excitement as she swayed back and forth, a welcome sensation she had often felt when she was a little girl sitting right here, swinging double with Isaac.

Chapter 16

Julia Ranck was setting the table for lunch when Ben wandered into the kitchen, young James hanging on to his knee as Ben pretended to limp and stumble. Looking at James roughhousing with their guest, Julia frowned and motioned to him, and her son quickly let go, then headed for the sink, where he put out his hands to be washed.

"I hope you like egg salad sandwiches," Julia said, glancing Ben's way with a smile, drying her son's hands with a dish towel.

"Sounds good."

Irvin appeared from the small sunroom off the kitchen, carrying his Bible. "Well, there he is! How was your night after so many hours on the road?"

Ben laughed self-consciously, having slept through not only breakfast but church, as well. "Sorry I slept so late."

"Not a problem."

The sound of squealing erupted from across the room. Little Molly came charging toward him, running right into his arms. "Mr. Ben's back!"

He leaned down and picked her up, swinging her high, then low again. This brought more giggles from the blond, blue-eyed cutie, and she begged for more. "Do it again! Do it again!"

"Now, Molly, let's settle down to eat," Irvin said, and she obediently, but not so happily, headed toward Julia to have her hands washed before joining her brother at the table.

After Irvin offered the blessing, the children became quiet. The adults discussed the weather, and then Ben inquired about Zeke, thinking he'd make additional small talk, taking the attention off any second-guessing the Rancks might be doing about the reason for his return visit. But he was stunned to hear that Zeke was being treated for depression and a mental disorder.

"There's a fine new center not far from here," Julia spoke up, and Irvin described the facility created specifically for Amish and Mennonite patients, to make them feel comfortable in a Plain environment, similar to their own homes.

Ben felt a twinge of sadness for the man who'd sought him out so faithfully while he had lived and worked here briefly—and for Zeke's family.

"And Annie Zook . . . I'm sure you know she's staying with Esther, for the time being," volunteered Julia, not making eye contact as she poured milk for Molly.

"I'd heard that, uh . . . from Annie. She wrote me."

"Ah, how nice," Julia said, now smiling.

"Was this Annie's choice to go to Esther's?" Ben asked.

Julia shrugged. "I think so. I don't know all the ins and outs of it, really. But Annie's all right. We see her several times a week."

Irvin seemed to agree. "She's figuring some things out, is all. I wouldn't be surprised if she's back home soon, when things blow over."

Ben wondered what things but assumed it had a lot to do with him and with her father's discovery of their dating.

"So, Ben," Julia began, giving him a knowing look. "What *really* brings you back so soon?"

Irvin chuckled. "Julia, he's barely recovered from his trip. Give the man time to catch his breath."

Irvin and Julia traded humorous glances, and Ben felt a subtle twinge of envy, admiring their close relationship.

For a moment, Ben considered telling them about his adoption bombshell but decided to wait. It hadn't occurred to him until now that he preferred to tell Annie his strange news first.

After the meal, he returned to the attic room to make his bed and put his few items of clothing away in the empty bureau drawers, as Julia had kindly instructed.

When he came back down, Julia mentioned that Irvin was taking a Sunday afternoon nap.

"Poor man's all tired out," she explained. "He helped a neighbor chop several cords of wood yesterday."

Ben was sorry he hadn't been there to help. He imagined Irvin walking through the woods, ax in hand, looking up, going from tree to tree, deciding which one to topple, which would make the best firewood. For a passing moment, flickers of just such an outing filled his recollection. Funny, he was pretty sure he had never done such a thing since, growing up, he and his family had lived in town. Still, the memory lingered. Was this something he'd done as a very young boy, before he'd been found in Kentucky?

Feeling the need for some fresh air, Ben could scarcely wait to drive the back roads with every window down, breathing in the rich scents, taking in the splendor of trees lining the road or the varieties of fruit trees filling the orchards. Most of all, he wanted to revisit the old covered bridge on Belmont Road.

Soon he was driving down the road, questions concerning his adoption plaguing him. There was no way of knowing his real birth date, nor his full name, beyond Zachary. He was like a dinghy drifting on foggy seas. And yet for some reason, he felt at home in Lancaster County. Being here was like a sigh of relief, and he was glad he'd made the journey back so quickly.

Spying the bridge up ahead, he pulled off to the side of the road and parked the car, more perplexed as he stared at the quaint yet picturesque site. What was it about this place that kept drawing him? And why had Annie Zook painted such a scene and had the painting so beautifully framed, only to hide it away from the eyes of the People? Did it have some special meaning to her? He knew he could not leave Paradise again without asking.

He thought of the swing in Annie's painting and the spotlight on what had appeared to be a peach stone. Why had she chosen to highlight it, as if that specific detail was in some way important?

Walking through the bridge now, Ben was not afraid. He experienced a nearly compelling sense of hope, though he had no idea why.

He turned to the left and strolled down the grassy slope, looking ahead toward the trees. He noticed a young woman—an Amish girl—sitting on a swing.

He looked again. He hadn't remembered seeing the long rope swing the other times he'd been here.

Ben stopped in his tracks.

Annie? Or is my mind playing tricks on me again?

Slowing his pace, he remembered the fear he had experienced the first time he'd come here. Only this time he was nervous for a different reason.

Is it really Annie?

Now that he was this close to the girl, he was tentative, not wanting to alarm her. So he made some noise, crunching some dry twigs under his feet, and saw that hers were bare. Naturally they were. This was the third week of May, and he'd learned quickly that Amish women and girls shed winter's shoes and ran barefooted, ready to embrace the warmth of the sun and earth, as soon as the first bumblebees were spotted.

Unexpectedly, she looked his way and frowned curiously. "Ben?"

A flood of emotions filled him at the sound of his name. "Hello, Annie."

She rose somewhat unsteadily from the swing. "It's *awful* good to see you again."

He could hardly believe she was standing there before him. "I didn't expect to find you here."

An awkward moment passed as neither seemed sure what to say and they just stood there smiling at each other. Ben didn't say he'd missed her, but he certainly had, and seeing her now brought it right home to him.

"I'm back . . . because I can't seem to stay away." He chuckled, offering a nervous smile.

"What could be so important that you traveled all this way?" She quickly told him that Julia had let her know he was coming, and how surprised she was. "My cousins seemed very pleased that you were going to stay with them."

Suddenly feeling comfortable with her, he reached for her hand. "It's so great to see you, Annie."

She grinned. "Did you get my letter?"

she asked, then added, "I almost didn't send it, because it was . . . um . . . too honest."

He was surprised at her candor. "Too honest? I didn't think so."

She looked down, cheeks pink. "I was afraid you might think I was too bold."

Ben shook his head. He had other concerns burning in his brain, but in her presence they seemed to slip away. He squeezed her hand before releasing it. Then he pulled out the carefully folded magazine cover from his pocket and showed it to her. "This is your work, isn't it? Your painting that won first place?"

She nodded, looking self-conscious.

"I recognized this spot as soon as I saw it."

She looked wistfully about her. "I guess I just love this place. My brothers and I used to come here to play when I was small. I used to swing on this very swing with my best friend in the world."

"Essie?" he asked.

She shook her head. "A little boy named Isaac."

Something within Ben whirled at the mention of that name. His mind seemed to cloud over, then clear with recognition. He *knew* that name. Or had Annie mentioned it before?

He forced himself to focus. "I know the last time I asked you about this place, it upset you. You said something bad had happened here, but you didn't tell me what. I need to know."

Annie looked at him for a moment. "This is where Isaac disappeared—kidnapped, most likely," she told him somberly. "Remember what Zeke told you, about the bones he thought were his little brother's? Zeke even thought he killed Isaac himself, but it turns out the remains the police found were those of a young girl. So we still don't know what happened to Isaac."

Zeke's missing brother was named Isaac?

Annie gestured toward the folded cover. "Where did you get that?"

"From a friend of mine who works for the magazine. I've carried it with me since last Christmas. . . ."

"Even before you came here?"

He nodded.

"Why on earth?"

"I think it's one of the main reasons I first wanted to travel here to Paradise."

"How so?" she asked, clearly perplexed.

"I didn't understand then, but I think I'm beginning to." He took a deep breath. "Annie, I need to tell you something I've learned . . . about my family."

Her face shone with concerned interest. "Jah? I hope everyone's all right."

"I just found out I'm adopted, Annie. I had no idea all these years, but Mom told me when I was home. It still feels like some weird soap opera—"

"Wait a minute," she stopped him. "You're adopted and your parents never told you?"

"I know. If it didn't hurt so much, it would almost be funny. My whole life seems like a cruel joke."

She stepped back a bit and, finding the swing again, sat down. "Jah, how strange for you, hearing it now. How did they come to adopt you?"

He shrugged. "Apparently I showed up on someone's doorstep one night and they took me to child services. I was traumatized, I guess—didn't speak for months. The authorities tried to figure out where I'd come from, but no one had reported a missing boy who matched my description and I couldn't—or wouldn't—tell them my name or where I was from. The Martins adopted me as soon as I became eligible."

He paused to breathe, to fill his aching lungs with air. He almost felt guilty, telling this innocent girl his unbelievable story. He looked over at her to gauge her reaction.

She was staring at him wide-eyed.

"Does this shock you?" he asked.

"No. Go on, Ben. It's all right; you can tell me." She tilted her head, her eyes following his every move.

He knew her well enough to know he could trust her with the full story. "I don't really remember much. My mother said I must have blocked it out. I have no idea when I was born or what my full name was. I don't know anything about my biological parents or if they abandoned me or what. I seem to remember some man taking me away in the night, but I'm not sure how much is real or my imagination playing tricks on me."

Annie frowned. "It doesn't sound like you were an infant. How old do you think you were? Does anyone know?"

"About four or five, I guess. As far as my actual birthday, I think they picked a month and day out of a hat and put that on my birth certificate." He paused. "At least I think that's what my parents said. I still don't remember much . . . just glimpses into the past."

He sat cross-legged in the grass, not far from the swing. "I have to level with you, Annie. I'm very drawn to this place . . . to your people, too. I often feel like a fifth wheel on the outside, in the English world, as you call it. Maybe this is why I never felt like I fit in anywhere. Because in some strange way, in the back of my mind, I knew I belonged somewhere else."

She began to swing a little. "You think someone took you away? Or you got lost somehow? What did your parents tell you about that?"

"They don't know much more than I do. But I do know one thing."

She stopped swinging.

He reached into his pocket. "This." He held up the smooth peach stone. "It was in my pocket the night I was found—the only thing I had in my possession that I recognized as mine."

"Oh, Ben!" Annie clasped her hand over her mouth.

He thought she might cry, she looked that distraught, but then just as quickly, amazement shone in her features.

"What is it?" he asked. "You look as if you've seen a ghost."

She rose swiftly and came to him. "Oh, I believe I have!" She placed her hands on his face, tracing his eyebrows and then his cheekbones. "What were you wearing that night . . . when they found you, I mean?

And how was your hair cut? Was it fancy-like?"

"I don't know. My mom said there wasn't anything unusual about how I was dressed, just that my clothes were large on me. Why do you ask?" He reached for her hands to keep them from probing his face any longer, baffled by her affectionate response.

"Ben." She swallowed. "My little friend Isaac carried a peach stone in *his* pocket all the time. He disappeared when he was four years old." Again she reached for his face. "It never occurred to me before but . . . you *look* like Isaac."

Ben shook his head. "Oh, Annie. That sounds crazy—"

"You recognized Pennsylvania Dutch, remember? And I've never seen Zeke seek out anyone's friendship the way he did with you. He avoids everyone. Here—" at this she led him back to the swing—"sit down a bit."

He complied, feeling both silly and intrigued.

"Look around you," Annie said. "Listen to the sounds. Do you remember ever sitting here before?"

He smiled, feeling foolish. "Annie—"

She put her hands on his shoulders.

"Ben, close your eyes. Just listen for a moment."

He did as she suggested, soaking up the pleasant song of birds and the rushing creek. And as he was silent, he *did* recall something: as a child, he had stood up on a swing. *Here.* He had looked down at the creek as he did so, seeing the trestle of the bridge just beyond. Other times he had twisted the rope and spun quickly round and round, making his head dizzy, till the swing came to a jerking stop . . . a little girl laughing as he did.

When he opened his eyes and looked at Annie, there were tears spilling down her face.

"I remember you, Isaac," she said softly. "Do you remember me?"

Chapter 17

Annie wanted to stand on the creek bank and spin around, arms wide with joy. She wanted to shout—to tell all of Paradise that Isaac was found at last. But, noticing Ben's reserve, she kept quiet, content to be near him, to savor this discovery alone. For now.

Heart still pounding, Annie was secretly thrilled she'd walked to Pequea Creek on foot, because when Ben offered to drive her back to Essie's, she was free to accept and ride along.

Together they walked toward the bridge while she kept sneaking glances at him. "I can hardly believe I'm here again with Isaac Hochstetler after all these years."

He looked at her intently. "How can you be so sure, Annie? Maybe there's some other explanation."

"What other explanation?"

He shrugged.

She grabbed his sleeve, and he stopped to look at her. "I knew there was some reason why you always seemed so familiar. Don't you feel it, too?"

Ben nodded. "Memories seem to be getting stronger than when I was here before."

"Like what?"

"For instance, I remember filling my britches pockets with bugs, especially daddy longlegs."

"Ach, you're foolin' me."

He grinned. "Now, why would I do that?"

"You honestly put creepy crawlers in your pockets?"

"Someone once told me that pockets were meant for hiding insects and caterpillars and such."

"Well, *that's* interesting. Do you remember who? Zeke maybe?"

They continued walking through the bridge, and Annie noticed how dismal it suddenly became as they reached the middle section—the light of the sky framed at both ends.

"I don't know," Ben said. "But I suppose if it's true that I *am* Isaac, I guess in time all of it will come back. I sure hope so."

"Me too," she replied. "It must be true,"

she said, repeating the facts that he was the same age as Isaac would now be, and that he had been found in Kentucky in the autumn of the year of Isaac's disappearance, at about age four. "I daresay the smooth peach stone seals the whole thing."

He handed the pit to her, but his manner seemed less sure. "I always wondered . . . because it seemed to have some connection to something I couldn't remember . . . but I somehow blocked out the trauma of what happened." He paused as if remembering something. "When I drove back here *this* time the strangest memories began to bombard me."

Annie felt the peach pit in her hand, like a pebble from a creek, its jagged surface washed smooth with time. "Did you ever know that Zeke—your brother—collected these, too? After you disappeared he did, that is."

"His daughter Laura told me that." Ben opened the car door for her. "To think that Zeke was so sure Isaac had been killed. And from what you told me—that he'd done it himself. Will he even believe it if his younger brother shows up now, alive after all?"

"You'd think he'd be glad, but as troubled as Zeke is, I really don't know."

He closed the door and Annie settled

into the front seat, the peach pit still in her hand. It felt peculiar sitting here in Ben's passenger seat again, though she wouldn't have traded this moment for anything. So much had happened since she'd last ridden in Ben's car only a few weeks ago. Here was Isaac! In the flesh.

Ben. *Her* Ben was Isaac! But now she had a job to do—to convince the People, beginning with her own father, that Isaac was indeed alive and well.

Once Ben was behind the steering wheel, she suggested that he not take her to Essie's as planned. "I suppose we ought to talk to Daed first, him being a preacher and all."

Ben turned toward her, looking hesitant again. "Well . . . okay. But first I'd like to see where Isaac—or . . . I—lived before the disappearance. Does the family still live around here?"

He wasn't convinced yet, she realized. "Not long after you were kidnapped, they moved away to Honey Brook. Then, following that, I'm not sure where, but they ended up in Canada eventually."

"Would you mind showing me the way to Isaac's . . . I mean *my* childhood home?"

"Wonderful-good idea. It might trigger more memories."

"Thanks, Annie," he said, face grim.

He's terribly nervous, she realized.

The pink light of late afternoon dazzled her senses, and just then she remembered her note to Esther. "Oh, I can't be gone much longer," she said. "I'm sorry, Ben, but I need to get back to help Essie."

"I understand."

"Maybe we should go and talk to Daed tomorrow instead. All right?"

"That might be a good idea. I need some time to process everything."

She could see how drained he was. "But it shouldn't take long to get to the house where you and Zeke lived with your parents, Daniel and Mary Hochstetler." She didn't mention the name Ichabod. "I know how to get there."

"What do you know about them?" he asked. "How many children did they have?"

"Just you and Zeke that I knew of." She'd never thought of this before. "They may have left the Amish life behind altogether, but I don't know for sure." She handed back the peach stone, wondering if she ought to tell him that his dear mother had passed away not so long ago. She didn't know how much to share, especially since Ben wasn't yet convinced that he was Isaac. But for her, there was no doubt.

Ben was amazed at how straightforward, even courageous, Annie was. She made her way right up to the back door, knocking hard and waiting till the owner of Daniel Hochstetler's former house came and answered. The woman who opened the door was middle-aged and clearly not Plain. Annie explained that her friend, Ben here, was visiting and wanted to see the house where he'd lived as a boy.

The woman looked curiously from Annie to Ben but invited them in anyway, saying they were welcome to look around as long as they didn't mind the mess. The woman herself left, saying she was on her way to the grocery store. "My boys are home, though, so no need to lock up—just let yourselves out when you're done." Ben had no idea where the man of the house was, or if there was one at all.

As he and Annie walked from room to cluttered room, they saw TVs flickering and blaring in nearly every one. Several teen-aged boys sprawled on sofas in the living room and barely seemed to notice two strangers giving themselves a tour of their house.

Heading to the relative quiet of the second floor, he and Annie found four bedrooms. Standing in the smallest of the four,

Ben had a sense of knowing this might have been his room. Annie seemed to detect his desire to be alone and excused herself quietly, going out into the hall to wait for him.

He walked the length of the floor, staring at the walls. Then, turning, he looked out the only window, wondering if he'd ever stood there, noting the low windowsill, only a few inches off the floor.

Looking into the closet, he imagined the kind of Amish attire he must have worn as a little boy. *Why doesn't anything ring a bell?* He looked at the bed, the way it was centered on the south wall.

A body sleeps best with the head of the bed facing north, someone had told him. When? Was that his first mother's opinion?

He turned and studied the north wall. *No, this couldn't have been my room,* he decided, going out to the hallway and finding Annie there, hands folded. "It seems only vaguely familiar."

"That's all right—could be the English furniture and such." She smiled encouragingly. "Maybe if you walk around the barn a bit?"

"There's a large pond, too." He'd noticed it when driving up. "I wonder if they stock it with fish."

Annie giggled at the notion.

They headed downstairs and out the back door, thanking no one, because the teenagers were now playing video games.

He and Annie strolled around, glancing in several of the outbuildings, seeing three big dogs running free. "Maybe this isn't the place," he said. "Is that possible?"

She shook her head. "This *is* the house."

He stopped walking and reached for her hand. "Annie, I think I know how much you'd like me to be your long-lost friend. But what if I'm not? What if Isaac isn't alive after all?"

She smiled. "You're Isaac—as sure as I'm Annie Zook, I know you are."

"Well, let's see what your father thinks," he suggested. "I'll go and see him first thing tomorrow."

Annie burst out laughing. "You want to help with milkin'?"

He shook his head, "Ew . . . bad idea."

She stopped and looked at him, wearing the cutest expression. Then she rattled off something in Pennsylvania Dutch. "Do you know what I just said?"

"Maybe. Say it more slowly."

She did. *"Es gebt viele schwatze Kieh, awwer sie gewwe all weissi Millich!"*

He concentrated. An alarm went off in

him. "I don't understand all of it, but some."

"Quick, tell me which part."

"Something about black cows and white milk?"

"Jah, that's right." She was laughing softly. "Yet another proof, Ben. Little by little . . ."

He wasn't as sure. It still seemed so *impossible*.

He spied an old climbing tree with a bent hook-shaped branch in the side yard not far from the white picket fence. At that moment, a genuine knowing clicked in him, like a falling into place. He knew without a doubt it had been the perfect spot to sit and play "riding horsey," remembering unmistakably a blustery springtime day when he'd climbed too high onto the unique bough, hoping to hide there so he wouldn't have to go to market with Mamma.

When his mother had demanded he come down right this minute, he'd lied and said he had a fever. So she'd scooted him into the house and stuck a thermometer in his mouth to see for sure. Ornery as he was, he bit down hard on it, breaking the thermometer and swallowing some of the mercury. Running to the kitchen sink, he gagged and spit while his poor mamma fretted something fierce, calling for Dat to come. He remembered the strange thickness in his mouth as it all came back to him—the fact that he'd willfully tried to make himself sick that day.

"Ben, are you all right?" asked Annie.

Maybe I am Isaac. . . .

He told her what had just burst across the years to him. "I remember that ancient climbing tree—old even back when I was a boy."

Her big blue eyes lit up. "Oh, this is ever so exciting."

He had the urge to scoop her into his arms but gave her a brief hug instead. "Well, let's see what your father says about this tomorrow."

She nodded in agreement, her face turning crimson from his touch.

They walked hand in hand across the side yard to his waiting car, but before opening the door for Annie, he paused to look again at the lofty tree, the silvery underside of its leaves gleaming suddenly in the breeze. Something told him he'd stood here many times before, or near here—possibly staring out his bedroom window at this tree, longing for the morning so he could climb it again.

"Unbelievable," he whispered. He could

not take his eyes off the massive tree, surprisingly aware at this moment who the stranger in his dreams had been all along. *My father knew all about trees. He loved nature and revered the Creator of all things.*

Annie touched his sleeve. "Ben?"

He looked at her and leaned down to kiss her cheek. He opened the car door for her and waited till she was inside to close it firmly. Going to his side of the car, he glanced up at the tree once more. "Dat . . . it was you," he whispered. "Where are you now?"

Chapter 18

Before dawn, Annie stood by one of the kitchen windows at Essie's, waiting for Ben to arrive. She felt the need to pray, to thank the Good Lord for bringing Isaac home. "I never really believed it possible, but you surely knew . . . all along."

When Ben's car pulled up, the thought crossed her mind that it might not be such a good idea to introduce him as Isaac to her father. For a moment, she contemplated Essie's desire to pray about everything. *Should I be asking the Lord God for His help today, as well?*

Opening and closing the back door quietly so as not to awaken Essie and the children, Annie rushed out to Ben, who met her on the passenger side to open her door. "Good morning, Annie. Did you sleep well?"

"It was a short night, I daresay."

He chuckled and hurried around the front of the car. She was glad for the waning moon. She had not forgotten how handsome Ben was, but seeing him now, hurrying around the car with such eagerness, made her heart flutter.

"Are you sure about going to see your father first thing like this?" he asked, buckling his seat belt.

She nodded, determined to press forward, though as the big farmhouse came into view, she wondered how to go about convincing Daed. She had a terrified twinge in her stomach, but there was no putting off something this important.

"I think it might be best if you stay put for now." She hated sounding bossy, but she needed to break the news to Daed slowly and carefully.

"Take your time, Annie. I'm not going anywhere."

The way he said it delighted her, and she got out of the car and headed straight to the barn, asking the Lord God for wisdom.

———

Zeke sat on the veranda at Philhaven, watching the moon fade in the coming sunrise. He still felt stunned. *I'll be caught with mud on my face with this new baby coming!*

One thing after another . . . all problems of my own making, he thought.

Yet he knew, if given the chance, he would not have done things any differently back after Esther's shun was announced. A man had certain needs—the Lord God ordained marriage for plenty good reason, for sure and for certain. There was nothing the brethren could say otherwise, and even though he was annoyed no end at Esther's baby news, he couldn't help hoping for another son. Laura and Essie Ann were fine where daughters were concerned, but for his plans to expand his hog operation someday he needed muscle and stamina—in short, another young man in the house. Zach would be a strapping fellow when he grew up, but little John was about as good as a girl, what with his asthma.

Zeke looked sadly at the chair where Esther had sat and kept him company a couple days ago, enjoying their first visit since his being admitted here. At least until he'd spoiled it by losing his temper. Such a good, pretty woman he'd married. He felt a lump come up in his throat. "We've got ourselves another little one on the way," he mumbled. "Where will that get me . . . with everything else I've done wrong?"

He was certain Preacher Jesse would

take this up with the bishop right quick, if Annie spilled the beans. Truth was, his time was awful short, and there was nothing to do about it but wait. If he jumped ahead and told on himself, he'd bring on the Bann faster than lightning. "Looks like it can strike twice in the selfsame place," he whispered, pulling hard on his beard, not minding the prickly pain he was causing his face. "It's my own dumb fault."

He moseyed indoors to wash up for breakfast. He would have to walk over to the dining room with the other folk residing here. He missed his own table, sitting at the head at every meal, hearing the smack of his children's lips as they ate, the burps that came, especially from the boys, showing their mamma how wonderful-good her cooking was.

If I'm to be under the shun, I'll be joining Esther at her separate table soon. At least in public. For a moment, the thought brought him a measure of satisfaction. For with or without Esther, he was to be alone—at least that's what was expected of him . . . if he were ever to be released from this place and allowed to return to his own home.

At the sink, he let the water flow through his hands, then splashed it on his face, getting his beard a bit wet as he recalled that awful long-ago night again.

Little brother has borne too much grief for one so young, he had concluded as he finished the task of burial. A muffled sob and running footsteps caught his attention suddenly, and quickly he straightened, catching his breath as he leaned on the shovel, looking about the grove. Isaac had disappeared!

"I killed Isaac," he muttered into the towel now as he dried his face.

Visions of that night continued to play out, confusing him. Even in his dreams the images appeared and disturbed him. One doctor had suggested Zeke felt too responsible for his brother—the reason for his tremendous, black guilt. Another agreed with the first doctor but implied Zeke was not carrying the blame at all but suffered, possibly, from some form of post-traumatic stress disorder . . . speculating that there was much more to the disappearance than met the eye. *"Perhaps you've buried the truth deep within yourself, for some unknown reason."* They had to dig out the reason, get to the bottom of things, so he could then heal and get home.

Some days he believed he was getting less fuzzy in his thinker; other days he just didn't know. But right this minute, he knew he should have abided by the separation requirements put on Esther and himself by the brethren. He should've waited till she confessed—whenever that time might be—before visiting her down the hall at night.

Just as I should've obeyed my father the night I took Isaac out to bury the puppy.

While Ben waited in the car, Annie searched for her father and found him hauling milk. "Oh, there you are."

Lifting the lid on the cooler, her father turned to her, his face solemn.

"I have some wonderful-good news, Daed," she said.

He did not crack a smile. "You must be comin' home where you belong."

"No, Daed. That's not it at all."

"Well, oughta be."

She forced a smile. "I want you to meet someone."

He eyed her suspiciously. "At this time of morning? Can't you see I'm awful busy? Your not bein' here has made a hole in things."

"It's important that you come with me," she urged, looking toward the driveway.

"What's more important than doin' needful chores?" His eyes were unsympathetic.

She bit her lip. He wasn't making it easy for her. Considering everything that had happened between them, how could she possibly break this to him? Gently? Or come right out with it? "Ach, Daed, what would ya say if I told you Isaac Hochstetler is alive?"

His brow furrowed in disbelief. He sucked in some air, staring at the cement floor. Slowly, he lifted his head and met her gaze. "Well, now, I'd say you're as crazy as Zeke, maybe."

"But I'm not."

"Say all you want, but if you think such a thing, then I have to pity you."

"Ach, Daed. Isaac's alive, and I can prove it."

He waved his hand and put his hat back on. "I've got work to do."

"No . . . wait. If you won't come out to the car, I'll bring him in, right here to you."

He stopped dead in his tracks, his back to her. "What on earth are you talking 'bout?"

"Isaac's here . . . sittin' outside in his car. Aren't you the least bit curious?"

Her father turned to face her. "I don't know what you're pullin', but I'm not interested in playing any tomfoolery or whatever this is."

"But, Daed—"

"Go 'bout your business, Annie. And I'll go back to mine."

With a heavy heart, she knew she had

been quite mistaken to think her father would listen. Maybe no one would. Maybe the People weren't ready to receive Isaac back.

Perhaps Esther was a better choice. *Jah, that's where we'll head next . . . and eventually out to see Zeke in due time.*

She turned to head back to the driveway, where Ben sat with the car still running, which was rather curious. Had he sensed Daed would not grant him a meeting? Was he prepared for a quick getaway?

Slipping into the front seat again, she said softly, "I guess I wasn't thinkin' clearly. This wasn't a good idea. Too much anger between my father and me." Then she began to cry, trying her best to tell him what her father had said. "I'm awful sorry, Ben." She brushed her tears away. "I thought things would go much better."

He reached for her hand. "I read something in the Bible the day I was so disappointed about the news of my adoption. I don't think I'll ever forget it." He paused. "The verse went something like this: all things work out for good to those who love God."

She perked up her ears, because she'd heard Cousin Julia say the very same thing. "Jah, I like the sound of that. And since we both love the Lord God—don't we?—well,

I s'pose we can hope in the verse, too."

Ben shifted the car into gear, and they drove in silence for a while. He seemed almost reflective as he stared straight ahead, as if suddenly sad. "I've been curious about the Amish tradition—why you live the way you do, seemingly locked in time. I guess knowing what I do now, my curiosity makes sense."

"Putting it simply, we do what our forefathers did."

"It's especially appealing in a world where things are constantly changing, you know?"

"Some things change, I s'pose," Annie said. "I hear some Amish read and study the Bible. Esther talks of a group called Beachy Amish and others, including the New Order Amish out in Gap, who memorize the Scriptures, and their bishop is all right with that."

Ben drove all over Paradise, past the Progressive Shoe Store, and then over east to the old mill. There, they got out and walked quite a ways before turning back and then stopping to watch a small waterfall across the road from the mill.

She thought for sure he was stalling, finding more places he wanted to see—such as the one-room schoolhouse, which he thought he remembered Zeke attending—before finally heading over to Esther's. Annie couldn't blame him, because the whole discovery was both peculiar and wonderful. She could hardly wait to share the news.

Finally, Ben asked her if she was ready to head back to Esther's. She was careful not to let her relief show as she nodded her assent.

"If Esther doesn't believe us, what then?" he asked.

"I can't imagine she won't. Everything adds up to you bein' Isaac."

To this, Ben chuckled, giving her a wink. "You're a pretty confident woman, Annie Zook."

Her heart pounded, and she knew she was smiling at him far too much. "I don't know if that's a good thing or not," she joked right back.

He asked about Zeke. "Has Esther seen him lately?"

"Once, so far. The People take turns visiting him, she says. As far as I know, he's doin' all right. Essie prays for him without ceasing, just as the Scripture says to."

Ben seemed to contemplate her remark, studying her now. "Prayer must be a powerful thing. I've wondered about communicating with God my whole life."

"So have I."

He turned the conversation back to Essie. "What does your father say about your staying with her?"

It still hurt to think of her father, especially as resistant as he'd been today. "My parents tend to think I'm taking sides with Essie—that I've abandoned them. There are big expectations on me, of course, which causes another rub. For one thing, I should've joined church by now, you prob'ly know."

He nodded, making the turn into Esther's drive. "Sam Glick hasn't joined yet, either, if I remember right."

"And he won't be," she said. "Oops . . . I don't think I was supposed to say that."

"He's leaving the Amish?"

"Maybe so."

Ben asked about Sam and Louisa. "What's happened with them, do you know?"

"Oh, I honestly think they care for each other, but they're miles apart." She didn't feel like going into any of that, not with her former beau—Isaac himself—sitting right here next to her, for goodness' sake! "Come on," she said as he stopped the car, "let's reintroduce you to your sister-in-law and to all your nieces and nephews. You'll love seein' Essie Ann again—she's so cute and growing ever so fast."

Ben got out and went around to open her

door. His manner seemed uncertain again.

"What's the matter, Ben?"

He shrugged. "Maybe we should take this slower. Maybe no one is ready to accept this. I'm barely used to the idea myself."

Disappointment and anxiety flowed through her. "No, Ben. . . . Daed's upset with me, but Essie's goin' to fall right over with this news." Then she remembered what Essie had told her about being in the family way again. "Come to think of it, I best be breakin' it to her slowly. I should do most all the talking, prob'ly."

Ben nodded, his eyes tender. "Are you sure?"

Annie took his arm, and they walked around the house together. "Remember that verse you told me—all things are working for good, jah?" More than anything, she hoped they could trust that Scripture.

Chapter 19

Louisa stood in the aisle at the art store, searching for the thinnest possible brush to create the fine details on her newest painting. She was working on an oil rendering of the Zooks' hay wagon—one of more than a dozen photos she had taken around the Zooks' farm. To bring the painting to life, she planned to include a litter of black kittens with the mother cat lying near, eyes closed while her young slept beside her.

She thought of her own beautiful Russian Blue cat, with his high cheekbones and angular face, deciding she wanted to paint Muffin and send the finished art to Annie as a belated birthday gift. *I need to get right on it*, she thought, eager to finish her current painting and contact a local gallery in Littleton, hoping for a sale. Her goal was to live within her means, refusing any help from her wealthy parents. The fact that she had done exactly that thus far made her quite proud.

Not in a wrongful way, as Annie might say.

There were times when she wished she could expedite a project, like the one that had come together so easily for her years ago: the ocean painting she had done at Great-Aunt Margaret's—near the beach, where the sweeping seascape had readily captured her attention. The setting had soothed her then and it comforted her now as she recalled its serene majesty. *Is it weird to miss a painting?* She often did just that, regretting it had ended up in London with Trey, who'd purchased it from her when they'd first met. *Never to be seen again by me.*

Spotting the perfect brush, she chose two exactly alike and made her way to the cashier's counter. On the way, she was distracted by the aisle where acid-free papers of every imaginable color were on display. One particular hue, a unique shade of green she'd come to know as "Amish green," caught her attention. Picking up the sheet, she held it next to her arm, pretending for a moment it was a sleeve, recalling the months of wearing such colors—deep blue, green, wine, and purple.

She thought back to a particular Monday. Wash day. She had been standing outdoors at the Zooks', helping Annie and her mother hang out dozens of articles of clothing, all lined up according to type and size. She remembered the first time she'd attempted to help, quickly learning the way things were expected to be done. Louisa noticed Annie was careful never to offend her by talking nonstop in Dutch with her mother, the way other women did at quilting bees or cannings. Yet another endearing thing about Annie: she was always conscious of Louisa's feelings, even to the point of not saying a word when Louisa happened to hang up one of the Zook boys' broadfall trousers inside out. Much later in the afternoon, when they were taking down the clothes, Louisa noticed the mistake, but Annie merely shrugged it off as nothing.

There were other appealing things about her pen pal and good friend that Louisa missed. It wasn't that she didn't care for her modern friends—she did and very much. Yet she knew that neither Courtney nor her other friends here could hold a candle to all of Annie's lovely characteristics, many of which were fostered by the Plain community she lived in.

Still, Louisa knew life in Paradise was

not perfect. If she'd learned anything from her visit there, it was that even the "simple" life could be complex. No matter where one lived, life was stressful. Even for those who chose a less hectic pace, it was impossible to escape the pitfalls of human emotion and the unavoidable problems that resulted. The Amish seemed to take this in stride and made the best of tough situations with help from their families, their community, and their God.

But I'm here now, teaching the students I missed, wearing my favorite clothes, and seeing my old fiancé. Thinking the latter, she felt herself shrug inwardly.

Carefully, almost reverently, she placed the "Amish green" paper back on its matching stack and continued to the front of the store to pay for her new brushes.

———

Long after her last students of the morning had left the studio, Louisa sat on the stool in front of her easel and added touches of texture and detail to her hay wagon painting.

She wanted the painting to not only depict the setting accurately but to draw the observer into the scene itself. She struggled to emulate something of the Dutch master

Rembrandt, who'd had the ability to create a sense of natural movement and a bold contrast between light and dark.

Sliding off her stool, she stepped back and studied the overall composition and feel. There was something she wanted to include and was struggling with its absence. *The exhilaration of walking on Amish soil.*

"Remember what it was like to sit on that hay wagon and be teased by Yonie. . . . *Think!*" she told herself.

Moving in closer, she gave the mother cat plenty of whiskers, being almost too generous with the brushstrokes in her rendering of one of the Zooks' barn cats—coal black with a sheen like none other.

To add interest in the foreground, she included a touch of wild tangled vines, then some dabs of purple blossoms and the enticing red of a cluster of berries.

"*Be* there," she told herself, again thinking back to the Zook farm.

She closed her eyes, but it was not Yonie's face she saw in her fond memory of Lancaster County. Sam's fine eyes and contagious smile were before her now, and she groaned. "When will I ever get over him?" she whispered, moving back to the painting, brush poised in midair. "Have you ruined me so completely, Sam . . . for my old life?"

A few more brushstrokes—a trio of distant birds in flight—and the painting was finished. She took meticulous care in cleaning her brushes. That done, she heard her Palm jingle—she was receiving a text message. When she checked, she saw that it was from Michael. *Wanna meet 4 lunch?*

Suddenly feeling guilty after her lingering thoughts about Sam, she sent a quick reply back to Michael. *Thx, but I have some shopping 2 do.*

Pushing her Palm into her backpack, she hurried to turn off the lights and headed out the door to her car, grocery list in hand, not waiting for a text reply.

She was pushing her keys into the ignition when she realized she had forgotten the reference book on Rembrandt that she'd intended to take home. She returned to the studio and located the treasured book. Rather than simply carry it out to the car, she thumbed through it there in the studio, finding the page she had often turned to and gazing at it once again.

Her heart had always been drawn to this haunting crucifixion scene of Christ. Her focus dropped to the crowd below the cross. The artist had painted himself into this scene, she knew from her studies. Why was that? Had he been as intrigued by this particular death as she was beginning to be?

She thought again of her great-aunt, who had once asked her as they sat sunning themselves on the beach, "What do you think happens after someone dies, Louisa dear?"

For whatever odd reason Aunt Margaret had pierced Louisa's thoughts with that unexpected question so long ago. Thinking on it now, Louisa hoped to talk again with Julia Ranck sometime soon. Louisa was eager for something else, as well. She felt she was ready to tackle a thoughtful response to Sam's letter, although she still wasn't exactly sure what she would say.

———

Annie found Esther busy in the kitchen, making sandwiches with some enthusiastic help from young Laura. The baby was crying, and Zach and John were pulling pots and pans out of one cupboard when Annie hurried inside through the back door. She'd asked Ben to wait out on the step, where she assumed he was gathering his wits. At any rate, she didn't want to barge in on Essie, not with the kind of information she was so excited to share.

She picked up Essie Ann and carried her upstairs, rocking her for a few minutes, and then when the wee one's eyes drooped shut, Annie placed her carefully in the crib across from the foot of Esther's bed.

Ach, gut. Now for the boys.

Whispering to Laura to take her little brothers to the sitting room and play for a bit, Annie stood before Esther, who was slicing the sandwiches in half, all of them piled on a single plate. "We've got us some company for lunch," Annie began, waiting for Esther to look up before adding, "and I have the most wonderful-good news to tell you."

Esther's eyes remained on her task. "Well, what?"

"You may not believe it at first, but it's absolutely true. Wait'll ya hear."

Esther stopped to look at her. "What on earth are ya babbling 'bout, Annie?"

"Zeke's brother, Isaac, isn't dead at all. He's sitting out on the back stoop." She motioned toward the back porch. "What's most amazing is you already know him. It's Ben Martin—remember Zeke's friend from the harness shop?"

Esther frowned. "I don't follow."

"Ben was adopted when he was four, the same age Isaac was when he was taken away. Ben is really Isaac." Annie led her to the back door. "Here, see for yourself."

Ben stood up and entered the porch. "Hello again, Esther."

"Ach, I don't rightly know what Annie's been tellin' me, but won't you come in and have some lunch with us?" she invited, clearly shaken.

He glanced nervously at Annie and then offered to shake hands with Esther, but she had already turned and was heading back into the kitchen. Scurrying about, she set another plate while Annie's heart sank.

"This is just ridiculous," she said softly, standing beside Ben and feeling terribly awkward.

What if no one believes?

Hurrying back to her apartment with her budgeted amount of groceries, Louisa stopped to say, "Hey, kitty," to Muffin before beginning the process of putting the food items away. She had become something of an organizational freak since her visit to Amish country, alphabetizing her canned goods, for example. She smiled as she placed her purchases in the small cupboard-style pantry, excited to bake from scratch again, as she had been doing since her return. She'd even taken several batches of cookies and muffins to her neighbors and an elderly couple who lived downstairs.

Finished with the chore, she made a salad and poured some freshly brewed sun tea before settling in at the small kitchen counter to eat. She had another hour before her next student arrived at the studio, and feeling an urge to connect with Annie, she pulled out a sheet of yellow stationery and began to write longhand.

> *Dear Annie,*
>
> *I'll be straight with you. I wish we lived closer, and I wish our worlds could collide more often. How's that for sappy?*
>
> *One thing I've wanted to tell you is that I'm basically at capacity with students and still have enough time for my own works in process. I'm finding it a really good balance.*
>
> *Something else—you may be surprised, but I've started seeing Michael again. It doesn't mean I've fallen in love with him. I'm warmly cordial, I guess you could say. Even though I'm reluctant to get anything serious going again, he's definitely letting me know he cares . . . a lot.*
>
> *Between you and me, though, I see Sam's face everywhere. Well, I should rephrase that—I see aspects of his face nearly everywhere I look. He's smiling back at me with those beautiful green eyes*

of his in the work my students do—in the landscapes and self-portraits, too. At first, when I arrived back here, I thought I might be in mourning, but that seemed too strange. The phases of grief are many—denial, sadness, anger. . . . But what do I really have to grieve about where Sam's concerned?

I'm rambling here. Sorry!

Hey, I'm sending you a calling card and detailed instructions. Will you use it and phone me from Julia's or from the neighbors' barn phone? You pick, but I really want to connect with you soon. Oh, while you're at it, please tell Julia I'd like to talk with her again, too. Her amazing faith and my great-aunt Margaret's prayers are definitely catching up with me. So, no, I don't think what you shared in your letter about your heart becoming tender toward God is strange at all. I'm right there with you, Annie!

Please write again soon.

> *Love,*
> *Louisa ("Lou")*

P.S. Tell Sam hi for me if you see him.
P.P.S. No, don't. Forget that, OK?
P.P.P.S. Call me!

Louisa had never been one to slam doors or throw things when upset like some out-of-control women she knew. But she had completely run out of stationery and wanted to write another letter—this one to Sam. Searching through her drawers, Louisa began tossing things over her shoulder, wishing she'd taken the time to organize her computer desk and files the way she had her kitchen.

Feeling nearly overwhelmed and hoping she hadn't waited too long to reply to Sam's thoughtful letter, she snatched some copy paper out of the printer and began to write once again.

Dear Sam,

It was really great to hear from you. I hope you don't think I'm rude for not replying immediately. I've thought so much about you since I left. As for your calling me, I would enjoy that a lot.

I guess I wasn't too surprised when you wrote about your plan to leave the Amish. I hope the transition goes smoothly. Congratulations on your promotion at work!

As for me, my life has sort of returned to normal, although I've made quite a few changes since my return here. I'm teaching a fine bunch of art students again, which is the thing that gets me going every morning. Ironically, many of my own paintings are of things I miss

*about Amish life—the life you plan to
leave. The grass is always greener, jah?*
*Please feel free to call, if you wish. I
think of you often!*
Your fancy friend,
Louisa Stratford

She didn't bother to look over what
she'd written. She simply folded the letter
and placed it in an envelope, addressing it
to his new home among Englishers.

Ben was talking with Laura and her
brothers at the kitchen table while Annie
helped Essie slice pieces of angel food cake.
"Walking in the dark is loads of fun," Ben
told the children.

"Ach, can ya see in the dark, like a cat?"
asked Laura, giggling.

Ben laughed, having a good time, and
Annie was glad of it. During the first few
minutes here, she had begun to doubt her
resolve, but now that the delicious chicken-
salad sandwiches had been devoured and
the tension had dissipated, she was hoping
to convince Essie that she and Ben hadn't
completely lost their minds. In the mean-
time, Esther had acted as if she hadn't even
heard Annie's declaration about Isaac.

She must think I've gone loony.

Laura piped up again, asking Ben if he'd ever gone hunting for snipes.

"Not recently." Ben caught Annie's gaze across the table.

"Do you know what they look like?" Laura asked, blue eyes shining.

"I've known some to appear under little girls' pillows."

Don't scare her, Annie thought, glancing at Essie, who seemed to be enjoying the entertainment, as well.

"That's mighty funny, Mr. Ben," Zach said, leaning forward, his elbows squarely on the table.

"Snipes don't like it inside the house," Laura declared.

"Jah, they stay up high in the trees," Zach said.

"Now, children, I think Mr. Ben is pulling your legs," Essie said, reaching over to wipe a smudge of food off Zach's face.

"Oh, for sure, Mamma. He's got us by the ankles!" Laura seemed more than happy to keep things going. She cupped her hands around her mouth and whispered to Zach loudly, "Look how one side of his mouth moves up higher when he smiles . . . just like Dat's."

Zach nodded. "Jah, I saw that. Same as cousin Nate, too."

Laura started giggling again. "He's got that smooth peach stone, too, remember?"

Annie jolted mentally. "Essie? May I see you in the sitting room?"

"Why sure," she said rather reluctantly.

While Ben kept the children laughing and talking, Annie told Essie again that her brother-in-law, Isaac, was no longer lost but quite certainly found. "The only thing he had from his Amish life on the night he was found was that worn down peach pit."

Essie looked away. "Oh, Annie, this is so strange for you to think this way. I mean . . . we *all* wish Isaac was still alive, and maybe he still is, but honestly . . . *Ben?*"

Annie rested a hand on Essie's arm. "I know what you're thinking, that this must be love talking and I'm making this up—"

"Well?"

Slowly Annie explained her reasoning— that Isaac and Ben would be the same age, that Ben had unexplainable but vivid memories that only Isaac could have, such as climbing the tree at the old Hochstetler place and swinging in the locust grove— "with me!"

Annie quickly told of all the places they'd stopped to visit that morning at Ben's request. And even though she desperately wanted her dear friend to accept the truth of a long-lost brother-in-law, it was painfully clear Essie thought Annie was quite ferhoodled.

"For one thing, I'd expect him to look more like Zeke. Wouldn't you?" Essie said.

"What about your in-laws—the Hochstetlers. What do you remember 'bout them?"

"Very little, really," Essie admitted. "They were not so keen on Zeke and me marrying, I do recall that. But as for looks, well, it's difficult to say."

"Esther, don't you believe me? Zeke's brother is alive."

"Oh, Annie, maybe he is . . . and maybe he isn't. Just because the bones—"

Annie felt her growing frustration. "Esther, no, listen." She stopped. Esther had turned pale and looked sad, as if she pitied Annie. *I've pushed this too far.*

She took a deep breath. "I'll prove it to you, Essie. Just give me time."

Essie, still white in the face, nodded, forcing a smile, and the two women hugged.

Esther whispered in Annie's ear, "I want to believe you, I do. If Isaac were alive, it would be amazing. But . . . it seems so . . . impossible."

Annie kissed Esther's cheek. "I hope I didn't upset you."

Esther shook her head, but her breathing seemed much too labored.

Chapter 20

Jesse took his time hitching up his driving horse to the family carriage. With the sun so warm that afternoon, he desired the covering of the gray buggy while making the trip over to Zeke and Esther's. He was mighty weary, what with Annie's strange imaginings, saying she'd discovered that Isaac was alive and all. It wasn't that he hadn't been curious; he was. Maybe too much so. And now that she'd left, he felt a twinge of regret. He hadn't even given the poor girl a chance to explain. Maybe if it had been anyone other than his willful daughter suggesting such a thing . . . Still, he was glad he hadn't succumbed, standing his ground . . . finishing his work instead of falling for Annie's wishful thinking. *Isaac alive? What on earth?* True, the bones weren't Isaac's, but to jump to such a conclusion?

He was headed over to Esther's, but not for the purpose of setting his daughter straight. He had other things on his mind—namely Esther's defiance. He'd thought surely by now she would have given up her close association with the Rancks and their church. He also felt responsible to protect Zeke's children—and his own daughter—from the onslaught of conversion tactics used by certain zealous folk. *My own cousins, for pete's sake!*

Something else consumed him—Ichabod's coming. Jesse had written back, but if the man came anyway, Jesse would have to do everything within his power to keep that visit in check. Zeke's father had often caused problems—even more than the thorny issues Zeke posed to the brethren. Who knew where it would end if Daniel actually showed up. Especially if the man had gone fancy, as Jesse feared.

If I'd just put off writing to him in the first place, Daniel Hochstetler would not be making plans to return here.

Jesse feared Esther was much too trusting and could be a prime target for half-truths. Annie, too, though for different reasons.

A shudder swept through him. Had Daniel already arrived? Was *that* why Annie had seemed so swept away with her strange notion of Isaac's return? Had Ichabod arrived in secret to stir up the brethren? *Has he already hoodwinked my own daughter?*

Aware of a newfound urgency, Jesse encouraged his best driving horse onward, before it was too late.

Esther offered Ben another cup of coffee. "Sure, thanks," he said, hoping to hear more about Zeke's growing-up years, or whatever Esther might be willing to share. After her short conversation with Annie in private, Esther looked visibly shaken and now seemed to be scrutinizing him. He felt terrible for not considering the emotional impact upon this poor woman. *Is it worth it? Am I causing more trouble?*

The three of them sat alone in the kitchen now that the younger children were off to bed for naps and Laura was outside playing with the dog.

"Zeke often talked with disdain about his father," Esther said softly, glancing at Annie. "I do know my husband was fond of his mother, who passed away a short time ago."

Annie spoke up quickly. "I knew 'bout this, Ben, but didn't want to put too much on you at once."

He felt sick at the news. Now he would never know his mother, nor would she know he had safely grown to adulthood. Taking a deep breath, he asked what had caused Mary's death, who'd received word, and where in Canada his birth parents had been living. More questions taxed his mind, but he decided to give Esther a break. *Give her time to think.* He was about to suggest as much when Jesse Zook drove into the lane with his horse and buggy.

Annie noticed right away, too, and rose immediately to go to the back door.

"It's all right, Annie," Esther said, going to her.

Ben could hear the two women talking quietly but made no attempt to listen. He mulled the information he'd gathered in only two short days. He knew it was finally time to discuss all he'd learned with Irvin and Julia. *Tonight at supper,* he decided. He had an urgent desire to call home, too. Perhaps his parents had recalled more information that would corroborate his discoveries.

Annie's father was being shown into the house. Ben stood to shake his hand. "Hello, Preacher," he said, instantly aware of the tension between them.

Jesse scowled and looked about the

room as if searching for someone. "I'd heard you left town."

"I did."

"But you're back."

"Yes, sir."

Esther asked Jesse to sit at the head of the table, and he did. She offered him coffee and some pie, as she had Ben.

They all sat down together, except for Esther, who stood as she had once before when Ben had come here for a meal with Zeke. He noticed the preacher send a dark look toward Annie, clearly aggravated to find the two of them in the same room together.

So now not only was Esther pale-faced, a reaction to their previous discussion, but so was Annie. Ben tried to catch her eye to alert her to drop the idea of pushing things with her father, but she didn't look his way and forged ahead. "I know you won't believe this, Daed," she said, "but in all truth, Ben here *is* Isaac, back from the grave."

Jesse gripped his chair.

Ben expelled a long breath.

A long moment passed as Jesse's eyes swept from Annie to him and back. The preacher's brow furrowed with obvious consternation. "Have you lost your mind, daughter?"

Annie shook her head. "Ach, Daed—"

"Now, you listen to me. Claimin' this Englischer is long-lost Isaac—just so you can keep carryin' on with him after I forbade you to do so, is that it? Never would I have believed you would sink to something so low."

Ben shivered. *This isn't going well.*

"Daed, I would never do such a thing," Annie said, pain evident on her face. "It's true, no matter how crazy it sounds."

"How's *that* possible?" Jesse looked squarely at his daughter.

" 'Cause it is," she asserted and then began to share all the things they had both learned since their meeting at the covered bridge.

When Annie finished, her father continued to stare at her without speaking, his focus darting back to Ben before slowly returning again to his daughter. His expression had softened some, but he clearly remained skeptical. Ben expected him to argue further, but instead he said, "Well, now. Haven't you forgotten something? If he's Zeke's brother, as you say, why was it Zeke never recognized him earlier?"

He turned to Ben. "Didn't you and Zeke spend some time together? At that mud sale, for one?"

Ben nodded.

"Well?"

The question lingered in the air. Jesse had a point, and Annie had no answer.

"Enough said," Jesse announced. "This is nonsense."

Esther looked more frail than she had before, and she moved toward the counter to get the coffee pot. When she did, Jesse asked if he might speak with her and Annie alone. "Why, sure." Esther looked weakly over her shoulder at Ben and said, "That is, if it's all right with you."

Ben took the polite hint, but Annie looked nervous, even alarmed. Excusing himself, Ben headed out the back way, deciding now was as good a time as any to disappear from view and phone his mom.

Worried that Ben had been offended by Daed's outspokenness, Annie poured cream into her father's coffee, listening as he told of having received word from Zeke's father in Canada.

"He wrote a letter in response to mine," said her father, explaining why he'd written initially. "So I wouldn't be surprised if Ichabod shows up, and soon."

Esther gasped. "He's coming *here*?"

Daed nodded. "He'll be lookin' for a

place to stay, I'm sure. But let's keep this mum. Don't need more troubles arising." He inhaled deeply and gave Annie another fierce look. She looked down, having recognized the utter disappointment on her father's face.

Jesse continued, "Your father-in-law ought to stay with me, Esther." He looked at them both. "Given the circumstances."

" 'Cause of my shunning?" Esther reached for her coffee cup, hand trembling.

"Ain't any good for two women to share one house, especially when both have such unchecked fancies." He darted another disapproving glance at Annie. "This Isaac twaddle is bad enough, but you both goin' to a church on the outside is creating a stir."

Annie wasn't too surprised, yet she hadn't heard much of anything from the womenfolk. Of course, she'd not been attending their work frolics since coming here to stay.

"The brethren expect you to return to Preaching services, Esther—you, too, Annie. These children are at risk."

"What're you sayin'?" Esther asked, her cheeks much too red.

"I'm speakin' of your souls . . . all of yous. Your children, Esther, are to be raised in the Amish church so that grace and peace may rest on this house. This is your husband's desire, as you surely know." He turned to Annie, "And you, the preacher's daughter, are helping this family right out the door. You should be ashamed of yourself."

He put on his hat. "I expect to see you come to your senses, daughter, and return home so God can finish His work of discipline. As for you, Esther, it's time to repent and put an end to this saving grace malarkey."

With that he headed for the door. Only when her father had left did Annie realize she had clenched her hands into fists so tight her palms were nearly bruised.

Sitting in the car, Ben called his mother on his cell phone. She answered on the second ring.

"Mom? Hi, it's Ben."

"Oh, honey, are you all right?" She sounded jittery. "I've been so worried."

"I'm fine, Mom."

He had debated how much to reveal to her, wanting to spare her feelings, but his own excitement got the best of him. "I think I know who I might have been, before I was found that night. Before you and Dad adopted me."

Silence filled the phone line.

Then the thin question, a single word. "Who?"

Gently he told her everything, filling her in on Annie's and his discovery. "You won't believe this, but I could have a brother and a sister-in-law, and two nieces and two nephews." He told of his first parents, that his Amish mother was deceased but that his father lived somewhere in Ontario, Canada. "I'm putting it all together, Mom. It's not as difficult as I thought it might be. Actually, I never expected to find out all this so quickly, or at all." He paused, sensing her anxiety.

"Oh, Ben, be careful. I would hate for you to get your hopes up."

"I know, but it seems possible at least."

She was silent for a time; then she said, "Don't forget us, Ben. We're your family, too."

"I know that, Mom. I hope you won't take all this wrong, but I needed to return here. I didn't realize why at first. It was as if something was *calling* me back. I needed to know about my past, my first family."

"Well, how long will you stay this time?"

"Haven't decided." From where he was parked, he could see Annie's father leaving the house, his head bowed as he strode toward his horse and buggy. "I'll be in touch,

Mom. Tell Dad I called."

"I'll do that. He sends his love."

"Please don't worry about me, okay?"

"You know me too well. It's what I do best."

"Yeah, right." He chuckled. "Bye!"

"We love you, Ben. . . . Good-bye."

Watching Preacher Jesse rein the horse around to make the wide circular turn at the top of the drive, new images emerged in Ben's mind. Indistinct and hazy ones of going to market and farm sales with a tall man. His father? Sitting on the tall man's knees . . . holding the reins with his small hands. He could almost smell the pipe tobacco now as he briefly closed his eyes.

Moments later, he saw Annie as she stood at the back door, waving, and he felt that familiar longing again, just seeing her. She hugged herself as if chilled, looking suddenly lost.

Getting out of the car, he called, "Take a walk with me," and she seemed relieved to accept.

Walking silently at first, they took the mule road out to the vast pastureland, where trees grew in random groves.

Annie was obviously discouraged; he couldn't recall having ever seen her so dejected.

Their eyes met and in spite of what he'd just told his mother, a renewed sense of doubt filled him. "Maybe we're wrong, Annie. Maybe we *both* have unbridled imaginations, as your father seems to think."

Her eyes filled with tears and she nodded. "I just wanted to believe it so badly."

"I did, too."

To redirect their talk to less volatile subjects, Ben pointed out various trees along the way. Then something popped into his head. "Say, Annie, Esther told me a little, but do you happen to know anything more about Zeke's father?"

"Ichabod?"

"What? Don't you mean Daniel?"

"He was always referred to as Ichabod from around the time of the kidnapping, according to Mamm."

Ben recognized the name from American literature. In high school, *The Legend of Sleepy Hollow*—the tale of the infamous and ridiculous schoolmaster, Ichabod Crane— had been required reading. "Why was Daniel called that?"

"Because he refused the lot for preacher."

Annie clearly felt uncomfortable talking about something that reflected so poorly on

Ben's true father. On hers, too, for that matter.

"Honestly, I don't know much about it," she finally said.

Ben didn't push for more details, and Annie quickly changed the subject. "Essie was plenty shook up when my father left. Still, she shooed me outside to find you."

Ben knew Esther had been stunned by the possibility of his being Isaac. Preacher Zook's fiery speech likely hadn't helped matters. "Maybe she can get some rest with us out of the house."

She smiled at him as they walked. In the distance, a farm wagon rolled by, pulled by a single horse. Suddenly he remembered an outing he'd gone on with the man he'd called Dat. There was a lingering embarrassment surrounding this memory that caused a strange pressure in his chest.

Annie held tightly to his hand and they walked in silence, enjoying the fresh air and the sounds of spring. Her nearness, the wide-eyed sweetness of her, brought the memory to him more fully.

He remembered riding beside Dat on the buggy bench on a trip to buy their supply of peaches at an Amish farmhouse, seemingly miles away. When they arrived, he recalled being made over by the very pretty young woman who sold the bushels of peaches. She touched his face and smiled sweetly—even gave him free peaches, saying if he squeezed a peach pit hard enough and long enough it would eventually sprout. He could still hear Dat's hearty laughter ringing in his ears over that one.

When they got back to the buggy, Dat said he had forgotten to pay for the peaches. He went back into the house but stayed longer than a curious boy could possibly sit. He followed Dat inside and peeked around the corner, witnessing a stolen kiss, until his father looked up and saw him standing there. Heart pounding, he had hurried back to the buggy and crawled into the front seat. . . .

"Ben? You all right?" Annie was staring at him. "You're breathin' awful hard."

He couldn't possibly share this confusing vision from the past with her, or anyone.

"Let's keep going." He pointed farther away from the house, wanting to embrace fully every moment they had together, because he had no idea how to continue seeing her, recalling the glare of disapproval on Preacher Jesse's face earlier.

They walked for more than an hour. "Should we be heading back?" he asked after a glance at his watch.

Annie smiled warmly. "I can stay out as long as need be."

Need be? He wanted to wrap her in his arms, carry her away to another world. But where . . . how? Could they possibly make this relationship work? He'd come back in part to solve the troubles he'd caused, and here he was, the source of even more troubles than he could have imagined.

Maybe he should have remained at home. What did it matter if he were Isaac? But he realized that he couldn't have stayed away. He had this intense connection to Annie, as if he had been born to know her.

He smiled wistfully. Were they soul mates, destined to be together? And yet they'd failed before. What was different now?

He considered this. For one thing, he sensed a freedom in Annie that had been missing before, and the realization of this suddenly spurred him on, giving him more fuel for hope.

Another hour later, they were met by Esther's daughter Laura running toward them, her bare feet pounding the dirt path that connected the field to the barnyard. "Ach, Annie, I'm ever so glad you're back."

"What's wrong?" Annie leaned over to

wipe the streaks of tears from the little girl's face.

"It's Mamma . . . she's *awful* sick. She's holdin' her belly and crying."

Annie picked up her skirt and ran toward the house. Ben followed. "Can you take her to a doctor right quick, Ben, if need be?" she called over her shoulder.

"Of course."

In a few minutes, Annie brought Esther out of the house and together they helped her into his car.

Zeke's wife is ill. . . . The realization of who he might be to frail Essie Hochstetler struck Ben anew. *My sister-in-law?*

Annie stayed with the children while he drove Esther to the hospital. They rode in silence as she closed her eyes and clutched her abdomen. On occasion she whispered, "Please help, dear Lord."

When they arrived, Ben offered to help Esther inside. Graciously, she accepted his arm as he gingerly assisted her in through the glass doors.

At the desk, a nurse smiled with concern as Esther quickly signed in. An orderly emerged, and Ben helped Esther into a wheelchair.

"You are so kind, Ben," Esther whispered before the orderly wheeled her away to another ward of the hospital. Ben followed.

Sitting down in another waiting room, he happened to glance up at the board. *Obstetrics?*

Then Ben remembered Esther favoring her stomach earlier, while Annie's father was drinking his coffee. *Esther must be expecting again already*. It struck him that Essie Ann, whom he'd held as a newborn—his own flesh-and-blood niece—was only four months old. *Doesn't Zeke have any knowledge of family planning?*

Chapter 2-1

Jesse noticed Yonie walking out on Queen Road with a girl who was not at all Amish. Of course, this being a warm, sunny day, a long walk with a pretty girl was in order at Yonie's age—*if* the girl weren't English. Jesse was wound up from his visit with Esther and Annie—and seeing Ben Martin there, too. He was tempted to pull the horse over and confront his son. *Ach, where will it all end?*

Yonie spotted him and waved, but Jesse also noticed the redness creeping up from his neck into his face. "Hullo there, Pop!" Yonie called, sounding a bit too flippant for Jesse's liking. But he knew better than to do anything more than wave back and smile. It wouldn't do to rile up that one—not the way the brethren were all in a tizzy about losing several young men to the world here lately. No, he'd keep his peace, bite his lip, and trust for the best.

But Annie, what another story *she* was. He wished he knew what to do. Sighing, he thought of Ben Martin and wondered why on earth he'd come back, trying to pass himself off as Isaac.

The whole thing was wild horse feathers, and Annie should know it. He divided his frustration between Annie's Ben and Yonie's girlfriend—and if she didn't look like the daughter of one of their neighbors, the Zimmermans! *Yonie and Dory—puh!*

These young bucks and their girls, he thought, wishing something could be done to eliminate all the nonsense the running-around years served up. Several fathers had wanted to address this subject in recent months, but Bishop Andy had said repeatedly, "It is our way." And that was that.

Truth be known, in Jesse's mind, the knowledge that he was the Lord God's second choice for preacher was ever before him. And he'd nearly convinced himself that was why he'd failed to rein in Annie . . . and evidently Yonie, too.

Annie was worried sick about Essie— scared she might lose her baby. This, along with Daed's reaction to Ben, continued to plague her. She was sure Ben's presence in the community would drive a greater wedge between herself and Daed. Yet why should she care? Hadn't she already cut herself off by not submitting?

She stewed till she was nearly woozy, wondering if Ben and Essie had arrived safely at the nearby hospital, worried that she may have actually caused Essie's pains somehow. Esther had become entirely too upset at the mention of Isaac, and Annie realized she could have handled things far better. *Was I too pushy?*

Annie second-guessed the whole thing while she walked the length of the upstairs with fussy Essie Ann. Now and then, she looked in on Zach and John, always mindful of John's breathing, making sure he was not close to having another asthma attack. Essie reminded her often that the coming of spring and summer were hard on John. *There's something difficult about the changing of the seasons,* she decided, thinking of Cousin Julia's children, as well. In April, James and Molly had had trouble adjusting to daylight saving time. Annie shook her head, thankful that the People did not switch over from fast time to slow time. No, staying the same was the best way to be.

Essie Ann's head popped up off Annie's

shoulder again and she began to cry. "Jah, it's all right, little one. . . . Mamma will be home soon." She hoped that was true, because this one would be needing some nourishment here before long, and there was nothing worse than a hungry nursing baby without its mother.

She stroked Essie Ann's soft head, sliding her hand down to caress the baby's neck, feeling the little wrinkles. "You're all right," she whispered. "Now go back to sleep."

Thinking that rocking might do the trick, she carried her to the big rocker in Essie's bedroom, glancing in Laura's room and seeing that she'd fallen asleep with a book on her chest. "Such dear ones," she whispered, and as she patted the baby, she thought of her father's argument regarding Zeke. Why hadn't Isaac's brother recognized him?

Because he's not in his right mind, Annie thought, but then reconsidered. Who says Zeke didn't recognize Ben? Not by name, maybe, but in a different sort of way. After all, hadn't Zeke been drawn to Ben? Sure he was. And Zeke rarely made friends with anyone. Maybe the whole unfathomable incident—his brother returning as an Englischer—had stirred up something awful in

Zeke's mind, compounding his problems.

Annie closed her eyes just as Esther often did, addressing the Lord of heaven and earth, less sheepish about it each time she did. "O Lord God, I ask that you hear my prayer. Thank you for bringing Isaac back—to all of us—and may it be possible for the truth of his identity to be received by the very ones who need him most. For this I am most grateful, dear Lord. Amen."

An undeniable sense of peace filled the room, and she basked in it, aware now that the sweet baby in her arms had gone limp with sleep. Not willing to take any chances with Essie Ann's awaking, Annie continued to gently rock, feeling the weight of this little one, thinking of all the good things the Lord Jesus, as Essie called the Son of God, had brought into her life. *All the blessings, jah, that's how Essie says it these days.*

She knew Julia saw things the same way. Blessings were a direct gift from the hand of the Father to His dear children. So if that was true, was Ben Martin—well . . . Isaac— exactly that? A divine blessing?

Smiling, she leaned her head back, resting in the truth, if that's what it was. *All things work together for good,* she thought, recalling Ben's words yet again. Why did that Scripture keep coming to her mind? Annie didn't know, but she knew her heart was more open to the things both Essie and Julia said now than a year ago.

Letting her mind drift to Essie's pregnancy, she remembered her mother having let slip once, to daughter-in-law Sarah Mae, that she heartily believed the Lord God knew she would be a better mother of sons than of daughters. Thus, perhaps, the reason why Barbara Zook had birthed six boys and only one Annie.

What made me think of that? she wondered. *Would Essie have many more sons and please her husband in that?*

After a time, she heard Ben's car pull up to the back door, and she rose silently to put Essie Ann in her crib, then hurried downstairs to see how Essie was doing. *Let her be all right, Lord,* she pleaded.

Esther was terrified. She had been bleeding for much too long, with intense pains across her abdomen and down her thighs. Suffering with deep dread and complete exhaustion, she longed to be warm . . . craved solitude. She knew her baby was in danger, and she must remain overnight in a hospital, far from her home and Essie Ann, who was dependent upon her for nourishment. *"A wet nurse,"* she had urged upon Ben, explaining how he must rush home to Annie with this request. *"But keep it quiet as to my whereabouts,"* she'd warned him, lest the news spread and the People guess her condition, though she had not come right out and told Ben what that was. Even now, she wanted desperately to protect her poor husband from a possible excommunication, which the brethren would surely put on him for breaking the rules of her shun.

The nurses were helpful and kind, yet she saw how curiously they looked at her. *Because I'm Plain.* She was different, and that was quite clear here in this fancy place, the blank television hovering nearly over her and all the worldly gadgets around her—an electric bed that moved up and down, of all things!

She set to praying for those who would be assisting her during the night, asking God to protect the young life she had conceived, even against the will of the People.

"Complete bed rest" had been the doctor's strict order. Oh, she'd give anything not to have been present at the house when Annie brought her friend over this day! If only there had not been such a constricting in her heart. She had felt instantly nauseated, then she'd stood all the while, serving coffee, wanting to honor the preacher by not sharing the same table.

But to think that Ben might be Isaac had been ever so startling. And if such news was able to upset her so, threatening the life of her precious little one, then what on earth would it do to Zeke? Surely she must not allow herself to fret this way, but, oh, she could not will herself to relax. Every muscle in her body was tense.

I must rest in the Lord. . . .

Earlier, after Ben, Preacher Jesse, and Annie had left the house, Esther had set about treating her symptoms with wild yam root—the most bitter of teas—then black haw root bark, homeopathic remedies she much preferred to drugs and this hospital setting. But her efforts had been in vain, and after a time, she had sent Laura to go and fetch Annie, who insisted she go to the hospital.

She could not let this baby die! *O dear Lord, calm my heart and prepare the way for Zeke, I ask. Help this most peculiar news not to disturb my troubled husband any further. . . .*

A couple hours later, when the telephone rang next to her bed, Esther scarcely knew enough to pick it up. But one of the nurses was on hand and did so for her. "Yes, Esther's right here. I'll let you speak with her."

The nurse covered the phone with her hand and said, "It's someone named Ben, calling about your baby at home."

Let it be good news. . . . She took the phone from the nurse. "Hullo?"

"Esther, I'm calling for Annie. She's with your children." Ben went on to say that a neighbor of Julia's had driven to the house to nurse Essie Ann in Esther's absence. "Annie's hoping this is all right with you."

"Oh my, yes." *I can trust Julia.* "It was so kind of you to let me know." She felt truly relieved and ever so strange speaking to Ben as though he were family.

"Annie doesn't want you to worry, Esther. She's comfortable taking care of the children and the house for as long as necessary."

"Jah, I know she'll do just fine."

He said a few more very considerate things to her before saying good-bye.

Though deeply grateful for their help, Esther could not stop the flow of tears, and as she wept, she prayed. *May your will be done, O Lord.*

Chapter 22

Ben didn't like to think about Annie all alone at Esther's with four little children, managing supper preparations on her own, though it appeared that young Laura was a willing and eager assistant.

Helping Julia set the table as Irvin arrived home, Ben was impressed by her abilities. His own mom was not so keen on putting on a big spread, or cooking in general, except for holidays or special occasions. Typically, she was much more happy having Dad get takeout. His standing joke was that he was the food-getter.

Happy is the man who marries a cook, Ben thought.

Irvin kissed Julia soundly on the lips, then hugged James and Molly when they came running to greet him.

"Hello, Ben! How are things?" Irvin

moved to the sink and washed up.

"Interesting," he said, glancing at Julia, who'd already heard the news regarding Esther, though he'd remained mum about his more personal news. "I happened to run into Annie by the old covered bridge yesterday."

Scrubbing his hands, Irvin turned and grinned. "Really now. What a coincidence!"

Ben smiled, too. James and Molly were getting settled into their chairs.

"I'm concerned about Esther. How's she doing?" Julia asked, carrying a platter of roast beef and baby onions to the table. She quickly filled Irvin in on the events of the day.

"When I left the hospital, she seemed to be in less pain and was resting," Ben said. He mentioned having called her later, at Annie's request, regarding the arrangement for Essie Ann.

"I'm glad Esther knows about the wet nurse. She shouldn't be worrying about her little one tonight." Julia paused. "Did the doctor give any indication how long Esther would be in?"

"Overnight is my understanding," Ben replied.

"I'll visit her first thing tomorrow, then," Julia said.

Ben nodded. "I think Annie would appreciate it. She'll be busy with the Hochstetler children."

Julia's eyes twinkled. "Well, why not give her a hand, Ben?"

He smiled at her. "I just might."

After the meal, when Irvin had finished helping in the kitchen and the children were off for their baths, Ben welcomed Irvin's company.

These had been a strange couple of days, and he needed to share his news with someone who might offer further wisdom. Someone whom he particularly respected, like Irvin.

As concisely as possible, Ben filled him in on having been told in Kentucky of his adoption.

Irvin listened quietly, nodding his head, his eyes registering empathy. But when Ben finally shared his newfound suspicion that he and Zeke's missing brother were one and the same, Irvin's eyebrows shot up. He scrutinized Ben for a moment, as if wondering if perhaps the young man were pulling his leg. "My, that's quite a leap." Irvin ran his hand through his hair.

"Isn't it, though?" Ben chuckled. "I still haven't had the time to fully digest it." He showed Irvin the magazine cover he'd carried in his wallet since last Christmas. "One thing is certain: Annie's painting led me to come here last winter. And it was also Annie who put it all together about my family history." He shared openly about the strange visions he had had since learning of his adoption, and of his own gradual realization that he was indeed who Annie had said.

"How does Jesse Zook take to this news, assuming Annie told him?"

Ben inhaled. "He doesn't buy it."

Irvin considered this. "Well, there are ways to *prove* that you're Isaac, you know. If you are, that is."

Ben nodded. He'd already thought of DNA tests, which were the obvious means to him, though they would no doubt sound like English mumbo jumbo to Jesse Zook. Likely the preacher would have to approve Zeke undergoing such a test with him.

"I would be willing, if it comes to that," Ben said. "But I'm not ready to push it yet." He paused, feeling tired. "Going from being the Martins' son to finding out that I might have been born here in Amish country has been a jolt to me, no question."

"So what will you do now?" Irvin asked.

"Take things one day at a time . . . if you don't mind letting me stay on a while. I'll pay you room and board—I sure don't expect a handout."

"Oh, we can work out the details later. Not a problem."

Ben thanked Irvin profusely, then excused himself for bed. He had to tread lightly, he believed, especially where Annie's family was concerned. Claiming his identity outright could blow up in their faces.

Yet there was no evidence of hesitation on Annie's part this time. The idea that something had changed in the way she viewed their relationship was both exciting and mystifying, although Ben wondered how long he could hang around before the Amish brethren ran him off again.

Time will tell.

Zeke was having a horrible night. Up and down, from his bed to the window he went, missing Esther, wishing for something to grab ahold of while he slept. *An extra pillow would do.*

He wandered out to the common living area and found a throw pillow on the sofa. Carrying it back to his own bed, he got in and pressed the pillow to his chest, all the while imagining Esther's supple and soft body. *I must get well. Must get out of this place and return home, and soon.* He felt desperately lost without his wife.

He propped his head up on his bed pillow and, still clutching the smaller one to his chest, mulled over his day. A long one to be sure, though not as physically exhausting as getting up with the chickens and plowing or planting for hours on end. Still, it had been stressful, with several sessions today including other troubled folk, some more disturbed than he, going around the circle talking about feelings—supposedly suppressed. His doctor had also talked of upping his anti-depression medication, which Zeke wasn't happy about—not that he had much say around there. *Will I ever be well enough to return to the People . . . to my family?*

By the way Esther had walked out on him when she visited, he wasn't too sure if she'd even have him back. But no, why should he think such a thing? He was in charge—always had been. She had no say, under God . . . nor under her husband.

But she *had* been somewhat lippy, standing up to him toward the end. Her attitude had stung him. He wouldn't allow his woman to have the upper hand next visit.

He gripped the pillow and began weeping silently. "Esther, my Esther, ach, how I miss you," he whispered into the darkness.

Ben lay awake as one childhood recollection after another pervaded his brain, as if the floodgates had fully opened. He squelched a laugh, recalling his rough, dry feet as a boy and his fascination with peeling thin layers of the skin—in strips—off the callouses on his big toes until his toes started to bleed. His father belittled him for it, but his older brother thought the habit quite funny. It was Mamma, though, who lovingly cleaned his wounds of the slivers of wood and dirt that sometimes found their way inside.

He couldn't resist the urge to reach down and touch the pads of his big toes, wondering if they were larger than they should be. He didn't feel anything unusual—no indication he had scarred himself for life. He did have one scar on the ball of his left foot, though he wasn't sure how he'd gotten that.

Scars . . . He wondered about his parents' decision to keep his adoption quiet. *How much better would it have been, knowing as a child what I know now?*

There had been plenty of adopted kids in his life while growing up. One girl in particular had parents who had made a scrapbook of the day they'd brought her home to be their own. All he'd ever had was his peach stone, although he didn't even know that was part of his secret past until recently.

Another memory popped into his mind, clearer than the rest. A summer day when his father had spent all afternoon in the barn "a-wrestlin' with the angels," according to Mamma.

"More like he's battling the devil," Zeke had spouted off to Mamma, who'd told Zeke to wash out his mouth with soap. But Zeke had muttered on the way to the sink, "Dat's in trouble with the brethren," insisting in a whisper that he'd seen the bishop and the preachers coming down the road, dressed in black.

Mamma had said, "Hogwash," but Zeke had kept talking about the new minister, Jesse Zook, who'd come "talkin' to Dat a-plenty. Before *and* after he got the preacher's lot."

Mamma had shushed him. And Isaac remembered sitting in the far corner of the kitchen, wondering why their father had skipped Mamma's dinner and would probably be breathing the same air as the mules all night.

Had someone else caught him kissing the peach girl?

Slipping out of bed, shaking his head at the memory, Ben found the print of Annie's painting in his wallet, folded so neatly along the same crease, he could see it was in some danger of tearing. Going to the window, he held it up in the moonlight, amazed again that even after all these years the peach stone held some significance to her, as well.

He placed the picture back on the bureau and reluctantly returned to bed, not tired enough to sleep. Tomorrow he would go and check on Annie and the children, and spend the day helping her with farm chores—the pigs, whatever was needed—if she wished. Regardless of his determination to spare her further trouble, he longed to see her again.

No, he *needed* to see her.

Jesse knew he'd be dead tired at the pre-dawn milking, but still he sat in the dark of the kitchen, drinking yet another cup of coffee. He craved time alone and was thankful for Barbara's willingness to retire for the night without him hours ago. Ben's return perplexed him no end. He wracked his brain, going over the events of the day and evaluating his memory of Isaac Hochstetler—what the youngest child of Ichabod had looked like. No unusual features nor distinguishing marks that Jesse recalled. For a moment, he realized how useful even a single photograph of Isaac might be, though, of course, such images were forbidden.

He contemplated again young Isaac's face. Daniel's younger boy was like all the other boys in the community—quick on his feet, mouthy at times, worked hard when told to, and played hard with his puppy dog and older brother. As for looks—the same deep brown eyes as Ben Martin's, that was certain, and light hair . . . much like Annie's.

But did this alone make him Isaac? Jesse didn't accept that for a minute. The fact that Ben looked to be about the right age wasn't especially significant, since any number of young men were just as old. So what was it about Ben that drove Annie to decide he was her long-lost friend? Was it merely a ploy to continue their courting? *Surely that's what we've got here . . . a desperate attempt.*

Exhausted now, he carried the cup over to the sink, left it there without rinsing it, and padded up the stairs.

He found his wife sitting up in bed. "Ach, Jesse . . . Jesse, I had another dream." He went to her and cradled her in his arms. "What was it, dear?"

"Isaac . . . and he wasn't just back, like he'd never been taken. This time, it was much more than that." She started to weep, and he feared she might awaken their sons.

"Shh, now, talk to me, love. Talk to your ol' Jesse. . . ."

She sighed. Then, after wiping her eyes on the sleeve of her cotton nightgown, she told him. "I dreamt the most peculiar thing . . . that Isaac was our own. Oh, Jesse, our very own boy. We'd lost him, just as Daniel and Mary had, and bore the terrible pain of it all, and then he was found. Found, I tell you." She wept like a broken-hearted little child.

What on earth? He held her even closer, stroking her long, long hair, whispering, "All's well, love. Simply trust that all is well."

Chapter 23

Not because she was terribly interested, but because she wanted to be polite, Louisa went with Courtney to the Park Meadows Mall in search of the "perfect present" for Courtney's sister's birthday. "You know how important turning sweet sixteen is, remember?" Courtney joked as they strolled through the vast food court, complete with river-rock fireplace and wood beams, creating a lodgelike interior.

But at the mention of the milestone birthday, Louisa let her mind drift to the Amish tradition of *Rumschpringe*, the years between turning sixteen and making the lifelong promise to the Amish church and to God.

"What would you think if your sister started running around now that she's sixteen?" Louisa asked.

"Berit already does." Courtney laughed. "We all did, from about twelve or thirteen on. Don't you remember?"

"I didn't get into guys till my last year of high school."

"Oh, that's right. Late bloomer."

Louisa shook her head. "Even so, I was pretty stupid. There's way more to life than all that. I wish I'd known before I gave so much of myself away."

"So you're judging *yourself* now?" Courtney wrinkled her nose and picked up the pace, her attitude changing.

Louisa kicked herself mentally. *Keep your mouth shut, Lou.*

They spent the rest of the afternoon going from store to store, window-shopping mostly. At one point, Courtney stopped to admire a skimpy skirt and halter top on a headless mannequin. "Hey, I could see you in this," she said casually.

"Yeah," Louisa said, sarcastically. "Too much of me."

"Seriously, it's so you."

"No it's not." *Not anymore.*

Courtney was visibly put out by the time they stopped for espresso and chai tea. "Maybe you should just go back, return to the simple hick life you crave so much, Louisa. Ever think of that?"

"All the time."

"So what's keeping you here?"

Louisa tried to laugh it off, but it wasn't funny anymore. Courtney evidently wanted a fight.

"Look," Courtney continued, "if you think everyone's messed up because they don't see things the way you do—the enlightened new you—then why do you bother with us pagans?"

Louisa wanted to set her straight, to tell her she *did* care about her, whether she understood her need for the simple life or not. But before she could say anything, Courtney's eyes began filling with tears and her pouty lower lip started to quiver.

"Hey, Court . . . what's wrong?"

Courtney struggled to compose herself, pulling a tissue from her small handbag. "You'll never believe it."

"Sure I will. Try me."

"The absolute worst possible thing . . ."

"You're not pregnant, are you?" Louisa asked, hoping she was wrong.

Courtney snorted with disdain. "Bingo."

Louisa studied Courtney, wondering if she was trying to put one over on her, but Courtney was definitely not kidding. "Oh, Court . . . Does anybody else know?"

"You're the first."

"Who's the father?" Louisa wondered if it was Courtney's housemate, Jared.

Courtney shrugged and shook her head. "I'm not exactly sure."

"Oh man . . ."

Louisa's mind jumped ahead. She began to ask, "So what are you planning to do?" but the firm set of Courtney's expression caused her to stop short. She felt sudden concern.

"You're not going to—"

"Abort? Oh, you bet I am."

Louisa grimaced. "Oh, Court . . . wait . . . think about this."

"You think I haven't?"

"Of course . . . I didn't mean that." Louisa realized it was nothing more than common sense that had kept her from being in Courtney's shoes right now. Would she have had a similar attitude had this happened to her? It was possible. At least *before* her talks with Julia and her sojourn in Amish country.

Louisa tried again. "I'm just saying you could marry some guy who likes kids. Or be a single mom like a zillion other women. I'll help you. I'll go to birthing classes with you. Baby-sit. Whatever you need."

Courtney wiped her eyes. "What I really need is for this problem to go away."

Louisa sighed. "It's not just a problem, Court. It's a life."

"Yeah, mine. Listen, I don't know why I told you. I knew you would judge me."

"That's where you're wrong. I'd like to help."

Louisa wanted to say so much more. But she knew it would do no good to charge ahead, not with Courtney being so defensive. She changed her tactic. "I love you, Court, no matter what, okay? But can I tell you how my visit to Annie's started me going in a whole different direction? You remember last fall, when I was getting ready to marry Michael?"

Courtney nodded, wadding up the tissue in her hand.

"There I was . . . by all appearances I had everything—money, education, a handsome fiancé—but inside I was empty. Something was missing."

"Like what?" Courtney asked wryly. "Horses and buggies? Aprons and bad hair?"

Louisa grinned at her friend but shook her head. "No. Truth. Meaning. God. I didn't even know it, but I was on a faith-quest. Sounds pretty wild coming from me, I know, but it's true."

It was obvious by the disbelief on her

face that Courtney didn't get it. But Louisa forged ahead. "You know, when I canceled the wedding and left here, it probably seemed that I was running *away* from love. But I was really running toward it. My friend Julia told me faith and love are really similar. You put your trust in the person you marry, giving yourself to them, knowing they will keep their vows. Love for a lifetime, no matter what."

Courtney snorted again. "Tell that to my dad. Divorced—again."

"Well, it's not a perfect analogy, since people aren't perfect. But God is, and I'm beginning to see that I can trust Him." Louisa hoped she was making some sense. She talked about God's Son, too, saying the name that was so often flung from Courtney's own lips, but Louisa spoke it with a reverence that seemed to put a curious light in Courtney's eyes. "All I'm saying is how can you refuse someone who loves you that much?"

Louisa paused, noticing the glints of tears in Courtney's eyes again. Then she added, "How can *anyone* say no to that?"

"So you must believe that this Jesus was divine or whatever?"

Louisa nodded slowly, realizing that she did, indeed, believe this. "Yes . . . I guess I do. But I have a lot more to learn." She wouldn't push. Not Julia, nor anyone else, for that matter, could have pushed *her* before she was ready. She'd had to come to the point where she longed for more than life had dished up. And she had been so ready while sitting in Julia's sunroom, eager for much more than Julia had time to give her that day. But since coming home, she'd started reading the New Testament. *Funny, my parents don't even own one!*

Courtney poked at her purchase absentmindedly, squinting as she tightened the tie strings on the designer shoe bag. "Maybe I'm making a mistake."

Louisa brightened. "Really?"

"Chill out. I'm talking about whether or not to keep these funky shoes for Berit's birthday."

Louisa sighed. Just when she'd thought maybe Courtney was seeing a glimpse of something significant. "Maybe we can talk more later."

"Later? Like when?"

"Whenever you want." She meant it.

They got up and walked out of the mall, their pace snail-like in comparison to the way they'd begun the hunt earlier. Louisa felt tense, wishing she might somehow explain the sort of freedom Courtney really needed without coming across as condescending.

"Hey, later," Courtney called to her as they pushed open the glass doors on the east side of the food court.

"Okay. Call me anytime."

Courtney gave a fakey little smile and hurried off to her red Porsche.

Great, Louisa thought, feeling as though she'd failed big time. Clicking her remote, she hurried toward her car. Once inside, she checked her Palm for messages and was not too surprised to see three text messages from Michael. "Uh-oh," she whispered. Backing out of the parking space, she promised herself to be a true friend to him.

She hurried home, looking forward to starting work on her painting of Muffin for Annie, knowing how pleased she would be. As for Sam, she was eager to write him again, although she would be careful not to encourage him too much, even though she really missed him.

———

The bishop had a big talk on about his youth, telling the brethren gathered in his barn about the gazebo his father had built "with all us boys helpin' out." With so much going on in his family, Jesse found

Bishop Andy's rambling discourse annoying, but he tried to appear interested.

Andy continued, "There was the homemade seesaw, ya know. Did any of yous have one in your backyards?"

Deacon Byler nodded, and by the look on his face it was rather apparent he, too, was wondering where on earth all this talk of childhood was leading. Preacher Moses, too. At least they weren't talking about Zeke. Or Ichabod, for that matter, as Jesse had already warned that the wayward one might be coming to town, much to the brethren's dismay. Jesse just wished he knew when.

The news the bones aren't Isaac's should change his mind, Jesse thought. *But what if my second letter doesn't reach him in time?*

The notion that Jesse had brought this on himself nagged like so many July mosquitoes. Yet something in him wanted to lay eyes on the man who'd renounced the lot, to see what the years had done to one so proud. And, come to think of it, he was exactly the person to declare Ben Martin an imposter, too.

"So, now we have this here problem with young Yonie Zook," Bishop Andy was saying, having switched the conversation abruptly. This brought Jesse back to attention right quick. "Your boy's got himself a rip-roarin' business, I'm sure you know, driving Amish round town and farther. Just what do you plan to do 'bout it?"

"Let it play itself out, that's what," Jesse replied, anxious to move on to other matters.

"Aw, let the boy have some fun," Moses said. "He'll get it out of his system sooner or later."

"Later ain't so gut, though," the deacon pointed out.

"I daresay he'll get himself so rich he'll decide he wants more than that one car of his." Bishop Andy squared his old, rickety body. "Ain't it what you think, Jesse?"

"Could be." Jesse didn't like the pressure. This was his son they were discussing, after all.

"So . . . while you're thinking on that, here's another predicament . . . in the same family." Here the bishop pushed up his glasses and blinked his eyes through them at Jesse before pulling a rolled-up magazine from his back pocket. "Here's proof we've got us some folk watchin' awful close on your household, Preacher Zook."

Jesse hadn't thought *this* was coming and braced himself for the bishop's remarks about Annie's art plastered on the cover of a worldly magazine.

"Just lookee here . . . the preacher's daughter has herself a talent. Don't that beat all?"

The men leaned in to see. The deacon was first to nod and then backed away, as if to say he'd already heard the murmurings from a bunch of the farmers who'd circulated the thing amongst themselves. But Old Moses kept looking at it, seemingly stunned. "What the world did she paint such a picture for?"

"That's what I kept wondering," Jesse piped up, "when first I saw it."

Bishop pointed to the swing. "Word has it that old swing got itself hung up again somehow, just here lately."

Jesse owned up to having given it to his daughter. "She asked Yonie to help her. It sure seemed mighty important to her to get it right back up there, and on the selfsame big branch—just like in the picture." He looked at the painting as it shook in the bishop's feeble old hands.

"I daresay we've got ourselves a dilemma." Bishop tapped on the magazine with his gnarled hand.

"What's that?" Deacon Byler wanted to know.

Moses tugged hard on his beard. "Jah, what?"

"Truth be told, she's mighty good at it," Bishop Andy said, "and if someone—well, the right person, or the *wrong* one—happens to see this here work of your daughter's, Jesse, she'll be pulled out of the People quick-like, I fear."

Jesse hadn't thought of that.

"How do you plan to rein her in before such a thing happens?" asked the bishop.

"Well, I've been workin' on that for some time now."

Old Moses harrumphed. "Sure don't seem so, not with her livin' over there with our shunned one, Esther Hochstetler."

Jesse didn't have much to defend himself with, because everything the brethren had said was true. And their eyes—all three sets of them—seemed more like fingers pointing his way. He'd failed the People. No, he'd failed his own kin.

Yonie and Annie . . . two free spirits, exactly alike. But by the way the men were looking at him, he knew he best be saying something. Anything would be better than this awkward silence. He cleared his throat, thinking of Ben Martin's return. That would get the attention off his family. "Well, Annie's got herself a fancy friend, if I'm so bold to say. And this here fellow claims to be Isaac Hochstetler." He watched their faces, and Old Moses teetered on his chair.

"Oh, now, that's the next thing to profanity, declaring such a thing," Deacon Byler asserted. "Everybody knows Ichabod's boy is long gone."

Jesse shrugged. " 'Course without his bones—"

"As for his claim," Moses interrupted, "is he serious?"

"Seems so."

"Timing's mighty odd," the deacon said. "What with Ichabod a-maybe comin'."

"More upheaval for the People," Bishop agreed, sadly shaking his head.

Jesse wished he'd kept mum.

"Well, if he's my kin, surely I'd know if it's him or not," Moses said. "Why don't you bring the boy over to me tomorrow?"

"I'll see what I can do," Jesse said.

The bishop rolled the magazine back up and asked if they all wanted to go inside and have something to wet their whistles, but Jesse thanked him and said he needed to head off to find Ben.

The others followed Andy into the house while Jesse headed for his horse and carriage, wondering why on earth he'd said anything. Then again, maybe having Zeke's uncle Moses look Ben over good would reveal this Ben to be the charlatan he was and put an end to Annie's foolishness once and for all. If so, maybe finally the preacher's daughter would join church.

Chapter 24

Annie stood in the cellar, holding the baby and watching the old washing machine dance across the floor . . . *chug-a-lug, chug-ga.* She'd taken the liberty of doing another load of wash, even though it was Tuesday, being extra careful when feeding the wet clothes through the pale rubber rollers at the rinsing stage. She'd heard of women getting their fingers caught in the wringers and for a fleeting moment wondered who would take care of Esther's children if such an awful thing happened.

She had carried Essie Ann's cradle down here, keeping a close watch on her while Laura was upstairs with Zach and John. Annie hoped Esther might return home today. If so, having some of the laundry done would be one less thing for her to think about. Annie knew she ought not hold her breath for Essie to come home for sure today, because she'd seen how terribly pained and pale she had been yesterday, and the memory of it dulled the joy she had experienced while walking in the meadow with Ben.

"My dear Isaac," she whispered, still marveling at the truth but also worried about what would happen next. Would the People accept her beloved as the grown kidnapped boy? Was there any hope that Zeke might recognize him now, troubled as he was? She shook her head in dismay. From what she'd heard, Zeke could barely recognize his own shadow these days.

" 'Tis a quandary." The words brought Essie Ann's little head up and she looked at Annie with a sweet, sleepy expression. "You know I'm talking 'bout someone, don't you?" She picked up Essie Ann and kissed her soft forehead. "Your uncle Isaac, that's who."

She heard heavy footsteps overhead. Someone was walking across the kitchen. Was it Ben returning already? He'd helped her all morning, bless his heart—slopping hogs and carrying wood for the old stove. He'd even shown an endearingly gentle patience with Zach and John. What's more, he'd offered to hold the baby for a while.

Her heart stirred at the possibility that he'd come back. *I must be in love,* she realized.

Opening the cellar door, she was startled to see her father. "Oh, hullo, Daed. What brings you here?" Annie stepped up into the kitchen.

Her father eyed her with the baby, then looked at Laura playing with the boys on the kitchen floor. "Isn't Esther at home?"

"No. But she will be." She thought she best not say where Essie had gone. She hadn't been instructed not to tell, but even so she didn't want to be the reason Zeke got in trouble.

"Is Ben here?" he asked, then quickly explained, "I stopped at the Rancks', but Julia told me he'd come here to help with chores."

"He did, but he went over to the harness shop. He's got friends—"

"I gathered that," he interrupted.

Laura wandered over, looking up at them. "Mamma's awful sick, did ya hear?"

Annie held her breath. *Don't say more . . . oh, please be still.* She tried to get Laura's attention, wishing she'd return to her brothers. "It's all right, dear one. Mamma will be just fine."

A frown grew on her father's face. "Esther's ill, yet she's gone from the house?"

"Jah" was all she said.

"Annie," her father said. "Time to fess up. What's goin' on here? Where's Esther?"

Laura answered for her. "Mr. Ben took her away . . . in his car."

"Where?" Daed's voice thundered through Annie, though he had not raised his voice.

"To the hospital. She's ever so sick."

Her father's harsh and knowing gaze held her own. Had he guessed their secret?

The baby began to whimper, and Annie moved past her father, asking Laura to come hold her sister a bit. Laura beamed at the chance to help, sitting right down on the table bench and opening her arms for the baby.

"There, now, cradle her gently the way you always do." Annie stayed near, watching, hoping her father might head on over to find Ben.

"I'm doin' all right here . . . really. If it's Ben you're lookin' for, you can catch up with him if you hurry."

But her father was smarter than that. "What're you hidin'?"

She felt her heart pounding through her apron.

"What's-a-matter with Esther?"

Laura piped up. "She's got a pain in her tummy."

Annie patted Laura's knee. "Jah, but I believe she's goin' to be better right quick." She bit her lip, trying to keep her composure.

Jesse leaned on the sink, glancing around the kitchen. "Annie Zook, you are the most difficult child ever."

"I've disappointed you, I know," she admitted.

"First your art . . . now this Ben Martin. And whatever you're not tellin' me about Esther." He shook his head, clearly put out.

"Ben is Isaac—of that I'm sure," she said, hoping to distract him from Essie's possible miscarriage.

"We'll know something today 'bout that rubbish." He turned to go. "If he's Isaac, then so be it." His shoulders drooped as he headed for the door.

Annie trembled. What did Daed mean?

Essie Ann began to cry again, and just then Annie heard a car pull into the drive. "Right on time," she said of the wet nurse, wondering if her father might accuse the Englischer of trespassing or worse.

Lord in heaven, help us all!

Jesse was exasperated. First Annie had

acted for all the world like there was something to hide, and then a strange English woman came driving in like she was expected somehow, hurrying around the back of the house and going inside without knocking! What was going on at Esther's?

When he arrived at the harness shop, Ben Martin was there as Annie had said, standing around with several Amish farmers and Sam Glick. Jesse watched the two of them talking together like they were old friends. He'd heard Sam had left his father's house and was staying in Gordonville with a former Amish family, looking to ease himself away from the People and into the world with some self-appointed missionaries, as they called themselves. The very notion further darkened his mood.

Jesse didn't go directly over to speak with Ben; he first went about his business, taking care to pick up a custom-made draft bridle prior to seeking out the man his daughter was obviously much too fond of.

"Hullo again, Ben." He nodded to both men. "Sam."

"How're you doin', Preacher?" Sam said, offering a greeting before saying a quick good-bye to Ben and turning toward the door.

Because they were momentarily alone,

Jesse decided not to mince words.

"Why did you come back here, Ben? The truth. Did you come to steal my daughter away?"

Ben looked shocked. "No, sir."

"Young man, I don't believe for one minute that you're Isaac Hochstetler. For you to make such a claim only confirms my suspicions about your character. Your return can only muddle my daughter's mind. Do you understand?"

"I do, sir."

"Don't you dare take her away from me. You left once. You can leave again."

"I don't want to cause trouble, but I truly believe—"

"Believe what?"

"That I *might* be Isaac."

Jesse shook his head with disgust. "Are you willing to put your belief to the test?"

Ben nodded.

"Fine, then." Jesse explained what he had in mind. When he was finished, Ben looked startled.

"Moses, you say?"

"That's right. It was his idea to have you visit him. He thinks he can identify you. Seems foolish to me, 'specially since Zeke would know better, but he's not . . . feeling so well these days." Jesse didn't know why he was telling Ben this. Likely Annie had already told him about Zeke's mental state.

"I'm willing to meet with Moses," Ben said, stepping back slightly. "But I want you to know something. I *do* remember growing up here. I remember going to a Christmas play at the one-room school, where my brother, Zeke, played Joseph. I remember you and the other brethren coming often to my father's house, too. Things like that . . . and more."

Jesse flinched. This was quite true. Especially after Daniel shunned the ordinance of preacher, he and the other ministers came in hopes of persuading Daniel to follow through with God's calling. Jesse was suddenly curious about how much of those visits Isaac . . . or *Ben* . . . recalled. But he sure wouldn't stand here in this public place to inquire. "I'll get myself over to the Rancks'. Then maybe you can"—it irked him to suggest it—"drive us over to Zeke's uncle's place."

"Sure. When?"

"Tomorrow, at first light."

Ben agreed, but there was more on Jesse's mind. "Let's get something else straight. Even if you *were* Amish, you're English now. And my daughter *belongs* in the church." Jesse's neck hairs stood on end.

"Promise me—no matter what—you won't take her away from her people."

Ben's face fell.

Jesse persisted. "Didn't you say you don't wish to cause trouble?"

The young man nodded.

"Well, then?"

"I have no intention of causing trouble," Ben said at last.

"Good man," Jesse said, somewhat satisfied. He tipped his head in farewell, plopped on his straw hat, and headed quickly for the door.

Chapter 25

I *should have stayed in Kentucky*, Ben thought, wishing Sam hadn't run off. He could use a friend about now. After the heated conversation with Jesse, Ben's head was reeling. *"Your return can only muddle my daughter's mind."*

Had he made yet another mistake? Caught up in a storm of emotions, longing to see Annie again and yearning to discover the full truth about his previous life, he realized he no longer had a choice. He had to see this thing through. *Am I or am I not Isaac?*

And what about Annie? Didn't she have the right to make her own choices? But no, not in her father's thinking. It was fairly clear she had been ruled with an iron rod, though so far she'd managed to escape it unscathed.

He'd forgotten how lovely she was, in every way. When he was with her, the entire world seemed to dissolve to nothing. Could he simply walk away from her because her father objected to him?

One thing at a time, he decided, heading back to his car. Tomorrow's visit with Preacher Moses might put a new spin on the truth for Jesse Zook. Ben was counting on it.

———

Zeke's head felt tight as he sat thinking about the early afternoon session with one of his several doctors. He couldn't keep track of them all. *Doctors . . . they're helping me, aren't they?* he thought, smiling to himself.

Just then he looked up and saw Irvin Ranck coming in the door. "How'd you make it past the front desk?" he asked, getting up to shake his hand.

"Oh, not to worry. One of my cousins works up there, so she let me in."

Irvin didn't make small talk this time. He simply pulled out his New Testament and began to read aloud. Zeke had no interest in stopping him or putting up a fuss; the sound of the Scripture soothed him, and he found himself rocking a bit to its lyrical rhythm.

Zeke listened quietly when his friend began to speak of God's sovereignty. He wasn't so sure what Irvin was getting at, but he didn't feel resistant today to the man who seemed to live to discuss Scripture.

"God knows the end from the beginning, Zeke. Do you believe that?"

"Why, I'd be a fool not to."

Irvin leaned back in his chair, looking relaxed. "Do you believe God has a plan for each of our lives?"

Well, he didn't know that so much. "Providence is what I believe in. Things happen when God allows 'em, jah."

Irvin nodded. "Mind if I pray for you, Zeke?"

Zeke was startled. "I don't know. . . . What for?"

"I'd like to pray a blessing of healing over you. Is that all right?"

Zeke had never been asked such a thing, and he didn't know why a feisty lump rose in his throat at the idea, but it did. He had to swallow hard, several times, to get his emotions back under control. "Herbs and bed rest are for healin'. And doctors . . ." He grinned. "Doctors are *supposed* to help folk heal. I don't think the Good Lord has much to do with any of that."

Irvin disagreed. "Our heavenly Father created foods and herbs and other good things that aid in our health, just as He gives wisdom to doctors and to the folks who established this place of healing. Wouldn't you agree?"

Zeke was tired and ready to quit pondering the questions and things Irvin seemed bent on saying to him. "Nice of you to visit me," he managed to say, struggling again to compose himself.

Irvin rose and put his hand on Zeke's shoulder. "I'd like to pray for you."

Not sure how to put a stop to it without offending his friend, Zeke relented. The words that came out of Irvin's mouth astonished him.

"Dear heavenly Father, I call upon you in the blessed name of my Lord Jesus to touch my friend Zeke with your healing power. Give him the ability to think and reason clearly, I ask. May he have the desires of his heart . . . to return home to his family, a new man and new creation in you. If it be your will, grant him a fresh start . . . and work a miracle in his life. Amen."

Zeke could not see Irvin for the veil of tears, but he heard him say, "I'll come see you in a few days—and I'll keep praying for you," before he left.

Wanting to shake his hand or give him some indication that he appreciated not only the visit but that mighty fine prayer, Zeke rose and stood at the door, watching Irvin head down the hall.

Annie stood at the window, peering down the empty lane once again. It was coming up close to suppertime and there was still no sign of Essie. Hadn't Ben said she would most likely be at the hospital only one night?

She heated up some of Esther's frozen homemade chicken corn soup for the children—and for herself, too, if she ever settled down enough to want to eat. The woman who'd come to nurse Essie Ann had left enough bottles of mother's milk to tide the baby over for the next couple of feedings. *Des gut,* Annie thought, having felt terribly nervous about being so dependent upon Cousin Julia's neighbor, nice as it was of her to drive over here.

Even though it wasn't appropriate for Ben to be in the house with her with Esther gone, she honestly wished he might return this evening, if only for supper. All day she'd thought of him, wondering how they might convince the brethren of Ben's identity. Truth be told, she was anxious to talk to him about anything, but she didn't expect him and he no doubt felt he was doing her bidding by staying away.

He's fancy, she reminded herself, but did it really matter? She hadn't joined church and, at this point, had no plans to—not as eager as she was to resume her art.

What must the outside world be like? She wondered how modern folk courted. Did they see each other only on the weekends? Whenever they wished to? Was it wrong in *their* families' eyes to spend time together alone in a house?

She didn't know why she contemplated such things now as she stirred the soup, preparing to fry the cheese sandwiches. Glancing over at the table, she smiled as Laura tried to show Zach how to print his name. John sat in his father's rocking chair, the force of his body keeping the chair going as the baby slept nearby in her cradle. All was well in *this* house.

Within her heart, an idea had sprouted, a way to show Ben her willingness to leave the Amish life for him. A way to prove she was ready to move ahead with their relationship . . . and her art, too.

It might not be best to tell him right out but to show him over the next few days. Hopefully he'd stay around Paradise long enough for the truth of the matter to sink in. She couldn't bear the thought of being without him again. "To think, in discovering who he is, he's found me, too," she whispered.

"What's that you said?" Laura asked, turning to look at Annie.

Quickly she brushed a tear away, hoping the dear girl hadn't seen, though it wouldn't have been the first time Laura had noticed her tears. "Ach, Aunt Annie's talkin' to herself yet again," Annie said, hoping to quell any worry.

Laura was nodding her head. "That's all right—you do that a lot. Though if I had such a good-lookin' beau, I think I'd talk to *him* instead."

Annie wanted to laugh, but she changed the subject to something more appropriate.

"Well, I think it's almost time to eat. Anyone hungry?"

Laura rushed to set the table while Annie quickly grilled the open-faced sandwiches, hoping Essie might sleep in her own bed this night. "Lord, let it be so."

"Now you sound like Mamma," Zach

said, still sitting at the table, making back-
ward *Z*'s.

" 'Tis a good thing," Laura said, helping
wash John's face and hands with a washcloth. "Mamma says we should talk to God
all day long."

Annie's heart swelled with love, and she
wondered anew how she could walk away
from the People she loved so dearly. *Yet if it
means a lifetime with Ben* . . .

"Come to the table now," she told the
children.

Laura helped John get into his booster
chair before sitting down across from
Annie. She asked to say the table grace, as
had become their new custom, and Annie
agreed.

"Where's Mr. Ben eating tonight?"
Zach asked afterward.

"I don't know."

"Can he eat with us again?"

"When your mamma's home, maybe,"
she told him.

Zach grinned, showing his gums. "I
hope she gets home right quick. I like him."

So do I! Annie hoped her blush wouldn't
give her away.

"I like *Mamma*," little John said, his
lower lip puckered.

"Aw, I know you miss her." Annie

tousled his hair. "She'll be home when she's better." *Dear Lord, please let it be soon.*

"Let's dig in now." She filled each bowl with a generous helping of soup, and as they ate, she tuned her ear to Essie's coming, praying it might be tonight.

Chapter 26

Esther remembered Julia teaching James and Molly a little song about letting their lights shine for the Lord. *"You in your small corner . . . and I in mine. . . ."*

She didn't know why she thought of this as she lay in her hospital bed. More than anything she wanted to be like a candle in the darkness, yet she viewed her life with Zeke as rather dark and dismal. She longed for her husband to "see the light," to share this freedom from sin and despair she'd experienced since discovering the lover of her soul, as one of the songs sung at Julia's church so aptly expressed.

Her concern for Zeke tugged at her heart as she settled herself in for yet another night away from her little ones and Annie. Oh, she desperately wanted this wee babe, caught between life and death, as much as she had wanted each of her other children. But she knew Zeke would suffer if God saw fit to let this child survive.

My wounded, defiant husband.

How could he say he loved her while treating her so? Was his harsh love an extension of his selfishness or another symptom of his disturbed mind?

She would not allow herself to think on how he might be treated by the brethren should their secret be discovered, even at this most precarious moment of her wee one's life. Of course Zeke could be reinstated as a voting church member if he were willing to repent. But their being found out was the sort of thing to set him off again, and she had no desire to cause a wedge between him and the People. He needed time to heal somehow . . . time to become readjusted within the family, too, if and when his release came. *If it be your will, O God.* And surely it was the dear Lord's will to reunite families and to mend broken hearts.

―――――――

The morning dawned while Jesse finished up the milking with Omar, Luke, and Yonie, the clouds giving way to rain.

"It's makin' down mighty hard," Yonie hollered to Luke at the far end of the barn.

"So much for heading over to Gordonville with the hay wagon."

Jesse wondered what his sons had cooked up but didn't ask. Better not to know too much these days, though after talking with the brethren it sure seemed like he ought to be coming down harder on them—especially on Yonie.

Still, sometimes taking a backseat to their bantering was better than saying anything. He carried the fresh milk to the cooler in the milk house.

The minute he was done here and had washed up some, he would head over to Irvin's, then ride with Ben Martin out to Moses' place. He didn't quite know what to make of it, but since talking with Ben, he'd become downright nervous about the meeting. If Annie was right and Ben was Isaac in the flesh, well, then he'd sent Ichabod's son packing back last month. And his headstrong daughter had been seeing the long-lost boy they'd all loved and missed for more than sixteen years. *If* Isaac were truly home.

Regardless of what he'd said to Ben about his being English now, he knew it didn't make sense to run off one of their own. The thought had already given him more than one restless night.

On the other hand, if Annie was off beam and Ben was an imposter, Jesse had already extracted a pledge of sorts that Ben would not take his daughter from the People. Once Old Moses confirmed the truth, Jesse would remind Ben of his promise, and surely if Ben had any trace of integrity left, he'd make for the door. Even if he stayed around, Annie would finally see him for the devious fellow he was, what with all those fake memories he was trotting out at will.

Sighing, Jesse headed for the house to change out of his work clothes, although he was sure to get muddy and wet heading down the road to his cousin's place in the rain. *If I weren't so upset at him, I'd ask Yonie to drive me over to Old Moses' place and be done with it.*

As it was, he'd soon be riding in an Englischer's car, so which was worse?

Scrubbing up in the kitchen sink, he noticed Barbara staring at him. "I'll be eatin' breakfast right quick," he said before she could speak.

"Oh, you off somewhere on this ugly day?" she asked, coming to him.

"Got me someplace to be, jah."

"Well, I hope you don't get indigestion like sometimes."

He sensed there was more than thoughtfulness behind her attention.

He turned toward her. "You all right, love?"

She nodded, but tears welled up in her pretty eyes.

"Aw, what's-a-matter?" He took her in his arms. "It's not one of those bad dreams again, is it?"

She struggled but could not speak.

"It sure must be." He kissed her cheek and held her even nearer, glad his elderly parents hadn't come over yet for breakfast.

When she'd managed to compose herself, she wiped her eyes on her apron hem. "No, not a dream. But livin' life without our girl . . . well, it's worse than any nightmare, I daresay." She began sobbing.

He should've guessed she was missing Annie. Jesse shook his head, feeling awful sorry, too, but not enough to say he'd go and seek her out again. What would his poor wife do if she knew of Annie's hopes for Ben Martin? He didn't have the heart to reveal his latest news—not till Old Moses had a chance to weigh in on the matter.

Even so he kindly waited, hoping he could calm his wife with his arms around her. "I'm no prophet, but things are bound to improve, don't ya think?"

She breathed in, her shoulders rising.

"Annie surely knows better, but then, so does Yonie. Word has it he's seeing a worldly girl."

There it was again: the judgment of God in those blue eyes. Not as steely as what he'd seen in the bishop's, but mighty close. Truth was, he had failed as a father on two counts, and two out of seven was a terrible proportion in the Lord God's eyes . . . and those of the People.

"Yonie's in the midst of running round." His words sounded hollow even to himself.

"Been mighty long enough, I'd say."

"Jah, but boys . . . they tend to take longer to get all that rowdiness out."

"I s'pose, but still. Everybody watches the preacher's children," she said, pausing. "What's your excuse for Annie?"

Where his daughter was concerned, he was more wary. She'd demonstrated her will, her ability to flit right over to Esther's as if his opinion didn't matter. "I'll think on it" was all he would say, much to her apparent dismay.

"There's more fuss," she said softly.

He clenched his jaw.

"Word is Esther's in the family way," she whispered.

"How do you know, love?"

"Sarah Mae has a friend who works over at the hospital."

Jesse groaned. "Bad news always travels fast, jah?"

Barbara made no comment. He would be sure to verify it when the time was right. Zeke was in a heap of hurt if true. For now, the crazy man was too ill to be shunned anyway. The brethren would simply wait. They would deal with Zeke's sin in Jehovah's time.

The rain rushing against the windows had lightened to drizzle by the time Jesse and Ben reached Moses' place. Jesse saw the aged man through the rain-streaked windshield, headed for the woodshed. Moses glanced over his stooped shoulder as Ben and Jesse stepped out of the car, and Jesse was sure he'd spotted them. But Moses continued on his way. *That's like him*, thought Jesse, somewhat amused.

Jesse glanced at the dreary sky, wondering if they might not get another downpour.

"This is the old homestead," he told Ben, "where Zeke's grandparents lived and raised a whole houseful of young'uns, including Preacher Moses and Daniel."

Ben took in the house, the big barn, and the surrounding land. "I think I remember this place. . . . Yes, that horse fence. I think I helped whitewash it once."

Jesse grimaced but kept silent. *How long will this charade go on?*

"The corncrib's in the same spot it was when I came here to play when I was young. Zeke and I both did, I *think*. I just don't quite remember being here with my brother."

Surprised he'd admit that.

Moses came back out of the woodshed and they wandered over to meet him.

When they neared, Moses offered a smile. "Wie geht's?"

"Oh, I'm all right," Jesse replied. "I see you're out workin' early."

Moses nodded, glancing now at Ben. "Is this here the man in question?"

"I'll let him speak for himself."

Ben stuck out his hand. "Ben Martin's my name. Good to meet you."

"Moses Hochstetler." He accepted the handshake and let go, looking Ben over, eyes lingering on his face. "I remember young Isaac well. I also happen to know he cut his left foot badly when he was three. Had to have a whole lot of stitches." The old man stopped and inhaled slowly. "Does that sound familiar to you, Ben?"

Ben wrinkled his brow. "Maybe so."

"Then there oughta be a scar to show for it," said Moses. "Somethin' else, too. Isaac always had a swirl in his hair, at the crown. Like a cow licked him hard one too many times and his hair stayed that-a-way."

Ben grinned. "Oh yeah, I've got that. When I had short hair back in school, my mom always tried to slick it down." He turned around and showed them his head.

"Well, I'll be . . ." Moses muttered.

Then, without being asked, Ben sat on a log and removed his shoe and sock and peered down at the ball of his left foot.

Moses leaned down a bit and, frowning, lowered his spectacles. "Sure looks like a scar there to me."

Jesse squinted at Ben's bare foot. "Where?"

Moses pointed to the faded scar snaking across the ball of Ben's foot. "There it is, for sure and for certain."

"How'd I cut it?" Ben asked, still studying the scar.

Straightening, Moses pulled out his blue paisley kerchief, wiping his eyes for a time before speaking. "On a broken canning jar . . . Isaac."

As Ben slipped his sock and shoe back on, Jesse grabbed Moses' arm. "Surely you must be mistaken?"

Moses shook his head, his voice thick with emotion. "Like Simeon of old, I have seen the hand of the Almighty. This here's a miracle of God, I daresay . . . bringin' our lost son home again." He smiled right at Ben; then, next thing Jesse knew, Moses reached around Ben and gripped his shoulders, shaking all over.

Jesse, stunned at this turn of events, couldn't hold back his laughter. *The joke's on all of us. This old man's too blind and senile to count five fingers much less find a scar!*

Ben stood up and smiled like they'd just given him a new horse and buggy. "Wait until Annie hears this."

Jesse shook his head in disbelief. "Proves nothing."

Moses crept closer to Jesse, his face solemn again. "Since we don't know if or when Ichabod is coming, take him to Zeke for a final say-so. I dare ya to."

"Zeke isn't in any condition to identify an insect, much less his brother."

"Perhaps you underestimate him." Moses turned to Ben. "That just might clinch it. I say it's a good idea."

Ben stood there, looking from one man to the other, like he scarcely knew what to do next.

Jesse crossed his arms. "I don't know

how that's possible—not anytime soon."

Moses rubbed his cheek thoughtfully. "Maybe you can get Zeke a pass to attend Preaching service here before too long." He turned to Ben. "You're not leavin' anytime soon, are ya?"

"I don't know what my plans are exactly," Ben confessed. "I'm staying with the Rancks for the time being, but I don't want to mooch off them for long."

"Well, you're always welcome over here," Moses told him. "Any close kin of my brother's is family to me." He slapped a hand on Ben's back and moved toward the house. "Come on in and meet some more of your relatives."

Moses was clearly convinced, but Jesse was mighty annoyed. Someone needed to put a stop to this drivel, and if it had to be Zeke, so be it.

Chapter 27

Annie tried to hold back her excitement but still let out a little whoop when she saw the hired driver bringing Essie home later that afternoon. "Guess who's here," she told Laura, picking up little John as Laura reached for Zach's hand. All of them went rushing out for the welcome.

A peachy glow had replaced Essie's sallow cheeks, and Annie set John down and watched him run to his mamma. "Ach, we're so glad to see you," Annie said, waiting her turn while the children hugged their mother.

"Oh, it's nice to be home." Essie was looking at the children as if she hadn't seen them in weeks. "Ach, I missed yous!"

Annie kissed Essie on the cheek. "And we all missed you. But come now, let's get you inside."

Essie let Annie help her into the house. "The baby's goin' to be all right," she whispered. "Thank the dear Lord."

"Oh, such wonderful-good news!" Annie suppressed her tears of joy.

"We must keep mum 'bout all this," Essie warned.

Annie was glad she'd tried to keep Essie's condition a secret from Daed yesterday. Still, she worried he might have guessed somehow.

Essie sat down to catch her breath, looking around the kitchen. "Everything is so clean," she said, smiling at Annie. "You must've had some help, jah?"

"Oh, just a little," Annie confessed, assuming Esther suspected Ben must have volunteered to assist with outside chores, freeing Annie up to work indoors.

Essie nodded her head. "And did Laura do her share?" she asked in Laura's hearing.

"You can be sure of that. Ain't so, Laura?"

The girl's eyes shone with delight, and she ran to her mother yet again, throwing her arms around her waist. "I helped all I could, Mamma. But Auntie Annie did most of it—and cookin' and taking good care of us."

Essie's grateful expression warmed

Annie's heart. "I was glad to do what I could."

"Well, I need to be holdin' my wee babe," said Essie, taking Laura's hand and getting up. "She must be napping?"

Annie said she was upstairs in her crib, and Essie headed through the sitting room to the stairs as Laura said, "You missed Essie Ann a lot, didn't ya, Mamma?"

Their happy voices faded and Annie heard only their feet on the stairs.

Eager to check the mail, Annie went outdoors, hoping for a letter from Lou. But there was nothing from Colorado. Even so there was a fat envelope that no doubt contained several "circle letters"—short journal-like correspondence where several ladies wrote about their activities and sent them around to one another—from Essie's five cousins in Wisconsin. Esther often shared these letters with Annie and Laura, reading them aloud, laughing as she did.

You heard my prayer for Essie, dear Lord, Annie said, thankfulness welling up in her. She walked back toward the house, where Zach and John had wandered into the backyard and were throwing a stick to Zeke's big black dog. Annie sat on the stoop to watch them and sighed inwardly. Not till this moment had she realized how much responsibility for Essie's children—and for keeping the house running smoothly in her absence—she had carried while Essie was gone. *Help me always to think first of others,* she prayed.

But she knew she would think of herself in *one* way. The tremendous joy she felt with Ben—the thrill that he was pursuing her again—was becoming habit-forming. And lest she wither on the vine again, as she had after his leaving, she determined to get a driver to take her over to the Englischers' outlet stores. Some new, fancy clothing should be just the thing. Without saying a word, Annie would let Ben know her eagerness to join his world.

After meeting Moses' wife, a handful of great-grandchildren, and an elderly grandmother, Ben wanted to rush off to Esther's and tell Annie the good news. *I am Isaac!* To think Moses had remembered the scar.

Equally amazing, Annie had somehow known all along.

When his cell phone rang, he hoped it was Annie calling him—from Julia's maybe. He was surprised instead to hear Julia herself, letting him know Esther was on her way home from the hospital. Thanking Julia for the update, he disconnected.

He wished he could phone Annie, but since there was no way to contact her at Esther's, he knew he must put off seeing her for a while. Annie and the children were most likely welcoming Esther home right now, and he didn't want to just show up, possibly intruding on her homecoming.

So he decided to call Sam Glick instead, grateful he'd keyed in Sam's new cell phone number when he last saw him at the harness shop.

Hungry now, he first headed for Route 30, looking for the nearest fast-food stop. Then, while enjoying a juicy cheeseburger, he called Sam and they exchanged small talk.

"More than ever, I'm interested in the Plain life," he told Sam.

"Is it the People or is it something else?" Sam asked, a teasing lilt to his voice.

Ben laughed. "You mean some*one* else?"

"Annie seems to like you well enough."

He wasn't inclined to discuss his affection for Annie by cell with a casual acquaintance—former Amishman or not. He changed the subject. "You'll never guess what I just found out."

"You like the smell of pig manure after all?"

Ben chuckled. "I found out that I am

Zeke's younger brother." Ben quickly filled Sam in on the telltale scar identified by Preacher Moses.

"No fooling? You're the kid who disappeared all those years ago?"

"That's what I'm told."

They talked a while longer about the kidnapping, Ben's memories, and the events leading up to his meeting with Moses today.

Then, after a time, Sam brought up Louisa. Ben was surprised, once again, at their similar situations, only reversed. Sam invited him over for supper, and Ben said he'd be all for it. Sharing a meal with Sam would be a distant second to taking Annie out, of course, but he also wanted to be sensitive to her needs and not rush things as he had before. Anyway, spending time with Sam might be a good idea for a while, a way to discover all he'd missed here while growing up in Kentucky. His past was calling him home.

———

Annie wasted no time getting started on her chores the morning after Essie returned home. She was outside in the pigpen slopping the hogs when Ben sneaked up on her.

"Oh, Ben, you scared me!"

He leaned against the fence and smiled

at her. "Hello to you, too, Miss Annie. Don't you smell good this morning."

She'd nearly become used to the hog smell, which was no doubt strong on her choring dress. She wrinkled her nose at him but couldn't help grinning at his teasing.

"You're out of breath, Ben. Where'd you come from?"

"I knew I'd find you out here this time of day, so I parked the car up the road and ran down. I didn't want to upset Essie again."

"That's awful kind, Ben."

"Have you heard?"

"Heard what?"

He was clearly excited. "Oh, it's the best news, Annie." Speaking quickly, he told her how Preacher Moses had identified him by the scar on his foot. "Now I'm sure, Annie. I am Isaac."

She wanted to go to him, let him wrap his arms around her, but she resisted, only smiling her best smile. "Ach, I'm ever so glad," she whispered, refusing her tears.

Ben looked over his shoulder at the house. "I'd better go. But I'll see you again soon."

"Jah," she called after him as she watched him hurry around the barn and out of sight. "But not soon enough," she whispered.

Finishing her chores, she headed inside and helped Essie get breakfast on the table. After the meal, she hurried to the neighbors' barn phone, calling one of the several van drivers. *This is the first day of a whole new life,* she decided. She wanted to see what she was up against as far as styles and prices went so she'd know how much money she would need when she was ready to do her serious shopping. Unfortunately, she had very little money of her own, having given much of her earnings to her parents all those years and now helping Essie with expenses. Annie longed to tell Louisa what she planned, having not shared a peep with anyone, even Esther, for fear she might try to talk her out of it.

When the driver dropped Annie off at the outlet shops, she instructed him to pick her up in an hour, then headed toward one of the stores she'd gone into with Lou and Courtney. There, she spotted several pretty pairs of shoes and made a mental note, dodging the startled looks from one clerk. Then she made her way to the next shop, hoping to see something like the skirt and blouse she'd borrowed from Louisa for her

date with Ben to the Sight and Sound Theatre last month. Within minutes she saw
three similar outfits, fixing her memory on
the location of each item, thinking she
might even be able to afford at least the
blouse right away. When she asked to look
at dresses, the clerk's eyebrows shot straight
up.

"We do not sell Amish apparel, miss,"
she said.

"No, I'm not interested in Plain clothing. I'm lookin' for something right perty, to
tell you the truth. Something you would
wear to have dinner with your best beau."

The woman's brown eyes brightened
and she winked at Annie. "Well, I'm happily
married, but I still remember those days.
Come right this way."

The clerk led her to a rack near the wall,
displaying a whole lineup of dresses in every
imaginable style and color.

"Are you looking for a particular size?"
she asked.

"I have no idea." Annie didn't want to
explain that she and her Mamm had always
made her dresses and aprons.

"Is the dress for you or someone else?"

"For me."

The woman scanned her quickly from
head to toe and said she was most likely a

petite two. Annie suddenly wished she had paid better attention to the size of Lou's skirt and blouse.

There were so many pretty things to look at, and she decided to try on several. She narrowed her search down to two dresses and one lovely skirt and blouse out-fit. When she asked if they could set the items of clothing aside, layaway was men-tioned, but she hadn't come prepared to pay a sizeable down payment. She left the store empty-handed, wishing she might take out some money from her savings account she and Mamm had set up together years ago, when first she'd started working at Cousin Julia's. But how on earth was she going to convince her mother to go to the bank with her . . . especially if she revealed her plan to slowly buy an entire Englischer's wardrobe?

All was not lost, though. She would find a way to make this very nice surprise hap-pen for Ben, even if it meant borrowing money, although she hated to. Daed's ad-monition to "owe no man anything" had been drilled into her. Still, seeing Ben's ex-pression when first he saw her in new, fancy clothes would be worth it all. *I can scarcely wait!*

Chapter 28

When Lou's letter arrived in the mail the next day, Annie discovered an extra thick envelope. Too excited to wait, she opened it and began reading even as she cut across the front lawn. Seeing a plastic card wrapped in paper, with an explanation for how to use it, she stood and leaned against the house. *Lou wants me to call her next time I'm at Julia's!*

She also found it interesting that her friend was again seeing Michael, the man she had nearly married last year. *Is she that lonely?* Annie wondered, not quite sure what to think, especially having seen how happy Lou had been with Sam Glick. She felt disappointed, really. She wanted Sam to win Lou's heart.

"With Sam going fancy, it could actually work," she mused. And now that Ben was back, she, too, hoped to move further and further away from the Plain life. She thought again of her plan to purchase English clothing.

Won't Lou be surprised!

Looking at the enclosed phone card, she could scarcely wait to get to Julia's and have her help place the call to Castle Rock, Colorado.

Later that same day, she did just that, with surprisingly little input from her cousin. Lou had given Annie her cell phone number, and the call went through ever so fast.

"Oh, Lou, it's wonderful to hear your voice again!"

"I'm right here in my art studio, between classes. How *are* you, Annie?"

"I'm fine . . . and you'll never believe who's come back to Paradise." Annie was glad to have the portable phone in her hand and made a beeline toward the sunroom lest she be overheard by Julia or one of the children. She was thankful Ben had evidently left the house before she'd arrived.

"You'll have to give me a hint," Louisa replied. "Is this someone we both know?"

"Ach, for sure."

Annie felt her heart pound just thinking about what she wanted to say. "It's Ben who's here! Can you believe it?"

Louisa was silent for a time, then she said, "Actually, I can. He came back for you, didn't he?"

"No." She had to set her straight. "He came back because he found out he's adopted. You'll never believe this, but it turns out he's Isaac, our kidnapped boy." Annie let the story unfold the way it had from the very beginning.

When she'd finished explaining, Lou said, "This is a shocker ... but a terrific one. You must feel stunned."

"Well, I am and I'm not ... if that makes any sense. I'm just ever so excited."

"Now maybe you won't have to jump through so many hoops to spend time with Ben."

"To be honest, I don't know how it will work for us to court, and he hasn't said a word 'bout it, either." She sighed. "My father is still not convinced he is Isaac. But Ben is. He's remembering more and more about growin' up here, and already word's spreading amongst the People about who he is."

Then Annie told Lou of her plan to buy some modern clothes. "Now all I need to do is find out where to sell my hair."

Lou let out a gasp. "What? You're kidding, I hope."

The idea had popped into Annie's head as she had contemplated the situation the night before. "No. Why? It's not so uncommon. I've read that hair this long can go for a perty penny . . . so I need you to find out where I should go here in Lancaster to sell it."

"Annie, this is silly. Does Ben know? I doubt he would want you to do that."

"Lou, listen. This is my big surprise . . . so he'll know how much I want to become fancy for him."

"It's hard to believe you really want to do this, Annie. Hopefully you won't be sorry," Lou said, as if Annie were making a horrid mistake.

"If I really want to be English, I don't need hair this long, anyway. Really, Louisa, I have plenty to spare."

"Well, if you're sure . . ."

Lou said she would "go online" and find out who was buying human hair for making wigs. "Surely I can locate someone there in Lancaster, or maybe in Harrisburg," Lou said. But then she had another idea. "Why not keep your hair and simply open a credit line for your shopping spree? You know, buy now and pay and pay and pay later?

Join the rest of frivolous America?"

Annie knew she was kidding.

"Better yet, borrow the money from me. How much do you need?"

"No, Lou. I know you're on a tight budget," Annie said quickly, "but it's awful nice of you to offer." She asked about Lou's art students.

Lou laughed a little. "Well, I know you're not that interested in my students. . . . It's Michael you're most curious about, right?"

Annie had to laugh, too. "I think we know each other mighty well. So have you been seein' him a lot? Like before?"

"Do you mean are we engaged? No. Will he ask me to marry him again? I don't know."

"Ach, do ya love him, Lou?"

There was an awkward silence, and Annie worried she'd offended her.

"Sorry. I'm pryin' too much."

"No . . . I think it's a reasonable question—one I'm trying to answer for myself." Louisa told her that Michael's potential law partnership with her father was a thing of the past and that because he'd given all that up—"possibly to impress me"—she was struggling with why she shouldn't be interested in him romantically for the long term.

"If you love him, then you'll want to be with him. Be his wife, have his children . . . jah?"

"The operative word is *if*, Annie. I'm still trying to figure out how I feel about him. I don't want to let my emotions sway me." She paused a moment. "You know, it's easy to look across the table at Michael and smile at him, listen to him talk, but I'm afraid he's going to fall in love with me again. I need to be more careful."

Annie wanted to ask about Sam in the worst way, but before she could, Louisa continued, "To be honest with you, Michael doesn't share my openness to faith."

"Does Sam?" Annie asked softly.

"I'm not sure. He's changing so much. It's something I'll need to find out."

They talked then about other things: how it was for Annie staying at Esther's, how fast cute little Essie Ann was growing, and how Annie missed her family at home. Annie also told of Ben's interest in her art. "He wants to see all of my work, not just the bridge painting in the Rancks' attic."

"He's seen the one with the old bridge and the long rope swing?" Lou sounded surprised.

"Not only has he seen it but he's been staring at it, I guess. Says it's the reason he

was drawn to Paradise in the first place."
She told Lou how he'd been carrying a copy
of it in his pocket since last Christmas,
when first he stumbled onto it.

"Wow . . . is that interesting or what?"

"He says it's a miracle how it all happened, and I'm starting to think it must be,
too."

"Oh, Annie, I have a feeling you and
Ben will end up together. I saw it in his eyes
that first time he asked me about you!" Lou
laughed. "I was actually talking to your future husband that day, telling him to ask
you out himself. What a riot!"

Annie couldn't help but smile. "Let's
not get ahead of ourselves. There's plenty to
work out 'tween us, but he found me for a
reason, and now he's found himself, too."
Annie felt completely overjoyed, sharing
such things with Louisa. "Just think, I was
being courted by my dear friend Isaac back
before we ever knew it."

"That's the sweetest story, and to think
it's true."

Ever so true.

Lou encouraged her to use the calling
card again. "Anytime at all. If I'm teaching,
I can always say so and set up a time later.
Okay?"

"Oh, this is so much fun. But I could be

in big trouble with the brethren if they knew I was using the phone for social purposes."

"But, hey, which is worse—cutting your hair and buying fancy dresses or calling me every few weeks or so?"

Annie hadn't thought of that. "Ach, I see your point."

"You're going to have to get used to this new life of yours."

Before they hung up, Lou said she'd call back in a few minutes with the location of a place to sell her hair, if Annie was sure about it.

"Oh, would you? I'm leaning that way, really I am."

They were saying good-bye, promising to keep in touch, when Annie added right quick, "I hope you won't marry for anything less than love, Lou. Honest, I do."

"And I wish the same for you. You and Ben . . . stick with love."

After Annie clicked the phone off, she sat there thinking about how satisfying it had been to talk to her pen pal so far away. *Nearly two thousand miles away.*

Chapter 29

Annie was finishing up her work at Julia's late that afternoon when Molly asked her to read a story. The two of them settled down on the porch swing out front, enjoying the balmy weather and the chirping birds. Annie opened the book to the beginning, reading the title page and the name of the author as she had been taught to do in school years ago.

Molly sat ever so still on her lap, listening as Annie read with expression, even taking care to change her voice to suit the animal characters. The story, which was about a puppy chasing a kitten into a schoolhouse, held Molly's interest and was coming to an end when a car pulled up. Before Annie could say anything, Molly whispered, "Oh, look, it's Uncle Ben!" And with that she hopped off Annie's lap and went running out to meet him, her skirt floating in the breeze.

Uncle Ben?

Annie watched as Ben leaned down to lift Molly high, his hearty laughter hovering in the air. She recalled how relaxed Ben had been with Laura, Zach, and John—even the baby—and her mind whirled forward to the possibility of a life with him. What would their children look like were she to marry him? And wouldn't he be a wonderful-good father? *A loving and kind husband, too,* she thought.

"Annie! Glad to see you're still here." Ben hurried toward the porch with giggly Molly in his arms.

Her heart leaped when he came near, and she wondered if Molly might run inside and play, leaving them alone momentarily. Ben must have been thinking along the same lines, for he gave Molly's cheek a squeeze and set her down, shooing her into the house. "I'm glad I caught you, Annie. Have a minute?"

"Why, sure."

He pulled up a chair and scooted it next to hers. "I want to tell you something. I've made arrangements to rent a room for a few months in the same house where Sam's staying."

"You did?" Annie was pleased as pie.

He nodded. "Sam and I are becoming good friends. He's giving me some pointers on starting a small business. Did you know he's got a day job, and his own carpentry and remodeling business on the side?"

Annie found this interesting. "Last I saw Sam, he'd talked of leaving the Amish life . . . before it was known. But I hadn't heard how he was doing on the outside till now."

"He seems to be fine. But he misses Louisa."

"He said that?" She smiled.

"Loud and clear."

"Well, I talked to Lou on the phone today, and 'tween you and me, I think she misses him, too."

"Do you suppose Sam's leaving will make a relationship with Louisa more likely?" Ben asked.

Not wanting to let on what she knew about Michael, Annie was noncommittal. "Hard to say. . . ."

She changed the subject. "Do Irvin and Julia know 'bout your plans to rent elsewhere?"

"I told them I plan to move out in a week or so—make space in the attic for whoever might need a place. You never know about Irvin and Julia . . . who they might want to help next."

Annie agreed, and then Ben began to talk of his work prospects. She said it was too bad he couldn't work over at the harness shop as he had before. In part she was trying to tell him she wished he'd never left. She hoped he was reading between the lines just now.

"I'm sure I'll come up with something," Ben replied.

They sat for a moment without talking; then he reached for her hand. "Will you have dinner with me next week? Celebrate the reunion of Isaac and Annie." He smiled broadly, eyes filled with hope.

"Oh, jah, that would be so nice." She was aware of her beating heart.

"How about Monday, when fewer people are eating out?"

"Monday's fine."

"We could drive farther away, too, if you like."

She knew he was being cautious, as they had been last winter—driving long distances so as not to be seen by anyone who might recognize her. "No, that's not necessary at all. Ever so kind of you, Ben."

Julia peeked her head out the door and invited Annie to stay for supper, all smiles.

Annie rose. "I best be goin' to help Esther. But nice of you to invite me, Julia."

"Hard to believe you're passing up my homemade noodles," Julia teased.

Annie laughed. "I guess I am at that."

Ben offered to drive her, but Annie insisted on walking. "I really want to take you," he said as he stood and grinned at her.

"Your supper will get cold," Annie said, glancing at Julia. "Tell him how much better those buttery noodles are *hot*, Cousin."

Julia wiggled her fingers in a wave. "Take your time getting her home, Ben," she said. "I can always reheat the noodles." She winked, then disappeared into the house.

"Not so subtle, is she?" Ben joked as they made their way down the front steps and toward his car.

Annie squelched a laugh, ever so happy to be escorted home by her handsome beau.

After taking Annie back to Esther's, Ben called Julia on his cell to let her know he would not be back for supper. He needed time alone to consider all the years he'd skipped over while in Kentucky, thinking his sisters and parents were his true family. Of course they were still his family, and he had everything to be grateful for regarding the Martins. They'd taken him in when he had needed a family most, making him their own son. Whatever lay ahead, Ben would never forget that.

In spite of his close connection to his Kentucky family, he hoped he could have a face-to-face meeting with Daniel Hochstetler, his birth father. There had been some talk between Annie and her father that Daniel might be heading this way.

Ben wished it would be sooner rather than later. There was so much rattling around in his head about the four years he'd spent living here as a child—nearly too long ago now to separate imagination from reality. Too, he felt he needed—no, *wanted*—to mourn the loss of his mother, that she hadn't lived to see his return. He had some vivid memories of her but not enough to satisfy him. He wished he could talk with Zeke about her and his childhood, hoping his brother might be able to dredge up more memories.

It annoyed him that no photographs were allowed by the Amish brethren. A picture of his biological parents would be a big help at a time like this. And how cool it would be to carry a picture of Annie in his wallet!

———

The blinds were wide open in the sitting area off her kitchen as Louisa enjoyed curling up in one of her favorite chairs. She loved how the evening's light filtered into the room, this place that had her personality and likes written all over it. She cuddled Muffin, who yawned and slapped his long tail, blinking his pretty eyes. Her cat felt as soft and warm as a feather bed, Louisa thought, recalling how warm and comforting the one at Annie's house had been. Tonight she was snug and cocooned away, soaking up the cozy feeling and glad to have this time to herself . . . and Muffin. She had often wondered what other single or widowed people did for companionship, having read how important the connection with people or animals was . . . and she was once again delighted to have such an affectionate kitty.

She exhaled slowly, contemplating the few times she had gone out on lunch or dinner dates with Michael since her return from Amish country. He had been attentive, endeavoring to woo her back. And she was becoming vulnerable to him, even though she often thought of Sam.

When the phone rang, she assumed it was Michael but was pleasantly surprised to hear Julia Ranck's voice. "Well, *hey*," Louisa said.

"I've been meaning to call you after our

last phone discussion. I thought I'd just pick up the phone right now, if this is a good time."

"It's really a perfect time, yes."

Julia explained that her husband was bathing the children and Ben was gone from the house. "Still out with Annie, I would guess."

But it was clear Julia had not called to talk about Annie and Ben, or her children in the tub. She wanted to continue their conversation about Louisa's "spiritual issues," she said. Louisa was amazed at the timing of the call. She was all set to live life to the fullest—to live for God and others, just as Julia and her husband, Irvin, seemed to thrive on doing.

"I'll tell you honestly," Louisa said, aware once again of her openness with this woman. "I've never been this interested in the so-called God of the universe before."

———

Esther sat up in bed, cradling her baby near. Annie had been so kind to take good care of her during the past two days since her return from the hospital. Now that she was better, she enjoyed picking up the baby prior to her time to be nursed just to hold her and enjoy the fading sky in the window across her bedroom. The days were growing longer with the coming of summer, and she was especially glad for this tender time between twilight and dusk.

Hearing a creak in the hallway, she turned and saw a glimpse of the white cotton nightgown Annie had recently sewn for herself in the crack where the door stood ajar. "Come in, Annie."

"Hope I didn't wake you," Annie said, silently slipping inside.

"Nee, I'm just thinking 'bout this day and the goodness of the Lord." She kissed her baby's head. "And my sweet one right here."

"You seem back to your old self." Annie sat on the edge of the bed.

"Oh, ever so much better, jah."

They sat quietly, looking at each other for an awkward moment, and it was clear to Esther that Annie had something on her mind. "What're you thinkin' tonight?"

"Truth be known, it's my art. I'm itchin' to start up again. Been waiting till the middle of July, which is comin' fast now." She sighed. "You may think this odd, but I feel only half alive without it."

"And yet you honor your father's request." Esther's heart went out to her.

"If it were up to me alone, I'd follow my heart, probably, and paint every single day."

Essie studied her friend's face, nodding slowly. "It's a wonderful-good calling, Annie. But surely your heart is calling you to more than art, ain't so?"

"Ben, you mean?"

"Could be. But I'm not thinking of him tonight. I've seen you changing, Annie, your heart softening to the Lord."

"Maybe so, but I still love to paint."

Essie wanted to share something she'd discovered from her talks with Julia and others at her new church. "I hope you can understand what I want to tell ya, Annie."

"Jah?"

"Sometimes when we love something, if we're willin' to give it up—'specially to God—it is given back. Ever hear of such a thing?"

Annie shook her head. "No . . ."

"Honestly, I think if we cling too hard, the thing we love can't blossom. But if it's released, sometimes it is returned. If it's s'posed to be, that is."

Annie pulled her robe together tightly, fidgeting, and Esther worried she had offended her precious friend. "Just think on it, all right? Don't fret."

Getting up, Annie nodded. "I'm awful tired. Good night, Essie."

"Sweet dreams, Annie."

After nursing the baby, Esther rose and carried her to the crib. She stood there looking down at her miniature angel swathed in the white of the moon, listening to the slow breathing. Her heart swelled with love for her family, and she thanked the Lord yet again for sparing the life of the next new babe. Then she prayed, "Oh, please touch my Zeke with your loving hand, Father. Prepare his heart for you, and call him to know and love you just as I do. This I pray in Jesus' name. Amen."

Ben sat in the Rancks' attic room and read and recited the Pennsylvania Dutch words from the book Irvin had loaned him. Again and again he practiced, trying for not only the correct pronunciation but the cadence of the words and phrases as he remembered hearing—and speaking—them.

Closing the book, he reached for the Bible he had slipped into his suitcase back home. Turning to the Gospel of John, he read all of chapter fifteen, contemplating the concept of Christ being the true vine, God the gardener, and he himself being a branch. *"If a man remains in me and I in him, he will bear much fruit. . . ."*

He had always wanted to be a "good guy," but he had failed, time and again. He struggled with temptation, like anyone, English or Amish. There seemed no way to be consistently kind, patient, loving, obedient—or good enough—while growing up in his father's house. In *either* of his fathers' houses. He needed to be connected with the "source," the true vine; he needed to be grafted in.

Continuing his reading, Ben realized he had never felt this inclined toward the Scriptures. They were telling him he belonged, that he wasn't alone. He did not have to guess any longer; in the fullest sense, he knew who he was.

Rejuvenated, he determined to read several chapters each day, as he knew Irvin did upon first awaking. He would talk to God, too—the real and personal way he had witnessed Irvin and Julia doing—because he was persuaded his being here, and the realization of his identity, had somehow been orchestrated by an unseen hand. Surely, God had called him not only back here to his Amish roots but into a relationship with Him, as well.

Chapter 30

Other than the letter, there had been no forewarning of Ichabod's arrival in Paradise. Jesse coughed abruptly at the sight of his old friend standing on the back stoop Monday morning, the screen door rattling with his knocking.

As lanky and dark-headed as Jesse remembered, Ichabod stood with broad shoulders, waiting. Not saying a word, Jesse made his way through the utility room and opened the door.

"Preacher Zook" came the familiar, raspy voice.

Jesse refused to say he had been expecting him or to offer his usual welcome. All the anger and bitter disappointment of the years filled him in that silent moment. As they exchanged glances, Jesse noticed the surprisingly congenial expression on Ichabod's ruddy face and saw neither pride nor resentment registered there.

"I've come to visit my son's grave, if it'd suit you to show me the way. Thought I might ride over to the cemetery with you and the missus . . . or however you'd like to do this."

"Daniel . . ." The name slipped out before Jesse could retrieve it. The brethren had agreed to call him Ichabod for a reason, and nothing had changed, far as Jesse knew. The man was still an exile. Yet he seemed markedly different. Was it the loss of Mary or had the years whittled away the ruthless edges?

Leading the man down the steps and through the wide yard, past the freshly hung wash, Jesse mustered up all the humanity he possessed. As they walked, he told of having plowed up the bones initially mistaken for Isaac's. Jesse revealed, as kindheartedly as possible, all the upsetting circumstances surrounding Zeke's shocking admission of guilt . . . then the sudden dismissal of evidence.

He felt wearied by the telling, but the father who had lost so much deserved some explanation. Daniel received the whole of the news at face value, which stunned Jesse further. This wasn't at all the demeanor he'd expected. "I'm awful sorry to be the one to tell you. I did send a second letter, but you must not have gotten it. Seems you've made the trip here for nothin'."

"No . . . no, I 'spect that isn't so." Ichabod tilted his head, looking hard at Jesse. "What with my dear Mary passed on and all my kin settled round these parts, I might just like to . . . make amends."

Jesse scratched his head. Was he hearing correctly? This was not the man he'd known. That man carried an enduring chip on his wide shoulders, ever seeking out conflict of some kind or another.

Aware of how distant they had become, Jesse asked how long he planned to stay in the area.

"Haven't thought it all through yet, Preacher. But I want to see my son and daughter-in-law . . . and their youngsters. How many grandchildren do I have?"

"At last count, four."

"I'll be moseyin' over there, then."

It was urgent for Jesse to catch him up on Zeke's fragile mental state, to say that his son was not presently living at home.

This news seemed to pain Ichabod, and he shook his head. "So much suffering in this old world, ain't?" He removed his hat and pressed it against his chest. "I have something to tell you, Jesse. Something I've played and replayed in my head. You see, part of why I've come is to repent."

Jesse shifted his weight from one foot to the other, hardly able to think, let alone speak. Who *was* this man?

"The Lord God has dealt bitterly with me." The man bowed his head for a moment before raising it with a sigh. "I kept myself afar off, resisting the Almighty. I let my conceit rule me, livin' for myself and breakin' my Mary's heart. Broke it clear in two . . . and then some." He struggled to speak. "I did the unthinkable."

Jesse was stunned, and when Daniel was finished confessing his sin with another woman, Jesse placed a hand on his old friend's shoulder and said, "So, then, will you be askin' forgiveness of the brethren?"

"First you, Jesse . . . then all the ministers, and finally the membership."

Moved now, Jesse extended the hand of fellowship. "I forgive you, Daniel."

A palpable power gripped the two friends as they shook hands. "I was a sinner, 'cept for the grace of our Lord."

"As we all are."

Jesse led him out to the paddock, where a thin haze hung near the ground as they walked and talked amidst the horses and mules, resuming their friendship. Jesse assured him that he would without question find mercy amongst the People. " 'Tis our way."

They talked more of Zeke and Esther and the children, although Jesse said nothing of Esther's shunning nor of Ben's claims, wanting to spare Daniel more grief just now. "I'll see if I can't get Zeke out to the work frolic later today . . . over at the bishop's place."

Daniel brightened. "Oh, that'd be just fine."

Right then and there, under the Lord God's heavenly covering of clouds and sky, Jesse offered to have the man called Ichabod hang his hat at his house, to rest up a bit and share a hot meal before heading out to chop wood with the men.

"Mighty kind of you, Preacher." And Ichabod smiled.

Not accustomed to doing so, Jesse had thrown around the word *preacher* quite a lot in order to get one of Zeke's several doctors to consent to a half-day pass. In the space of a few hours, from the time Ichabod had appeared on his doorstep till now, a whole group of hardworking men had gathered to cut wood at the home of their elderly bishop.

Jesse helped Zeke from the van, then paid their driver. Zeke's face shown with appreciation as the men spotted him and began coming to greet him in clusters of threes and fours. In spite of all Zeke had been through, the men were enthusiastic to see him.

Thankfully so, thought Jesse.

Suddenly he noticed Ben over by a pile of uncut wood. "Ach, of all the nerve," Jesse muttered, guessing Moses must have let the cat out of the bag about today's work. He hoped Ben would stay put behind the stand of trees, working a two-man saw with one of Jesse's nephews. No need to spoil such a wonderful-good thing as this, a man and his son reconciled on Amish soil. That is, if it didn't backfire. Jesse prayed it wouldn't.

Still observing Ben in the distance, Jesse let out a sigh. There was no point putting it off. Even if Moses couldn't recognize Ben for the imposter he was, surely Daniel would. Despite the inconvenience of the whole thing, they could kill two birds with one stone—be done with the whole foolishness.

Jesse led Zeke around the side of the house, on the look-out for Daniel, wondering if he'd arrived yet. Meanwhile, Zeke was thirsty; he'd like to get his hands wrapped around the well pump in the backyard.

Jesse walked with him to the well, hoping Daniel hadn't changed his mind about coming.

Zeke finished wetting his whistle at the pump, wiped his face on his shirtsleeve, and looked up to see Jesse wearing a relieved look on his face. Zeke turned to see what on earth the preacher was staring at over yonder.

Squinting hard, he set his gaze on a man swinging his long arms, coming up the lane with a downright confident stride. The man seemed familiar somehow, and Zeke wondered why. Then he knew. *Am I seeing things?*

The man resembled his own father, or at least what Zeke recalled of the sternest man he'd ever known. Fact was, there was a good measure of recognition in Preacher Jesse's eyes, too.

Zeke let out a low groan. "Is that my ol' Dat—and if so, what's *he* doin' here?"

Jesse quickly explained about the letters he'd sent regarding Isaac's remains. "He didn't get the second letter from me, tellin' him there was no need to come."

Zeke's father walked right up to them, and Zeke felt his intense gaze. No question, his father had recognized him, too, despite the passage of years. Zeke felt fireworks exploding in his chest.

Dat spoke first. "Zeke . . . son, mighty gut seein' ya again."

Zeke stepped back, eyeing his father warily. "Been a lot of years."

"No doubt you're surprised." His father let out a nervous chuckle, extending his hand. "I've come to apologize, Zeke."

He stared at his father, refusing the handshake, and an awkward moment passed.

"Son . . . I—"

"No," Zeke sputtered, coming uncorked. "You just listen to *me*. You've caused nothin' but hardship my whole life long . . . even long after you up and hightailed it out of here." Angry tears spilled down his face. He shook his head again and again, unable to control the resentment, the bottled rage. "Don't ya see? This here's a result of your scorn." Zeke pounded his chest. "*This* . . . me."

His father pursed his lips. "I did you wrong. I know this . . . and have no right to ask you for anything."

Zeke frowned, somewhat taken aback.

This wasn't the man he remembered. The father who had raised him would have lashed back with similar fury, raising his voice and hurling insults.

Dat extended his hand again. "I've come to see if you'll receive me into the fellowship here, and perhaps someday . . . as your father."

The older man fell silent, looking at Zeke with surprisingly tender eyes. Preacher Jesse said nothing as Zeke studied his father's face. Those eyes . . . that face that had disapproved of him for countless months and years. All the memories of belittlement.

How can I forgive him?

Zeke looked down at his father's outstretched hand, now trembling with the effort, and something within tugged at him. He was still that little boy who'd always longed for his father's love and approval. And now . . . was his father truly offering it?

Zeke sighed and brushed his tears away. Irvin's long talks had taken a foothold in his heart, preparing the soil for such a moment. He wasn't the same man and, apparently, neither was his father.

It's time, Zeke realized, as years of resentment suddenly gave way. Forgiveness broke loose within and he did the unthinkable: he reached for his father's hand and gripped it. His entire soul shuddered, and he was instantly caught off guard, pulled forward into his father's embrace.

Zeke could not resist, and he wept.

Moved by what he'd just witnessed, Jesse grunted his exit, leaving Zeke and Daniel alone to work things out between them. Scratching his head, he wondered, *Who would've thought?* Daniel had been the harshest of men. A brutal father . . . absent in the flesh and otherwise, for sure and for certain.

Jesse smiled, almost wishing he might pat himself on the back for the part he'd played in this rather unplanned reunion.

The brethren would begin the process of bringing Daniel back into the fold. Such would take little time, as a sincere repentance on the part of the wayward one was the only requirement. Immediately following Daniel's kneeling repentance, the People would receive him back, no questions asked.

Our way . . .

He chuckled, resisting the urge to look over his shoulder once again. But he could hear Daniel and Zeke talking quick-like now, catching up on all the years, no doubt. The sounds of a son granting his father forgiveness.

Hopefully things would be settling down by the time Zeke spotted Ben. Then the man he'd once called Ichabod could finally and fully unmask Ben's foolishness. The event was inevitable. He would merely wait for it to unfold.

Isaac indeed! Jesse muttered as he continuing observing from afar. Several men now approached Daniel and Zeke, offering their friendly welcome as father and son began to work side by side.

Later, during a short break from their labors, Zeke looked up and happened to see Ben Martin. "What's he doing back here?" he wondered aloud, awful glad to see him. Zeke turned to his father, who was sipping a cup of water. "I want you to meet an English friend of mine."

Zeke hurried his pace as he made his way down the slope toward Ben, his father following beside him.

"Heard you'd gone home," Zeke said, offering a smile.

Ben seemed startled, his expression a mixture of surprise and shock. "I . . . well . . . I'm back, yes."

Despite Ben's strange reaction, Zeke extended his hand and Ben shook it.

Zeke was about to introduce his father

when Ben cleared his throat. "I've been wanting to talk to you, Zeke."

"Well, here I am." Zeke chuckled.

A small smile traced itself on Ben's face. He turned to Zeke's father, and a look of confusion crossed his brow.

Zeke's father squinted his eyes, shielding them against the sun. A look of puzzlement crossed his own features. "Do I know you, young man?"

Ben was silent. For a moment Zeke stood back, curious as the two men awkwardly observed each other.

"Ach, sorry. This here's Ben Martin," he said. "And, Ben, this is Daniel Hochstetler, my father."

Ben reached to accept the older man's handshake. "Good to meet you, sir. Very good . . ."

Shaking hands, the two men seemed tongue-tied, eyes locked upon each other. Zeke noted his father's pale face. "What is it, Dat?"

His father stepped closer to Ben, gripping the younger man's shoulder. "In all my born days . . . If you don't look like . . ."

Dat stopped and shook his head, and Ben gave Zeke a quick, almost guilty glance.

Look like who? Zeke wondered, following his father's unrelenting stare at Ben's features.

Dat released his handshake and stepped back to appraise Ben. "All this time, I've wondered what the world my Isaac might look like all grown up. And here you are, the spittin' image of my own imagination."

Zeke shivered. "What're you saying, Dat?" He looked back at Ben, who instead of brushing off the strange comment was nodding gravely.

What's going on?

Just then Preacher Jesse walked over, looking at them as if he might object to this strange meeting. But he said not a word when he stood alongside Zeke, his brow furrowed with something akin to fear.

Dat chuckled. "Ben Martin, you say? There's no way you might be mistaken on that?"

Ben returned the smile, but his eyes were serious. "I was mistaken for years, but not anymore."

"What's that you say?" asked Zeke's father.

"I have the memories to prove I'm someone else."

His father crept closer, his face displaying a mixture of disbelief and hope. "Isaac?"

Ben simply nodded.

"I knew it!" Dat exclaimed. He burst out laughing and grabbed Ben by the shoulders.

Zeke's mouth dropped open, unable to fathom what was happening right before his eyes. Was this another mental trick? Or was his father as deluded as *he* had been? It made not a whit of sense. And by the incredulous look on Preacher's white face, it made no sense to him, either.

Preacher Jesse spoke up. "So you actually buy this nonsense?"

Grinning from ear to ear, Dat released Ben and turned to Jesse. "This here is my lost boy, I'm tellin' you."

Jesse's face clouded. "He'd like you to believe that."

Dat's eyebrows rose, apparently taken aback at Jesse's objection. He turned to Ben, scrutinizing him further. "So . . . Preacher Jesse thinks you're an imposter? Is that what I'm hearing?"

"Yes, sir," Ben said. "He does."

"But you have . . . memories?" Dat continued.

Ben nodded.

Dat glanced at Preacher Jesse. "Well, then, let's put this to the test and be done with it."

The preacher seemed to momentarily consider this, then sighed softly. "Fine."

Dat cleared his throat and fixed an intense look on Ben. He took a deep breath, as if regretting the words to come, though he spoke them anyway. "My young Isaac was aware of my terrible secret—the dire sin that kept me from accepting the divine lot." He looked at the preacher. "Jesse Zook knows what I'm talkin' about."

Jesse nodded, but Zeke was confused again. *Isaac knew our father's secret? Who remembers much, if anything, from the tender age of four?* It seemed an impossible test.

Dat chewed his lip but didn't speak, as if trying to bite back the tears filling his eyes.

At last he pulled himself together. "When you were young, you loved to carry around a peach stone. . . ."

Ben brightened as he slipped his hand into his pocket and brought out a peach pit, holding it up. "Like this?"

"Means nothing," Jesse interjected.

Dat raised a hand before continuing more soberly. "And do you remember where you first received a peach?"

Ben's grin faded. He glanced first at Zeke, then at Jesse.

"Speak the truth as you remember it,"

Dat said gently but with conviction.

Ben looked down at the ground, appearing oddly embarrassed. *Or maybe he doesn't remember,* Zeke thought, as Ben seemed to struggle.

"He doesn't know," Jesse said. "Because he's not—"

"The peach girl," Ben finally replied. "The one you . . . liked."

Zeke expelled a nervous breath, and Preacher Jesse's eyes grew wide in apparent amazement.

Nodding sadly, Dat looked at Jesse and said, "My foolish sin was known only by my young son. Mary, bless her dear heart, forgave me in the end. Took me back even though I didn't deserve such love."

Embracing Ben's shoulders again, Dat held on as if he might disappear. "Can there be any more doubt? This young man, this Ben, is my own Isaac . . . in the flesh!" Suddenly Dat laughed robustly, even hilariously, pulling Ben hard into his arms. "My dear Isaac . . . my son."

For a moment, Zeke simply stood there, stunned. *Isaac . . . alive?* Even Preacher Jesse was speechless, stepping back in disbelief.

Zeke felt himself go rigid at the thought of his brother still alive, barely noticing the small crowd of men now gathering around them. And yet . . . hadn't he, too, on some level, felt drawn to Ben? He had always felt strangely at ease with the younger man. His thoughts flew to his previous conversations with Irvin. *God can work miracles!*

Unable to resist any longer, and in a flood of bewildered relief and thankfulness to his sovereign God, Zeke joined his father and Ben, the three of them spontaneously connecting in a circle of love regained.

Chapter 3-1

After hanging out the wash at Essie's, Annie phoned Yonie from the neighbors' and asked him to drive her to town for her hair-cutting appointment. He seemed surprised she'd called him, but she felt it better to use his driving services than to have someone outside the community see her looking all skimpy and nearly weightless, like a frail flower, with hair only to her chin. Well, maybe she would have it cut slightly longer than that so she could still pull it into a ponytail for the hot summer months. Even if she did that, she had a good thirty-five inches or more to sell for a wig, which Lou had said should fetch between two hundred fifty and three hundred dollars. "Virgin hair" like hers that had never been cut or colored was particularly valuable.

That sort of money will go a long way, she

assumed. At least Annie was determined to make it stretch for those shoes, dresses, and maybe even that skirt and blouse she'd seen at the outlet shops. "Or I could always buy some English clothes patterns and sew some up for myself."

She honestly could not wait to see Ben's reaction to her new modern look. She wanted to please him . . . and to please herself, even though she felt jittery at the thought of losing the long, thick hair she'd had since she was a little girl. Yet she had contemplated this moment long enough. It was time for action and she would grit her teeth, if necessary, to get through it.

While sitting on the front porch waiting for Yonie to arrive, she enjoyed the sunshine and watched Zach teach his little brother to play tug-of-war with an old rope. She was reminded of the long rope swing over at Pequea Creek. "Yonie put the swing up just in time," she whispered to herself, still stunned at how things had fallen into place where Ben was concerned—at least in her mind they had.

Yonie's car pulled into the driveway, and she lifted her skirt a bit to hurry to meet him. "I thought you'd never get here," she said, grinning.

"Me too." He told her he'd had to stop off at Dory's.

She laughed. "Well, you're not runnin' much of a driving business, then. How're you ever going to make a dollar if you're such a slowpoke?"

He bantered back in kind, talking cheerfully with her until he pulled up to the beauty salon. He turned and looked at her, frowning his disapproval. "What're you thinkin' of doing, Annie?"

"Oh, you'll see." With that, she opened the door. "I'll call from here when it's time for you to come get me."

He was plainly concerned. "Bye for now," she said, her heart pounding as she waved and headed into the shop.

Sam leaned forward at the restaurant where Ben had gone to meet him for lunch. "What do you mean you want to return to the life you missed?"

"I want to give my life back." *To my family who lost me,* Ben mentally added.

"It would be a huge adjustment."

"And I can't imagine it," said Ben. "But I can't let it go all the same."

Sam mentioned the dawn-to-dusk hard work, giving up a car for a horse and buggy, wearing homemade clothing . . . all the things that would be required of Ben should he choose to become Plain. "Unless, of course, you were to join up with the Mennonites. Most of them drive cars." Sam wore a mischievous grin. "I'd say keep that nice car of yours, ain't?"

"Well, I was born into an Amish family. . . ." Ben hadn't said it aloud before, and the declaration sounded foreign to his ears. He wondered what the implications might be for his adoptive family—how they would react and whether it might ultimately hurt them—and himself, as well.

But he was curious to know more. "The language barrier—what about that?"

Sam shook his head. "I think you could learn to speak fluent Dutch pretty quickly, Ben."

"It's funny, I still remember some words and phrases . . . and I understand more than I can speak."

"Not surprising, really," Sam replied. "It *was* your first language."

Ben asked if Sam would be willing to coach him, and Sam chuckled.

"I'll trade you. You teach me how to drive a car, and I'll teach you Dutch."

"Thanks," Ben said, laughing.

Sam leaned forward. "Uh, just a suggestion, Ben. You'll be wantin' to quit saying thanks so awful much." Sam explained that the use of *thanks* was looked on as suspect and wasn't part of daily Amish conversation. "You can show your gratitude in other ways. But we say it less . . . and show it more."

Ben smiled. "You just referred to yourself as one of the People."

Sam laughed, nodding his head. "I s'pose once Amish always Amish. I've heard that repeatedly from folk who leave the community. You can't take the Plain out of a person. It's next to impossible."

"So what are you going to do about clothes and cars and such, here on the outside?" Ben asked.

"Oh, I'll look and try to act English, but inside, I'll know. I'll always know who I am." Sam looked solemn. "I daresay, you had better have a good reason to leave your modern life behind. But you, and only you, must count the cost on that."

"I'll miss my car, no question. My cell phone, too." Ben found their talk fascinating, especially since Sam was on the way out. "What about my family back in Kentucky? Would I be allowed to stay in contact with them?"

"I don't see why not."

"Ever think of letting Louisa know

you've gone fancy?" Ben asked.

Sam lit up. "Oh, I wrote her, all right. Just heard back from her, too."

The fact that Sam didn't volunteer more about Louisa made him wonder.

Surrounded by bright lights and electric gadgets, Annie stared into the wide mirror, feeling guilty as all get out and tempted to flee. She watched as the stylist divided her long hair into several lengthy ponytails, then lopped them off, one by one. *I can't turn back now. . . .*

She hoped against hope that Ben would appreciate her new look. No, she was holding her breath that he would understand what she was going through to become the modern young woman he could wholeheartedly embrace as his own beloved wife.

After the stylist finished cutting, she used a blow dryer on Annie's now barely shoulder-length hair. *Will Lou be surprised I actually did it?* she wondered.

She knew she would have no time to run to the neighbors' phone later today or to sit down and write to her pen pal. Truth was, she wanted to look extra pretty for her dinner date with Ben tonight. She had even purchased a light pink lip-gloss and a compact of pressed powder to take away the everlasting shine on her nose.

Once her hair was fluffed and swinging free when she moved her head, Annie received payment for her hair and went to sit near the window to wait for Yonie to return for her. The blond woman sitting nearby was thumbing through a magazine, and although Annie couldn't see the cover completely, it looked to be a craft magazine.

Not wanting to be nosy, but unable to quiet her interest, Annie asked about the magazine, and the pretty woman spoke right up, obviously happy to chat with her. The woman said she enjoyed creating art from cloth patches and items like bottle caps, soup cans, and paper clips, all arranged in an imaginative design. "It's something like quilt making. All you need is a mental blueprint," the blonde told her.

Annie couldn't help but contemplate her own art—and life. Did she have a plan? Julia called the Bible such a blueprint, and Annie was sure she ought to be following the Scriptures more closely, too. *Why do I resist it so?*

Yonie was not only unmistakably aghast, but seeing Annie with her hair barely touching her shoulders seemed to unlock something in him.

"Nice," Yonie said simply.

"You think?"

"Well, nice for an Englischer, that's for sure," he said. "Not so much for *you*, Annie."

At least he didn't shame her, as she'd braced herself for, even though he'd been nearly as bold not long ago, getting his own hair cut in a modern style. Of course, it wouldn't take much for him to grow it back into the cropped, nearly bowl-shaped cut, though thus far he'd made no attempt to do so.

On the drive back, after a stop at the outlet stores so Annie could make her purchases, Yonie began to talk of college and how he'd been thinking about going. "To make something of myself, ya know . . . besides bein' a farmer."

"This is the first I've heard of it. I guess you'll have to take a qualifying test, jah?"

"The GED. I've heard enough about how mighty hard it is, so I think I may have to get some tutoring in order to pass."

"You might have to study. Imagine that." She grinned at him.

"Sometime next fall, after the harvest, I'll start lookin' for my own place. I'm a noose round Daed's neck." He fell silent for a time, driving with one hand on the steering wheel, one arm leaning on the open window.

His light hair rippled in the breeze, and Annie tried to envision him dressed like Ben or any of the other fancy men she'd seen, with an open-throated shirt or T-shirt and jeans.

"I suppose you'll be marryin' fancy, too?"

Yonie chuckled. "You and your romantic notions."

"Well, you've been seein' Dory for a good long time."

He gave her a fleeting look. "And you've been seein' an Englischer again, too."

"Jah." She wouldn't hedge on that, at least not with her favorite brother. "I hope we won't lose touch with each other, you and me." She felt a lump in her throat at the thought of his leaving. "Where will you go to college?"

"Maybe where Sam attended, at HACC, on the Old Philadelphia Pike."

Annie didn't dare speak for fear she'd start to cry.

"Nothin' stays the same, Annie. It's a rule of thumb . . . of life."

He could say what he wanted, but she didn't quite agree. After all, there were plenty of things that *did* stay the same. Even though she wasn't exactly a good example, what with her new hairdo and published painting, Annie knew lots of folk who embraced the time-honored life of their ancestors. In some ways, the People as a whole had remained similar for hundreds of years. In other respects, all of them were on a path to change. She thought of the people dearest to her and hoped Mamm would be all right, not despairing over Yonie's startling news—and Annie's own new look.

"Poor Mamm," she sighed.

"Jah, I know what you mean," Yonie agreed, seeming to have something of a lump in *his* throat, too.

Picking up the small hand mirror on her bureau, Annie prepared for her special evening with Ben. She removed her head covering first, realizing anew how terribly difficult it would be to continue putting up her hair into a bun with it cut so short. Somehow she had managed to wrap it up—if only for Essie's sake—upon her arrival home today. She had decided to reveal herself as quite fancy this evening to Esther but wanted to be more discreet about prancing around in front of the children. Prior to going out, she truly needed Essie's reaction to her modern outfit and dressy shoes, not to mention the face powder and pretty pink lip-gloss.

Annie knew she looked completely different even to herself. She'd heard of other Amish girls cutting their hair to make bangs and living to regret it, but not her. She was on the way to jumping the fence, and if she got a good response from Ben, she felt sure she might even beat Yonie over to the outside world. Truth be told, everything she did now was either with her art or Ben in mind, and Annie could hardly wait to have both. No need to chose one over the other as she had with her former beau, Rudy.

I can have it all.

Worried and excited about his impending decision, Ben knew he couldn't put off telling his family back home. He and his sisters were exceptionally close, and even after the recent tensions between him and his adoptive parents, he still couldn't exclude them from such a monumental life change. They might try to talk him out of it, but better to hear their objections now and give them time to get used to the idea.

When his mom answered the phone, he asked, "Is Dad around? I've got something important to tell you both."

"Uh-oh. That sounds ominous. Hang

on. I'll get Dad on the other phone."

Ben waited until he heard the click of another phone being picked up. "I'm here," his father said.

Filling his lungs with air, Ben said, "I'm thinking of going Plain—returning to the Amish."

No one spoke.

He'd thought at least his mother would protest, but he heard nothing.

"You must be freaked, and who could blame you," Ben said, filling the silence.

Finally his dad spoke up. "After everything you've found out about your first family and all, I guess we shouldn't be so surprised."

"I'm already learning Pennsylvania Dutch. It's coming surprisingly easy."

"That's because it was ingrained in you at a young age," Mom suggested. Her voice began to shake. "I always felt you suffered from being cut off . . . longing for your original family. But we don't want to lose you, Ben."

"You won't, Mom. You couldn't get rid of me if you tried."

"Though I suppose you won't be calling us on your cell phone quite so much, huh?" Dad said, attempting a weak joke.

Ben chuckled. "You're probably right.

But there's always snail mail."

"Well, we hear the excitement—the confidence—in your voice, son," Dad offered. "We're behind you, if this is what you want."

He's too polite to say, "You're out of your mind!" Ben thought. Still, he was relieved they seemed to be accepting his decision so well.

Chapter 32

Annie's heart was beating fast as she called to Esther to come upstairs. "What's-a-matter?" Essie asked as she entered the room. Her mouth dropped open. "What the world, Annie Zook!"

"Don't be alarmed . . . it's for Ben. It's a surprise."

"You can say that again." Essie shook her head. "Ben's here early. I saw him pull into the lane just as you called me up here." She eyed Annie yet again. "Goodness me, you're a brave one."

Annie smiled. "Look who's talkin'!"

"You're right perty, Annie."

At that she hugged Essie and hurried down the steps, more than ready to see what Ben had to say about her appearance.

It didn't take long for Annie to find out, because Ben was already standing at the back door, ready to knock, when Annie walked out through the kitchen and met him. "Hullo, Ben!" she said, trying not to grin lest he think she was showing off.

He started talking, saying, "I have the best news—" But he stopped and went momentarily silent, staring at her. "Whoa . . . Annie." His gaze lingered on her short hair.

They stood there awkwardly, Ben obviously stunned by her fancy getup.

"Do you . . . like it?" She touched her hair.

"You're very pretty, no matter how you dress or how long your hair is."

She sensed some hesitancy on his part. "What were you about to say? What's your news?"

He told how his father—Daniel Hochstetler—had come to the work frolic and identified him, and of the wonderful reunion with Zeke, as well.

"I think seeing the three of us together blew your father away . . . though now there's no question in *anyone's* mind that I'm Isaac." He smiled broadly.

"Oh, Ben, I'm so happy for you! For all of you!" She reached for him and he returned her embrace.

Stepping back, he cleared his throat. "Are you ready for a nice dinner?"

She nodded, still not sure if he was as pleased as she'd hoped about her new look.

Annie took in the soft lighting and candles as she and Ben were directed to an intimate table for two at the Olde Greenfield Inn. The 1780s farmhouse was well known for its romantic setting, and Ben had told her on the drive that it was consistently ranked as "Lancaster's Best" in several magazines. As they were seated in the well-appointed dining room, a waiter placed a large white napkin over her lap before doing the same for Ben.

Ben winked at her and continued to look her way while she opened the lovely menu. So many choices, from appetizers to desserts.

Glancing over the top of the menu, she saw him staring at her. "You're making me blush," she whispered.

"Annie, you look so beautiful. You always do."

She felt sure he'd added the latter so as not to indicate she'd looked less than pretty in Amish attire. Not accustomed to being looked at so fondly, nor complimented in this way, she suddenly felt tongue-tied.

Hoping to hide her red face, she attempted to read the menu. She couldn't help but notice another couple across the room. They seemed nearly too affectionate for being in public, and Annie felt distracted by the woman's soft laughter and the man's constant reaching over to touch her hands or face. It was as if they ought to be talking somewhere privately together, not being observed in public.

"Are you all right?" Ben asked.

She focused her attention on her handsome beau. "I'm fine. Such a perty place you picked for us."

"The food is supposed to be superb, too. I guess we'll find out, won't we?"

When he smiled, his eyes shone with unmistakable affection. She had not the slightest inkling why he continued to look at her, unless it *was* her lack of head covering or any Plain apparel. She could easily have passed for an Englischer.

She was glad Ben seemed more pleased with her new look now than he had earlier. She was also relieved he hadn't shown any dismay at her decision to cut her long tresses. Of course, she never would have wanted to confide in him why she had done so, because in less than the space of an hour, she'd spent every last penny of the money she'd earned for her "perfect hair," or so the stylist had called it.

When the waiter returned, Ben politely ordered for her the lamb chops she had chosen and then ordered the prime rib for himself. She paid close attention as Ben spoke, soaking up every nuance of the way she wanted to speak and act. *Like I'm English.*

They soon fell into comfortable conversation. Ben talked of having met with Sam several times, his upcoming move, and of wanting to learn to speak Pennsylvania Dutch.

"I've even begun to memorize some basic Dutch words," he confessed.

What he seemed to imply began to dawn on her. "You're more than captivated by our Plain customs," she said. "Ain't so?"

"I think it's safe to admit it, jah."

She smiled quickly, but his eagerness to use her words, even occasionally, was beginning to worry her. "You're sounding like Lou when she was here, Ben."

Suddenly she wondered what he was really trying to say. She noticed his tan suspenders, but he'd worn them before, back when they'd attended the passion play at the Sight and Sound Theatre. He had often worn more simple clothing. She fingered the tablecloth. "You're more taken with Amish ways than ever."

His smile faded. "I thought you might be pleased."

"It's a bit unsettling."

He nodded. "And you're moving toward the English world." His eyes traced her face, her hair.

"I'm eager to paint again. It won't be long now and I'll be free of my promise to Daed." She pressed onward, finally telling him of the momentous handshake, the six-month vow she'd made to her father after all the years of hiding what was said to be a sin. "In spite of what the brethren say, I want to resume my artwork. I hope to set up a studio at Essie's once I'm free to draw and paint again. That'll be a wonderful-good day. I won't tell you otherwise."

She felt nervous as his countenance dimmed. "What is it, Ben? You look upset." She didn't want to spoil this evening, but his reaction worried her. She struggled, unable to explain the incredible pull toward what she'd missed so long. "I can't turn my back on it forever. It's part of me." She sighed. *Why is this so difficult?*

He fixed his gaze on her. "So . . . you're not planning to join the Amish church, Annie?"

She swallowed. "Maybe not."

"You'll stay on the fence forever?"

"Well, no. I'll be jumpin' it."

He leaned back in his chair, cheerless now. His shoulders seemed to sag, and he looked all in. "There's something I want you to know." He reached for his water glass and held it. "What I have to say may astonish you, Annie."

"What?"

"I want to join church, as you say. Here in Paradise. I want to become Amish."

She was stunned.

"In fact, I've already told my family back home. They had about the same reaction." Ben continued, "I have no right to ask this, but I will anyway, in case there's the slightest chance you haven't made up your mind." He stopped, looking at her intently. "Annie, I know you have an amazing talent, but you're also of the Old Order Amish. This is your background, your family . . . but not only that. It's your life."

She would not cry. "Lou said the same thing last year."

He reached across the table to hold her hand. "I believe Louisa's right. And if there is any chance you might finally become a member of your father's church, I would like to ask you to consider something else." He paused, his face registering some hesitation, but just when she thought he was not going to speak again, his expression exuded great joy. "Annie Zook, will you be my bride? Will you marry me?"

She could not speak for her tears.

"I know you're a gifted artist, Annie. But I also feel drawn to the Plain world, the life I've missed—the life I want to return to. Can you understand?"

She shook her head. *Will we always be heading in opposite directions?*

The tinkle of crystal filled the place as Louisa slowly scanned the leather-bound menu of yet another fine restaurant. Michael was talking of driving to Aspen, spending the weekend—booking separate rooms, he'd said—wanting to get some time alone with her away from the busy city.

She should have seen it coming, and she quickly objected, knowing to agree would send the wrong message.

Later, when they were between courses, enjoying the palate refresher of a rounded dab of mint sherbet, Michael took her totally off guard and pulled out a ring-sized box from his sports coat. "Louisa, I'd like to return something of yours."

She blinked, not sure what he meant.

He flicked the box open, just like in the

movies. "Remember this?"

Her lips parted when she saw her extravagant engagement ring—a two-carat diamond in the exquisite setting she had chosen when they'd first looked at rings together. *When we were naively in love.*

"Oh, Michael . . ."

"You can make me the happiest guy on the planet if you'll consent to be my bride."

She could not believe he was ready to ask her again. She also could not believe she wasn't leaning forward, removing the ring, and putting it back where she'd worn it for so long. The sight of the glamorous rock made her think of the ringless weddings in Amish country.

The last thing she wanted to do was hurt Michael's feelings. Surely it had taken plenty of guts to dig out this ring she'd not so graciously returned to him last fall when she'd abandoned her engagement promise.

"I'm asking you to marry me, Louisa. This time, like the last, because I love you . . and for no other reason."

He does care for me. . . . He really, really does.

She could not look into his passionate eyes for a single minute longer. She needed air, but now their entrées were coming. She could see the wait staff heading their way, bringing the celebration dinner.

Oh, what should I say?

Chapter 33

Annie's eyes had been pink and teary all day, and even little John seemed to notice. He'd crawled up onto her lap while she sat in Essie's front room, staring sadly out the window.

Ben's going to make his vow to God and the church . . . if the brethren feel he's ready.

John nestled himself in the crook of her arm, rubbing his eyes with his fists. "I think someone's ever so sleepy, jah?"

The little boy shook his head quickly. "No . . . no, Auntie Annie."

"Well, when Mamma says so, you must go up for your nap." She kissed the top of his head.

And there she sat, thinking about Ben and the fine meal they'd shared several nights ago. She felt guilty for not giving her answer to such an adoring beau. Yet she had withheld it out of sheer necessity, all the while seeing the hurt of rejection in his eyes . . . something she'd not been present to witness the day he'd received her letter.

Essie called sweetly for John to head upstairs, and Zach came in and stood in the doorway, waiting for his younger brother. "It's that time," Essie said, appearing with her hand on Zach's small shoulder. "If yous promise not to talk the afternoon away up yonder, I'll let you have your naps together."

Annie chuckled at trusting Essie. She knew, and so did Annie, that there was no possible way to get these two settled down if they shared the same bed. Even so, Essie shooed them off, following them on the stairs.

Leaning her head back, Annie thought she ought to be ashamed of herself. Holding tight to her passion for drawing—her treasured paints and brushes, her precious easel and canvas—while such a wonderful young man as Ben wanted to spend his life with her.

What's wrong with me?

In her memory, she flew back to the years Rudy Esh had courted her. He had also declared his love . . . had shown her, too, by putting up with her procrastination.

She'd hurt him terribly, but once she had set him free, in a short time, he had found a new love.

Was that to happen again? Would she be so foolish as to give up the chance to belong to Isaac Hochstetler? All the People knew who he was, now that word had spread rapidly of Daniel's verification that Ben was his own. *The man who could always identify trees!* She had to laugh at that.

Essie strolled into the room. "We'll see how long the boys talk, won't we?"

Annie smiled. "Laura's playing in her room?"

"Actually, she's asleep, and so's the baby."

"You should quick take a good rest yourself," Annie suggested.

But Essie sat herself down on the chair near the window and folded her hands, looking so peaceful. "I think you need a listenin' ear, Annie. Am I right?"

Annie sighed. "Jah, ain't that the truth."

"Something awful happened. It's printed on your face."

Annie nodded. "You know how fond I am of Ben."

"I assumed as much."

"It might seem peculiar if I told you I could marry him, but only if he remains

English." She explained how Ben planned to join church, while she didn't know how she could stay Amish when her heart was so tuned to painting. Truth be told, she had been longing to share her work with the English world like Louisa had when she had been there.

Essie smiled suddenly. "Well, if you *did* marry Ben, we'd be sisters-in-law—now, what about that?"

"My goodness," Annie said, but she knew that was not a good enough reason to give Ben the answer he desired. "But how can I not follow my heart to the outside?"

"There is such a thing as giving up your will. . . . Remember what we talked about before? About being willing to give up the thing we love?"

Not expecting this, Annie listened, surprised at how strongly Essie felt. "Laying down your desires may be hard, but asking the Lord for His guidance, His will, is a good way to live, I daresay."

Annie pondered that, even long after Essie got up and headed back to the kitchen to check on several baking pies. Annie was sure Cousin Julia would have said something similar were she to ask.

Sighing and wanting to walk after being inside much of the day, Annie headed outdoors, miserable at the thought of living her life without Ben and nearly as sad at the idea of turning her back on art, too.

No matter what choice I make, I lose dearly.

———————

Louisa wished she could fly out to be with Annie, who was in a catch-22 over Ben's intention to join her father's church. When Annie had called from Julia's to explain her painful dilemma, Louisa felt terrible and had racked her brain, trying to think of some way to help. But really, what could she do? What could anyone do?

Sighing, she put the finishing touches on her oil painting. She was pleased at her realistic interpretation of Muffin. "Fantabulous," she said, eager for it to dry and be framed. She had not made arrangements to mail the large painting, because now that the final brushstrokes had been made, she wondered if she could even part with it.

But she'd set out to give it to Annie, and that was still her plan. She realized that the painting would make a fine wedding gift, if ever Annie were to bring herself to marry. Louisa hoped so, for Ben's sake—Annie's, too—but knowing her Amish friend, that sort of commitment was rather up in the air for now, much as Annie's reluctance to make the lifelong kneeling vow to the Amish church had nagged her all this time.

"What will it take for Annie to take the plunge?"

She laughed, hugging herself. *What will it take for me?*

———

Zeke had not ceased talking about his father and his "newfound" brother to anyone who would listen, especially the folks in his therapy group. He knew he was jabbering on and on as he clapped his hands and paced the floor, describing yet again the impromptu family reunion. Ach, such a day it had been! The nurses smiled and listened, no doubt assuming he was obsessing on something new . . . something other than his dead brother.

But he knew he wasn't obsessing. Not, at least, to the degree he had been. After all, hadn't Irvin talked of miracles? And Zeke had witnessed one firsthand that day at the work frolic. "Isaac *is* alive," he said repeatedly. "My brother was never dead."

And when the nurse came in to check his blood pressure and take his temperature several times a day, he would simply shake his head. He was growing weary of being here. "I want to go home, and as soon as possible," he told one of his doctors. That afternoon, he said the same to his group leader, too. He was whole now—no need to be here when his family needed him at home.

More tests were administered under the advisement of the doctors. Zeke was terribly frustrated but kept his story straight—he knew to do that much—when telling about Isaac's return.

After additional tests and many further discussions, it was decided that indeed Zeke was much improved. So much so that when both Irvin and Preacher Jesse showed up together, they agreed to look after Zeke for a few days before allowing him to live at home. Jesse and the doctors believed he might be ready to take this next step toward resuming his life. But he must continue his medication. That was imperative.

———

The nights were taking their toll on Annie. Each night she was unable to fall asleep for hours and lay awake on her side, staring out the window at the night sky . . . or flat on her back, staring at the dark ceiling. In her dreams, her father's house had vanished and Yonie was nowhere to be seen, nor were Daed and Mamm. Ben, too, was out of reach. Often, she found herself falling, arms flung wide, feeling the air billow out her long Plain skirts before landing hard on her bare feet, the grass poking against the callouses on her toes. Annie dreamed of wandering up and down Pequea Creek, seeing it bone dry and grieving the loss of it. Her heart was always pounding as she awakened. Soon Annie began to dread going to bed, let alone falling asleep.

Tormented, Annie asked to read Essie's Bible. Not knowing where to begin, she opened to the book of Proverbs, reading each pithy verse from the beginning forward.

When she came to chapter twelve, verse fifteen, she read the words aloud: " 'The way of a fool is right in his own eyes: but he that hearkeneth unto counsel is wise.' "

Who wants to be foolish? In the sight of God, is that what I am?

She didn't wish to follow after her own heart, her own way, as she long had. She knew that much. But she *did* want to paint again, more than nearly anything, though she was losing interest in the hectic worldly ways of the English. If being fancy had anything at all to do with the emptiness, even despair, she'd felt in her dreams, then perhaps she was being foolish as the Scriptures stated. Were the nightmares the Lord God's way of guiding her, as Essie liked to say? Was it the will of the heavenly Father for her to join church and marry Ben Martin?

She contemplated how God achieved His will amongst the People. The most familiar was the drawing of lots, their custom for filling the offices of bishop, preacher, and deacon. The idea struck her that she was on the right track, somehow, in considering this.

She continued her reading and was spurred on when she spotted the verse in chapter sixteen, verse thirty-three—*"The lot is cast into the lap; but the whole disposing thereof is of the Lord."*

"What's that mean—disposing thereof?" she said aloud, wondering whom she might ask.

Marking her place, she headed outdoors to feed the hogs, wishing she were on better terms with her father. It bothered her that they had been barely on speaking terms for all this time. What could she do to bridge that gap?

Thinking about whom to approach regarding the Scripture, she remembered that Ichabod was back in town. He'd refused the lot once, long ago, according to Mamm.

Maybe she would know. Jah, sure she would!
Perhaps later in the day she could get her
Mamm alone to ask.

Knowing they would not be invited to
any canning frolics this summer, she and
Essie put up several dozen jars of strawber-
ry preserves on their own. When they were
finished, Annie set out to walk to her father's house. Past the towering white pine
tree she walked, where Ben had often
parked to meet her last winter. Now the sun
was a lone fireball in the sky, and she felt
glum. She recalled hearing Cousin Julia describe to her children how to know God's
will by listening to His still, small voice—
that knowing in one's heart. It had to do
with opening doors and walking through
them as guided by a divine and loving hand,
just as Abram of old had trusted God to
lead him when the path ahead had seemed
so uncertain.

All that aside, Annie understood in part
why the People chose to adhere to the age-
old tradition of drawing lots, as illustrated in
Scripture. She hadn't known that verses
pertaining to the lot were embedded in the
Proverbs, as well as the New Testament,
where she was most familiar with them. In
the Acts of the Apostles, drawing lots was
the process by which the Lord God had

chosen the successor to Judas.

"What if I were to cast lots between my love for art and my love for Ben?" she whispered as she made her way along the narrow road toward her childhood home. Of course, she realized her passion for color and texture on paper or canvas was a very different kind of love than giving one's life away for another. Truly, she believed that was what marriage with Ben would be—giving up her singleness for the sake of joining her heart with his, birthing their children and establishing their place in the family tree.

She had to smile, thinking there were two branches to Ben's "tree" and wondering how she might ever do a counted cross-stitch sampler for their front room if ever she were to give him a yes to his dear question. *He deserves an answer ever so soon.*

Hurrying along the grassy area beside the road, she saw several buggies coming her way. She considered what it might be like coming here to walk as an Englischer, many years from now. No doubt, she would be wearing her hair this short, though free and swinging against her cheek instead of pulled back into its present low, tight bun. And she would be wearing shoes—possibly some stylish sandals—her toenails painted a pretty, deep pink. Where would her husband and children be? *Who* would they be?

She waved at her older brothers Christian and Abner, and they waved back, their faces turning to flabbergasted frowns. No doubt there were strands of her hair too short to stay in the *schtruppich* bun, but she kept going, mussed up or not, and so did they. "Soon all the People will know." Yet she felt no sadness for what she had done.

When her mother laid eyes on her, there was fire in her eyes. "Oh, my daughter . . . my only girl. What on earth has possessed you to cut your hair?"

Annie knew there was to be no talking about divine lots or God's will today, not the way her mother stared and frowned so awful hard at her now.

Annie couldn't bear to see Mamm so upset. "I was thinkin' of Ben," she admitted.

Her mother's face softened. "Well, I can see you're more than sweet on him. I shouldn't be surprised." She spoke of Isaac's and Annie's childhood days again. Then she said, "It was the dearest thing— 'tween you and me—when your father came home with the wonderful-good news. He was nearly speechless, completely overjoyed to know our Isaac is alive and well."

"Daed's overjoyed?"

"Why, sure he is. We all are, for goodness' sake." Mamm studied her for a moment. "It is a sign, I daresay. From almighty God." She told of her dreams, especially the most recent one. "I just hope we can bring him back into community once again."

Annie listened, taking it all in, but she was especially pleased to know how her father had responded to Ben being Isaac. She and Mamm sat and talked for a while longer, then she helped her roll out a few piecrusts, just as they'd always done together.

Later, when the pies were scooted into the oven, Annie left the house to go looking for Yonie. She found Luke first. He looked at her nearly cross-eyed before telling her, "Yonie's in the barn, all dressed up. Ain't that awful silly?"

When she located Yonie, he was pulling hard on his long, colorful necktie, which one of the cows had chomped on and was right this minute chewing.

"Oh, Yonie! For goodness' sake!" She hurried to his side, trying not to laugh, but giggles spilled out of her anyway.

Her brother struggled and at last managed to get the dandy thing yanked away from the cow. "That'll teach me, jah?" he said, not at all happy.

"Were you thinkin' of goin' out dressed

like this?" She eyed him suspiciously. "You're not getting' hitched today, are you?"

He shooed at her, but there was a grin behind his eyes.

"Well?" She stared at him, pointing at the mess he had hanging around his neck. "Best be takin' that off before Dory sees ya like this."

Scowling, he fumbled to unknot the slobbery, torn tie. When he did, he wadded it up and tossed it into a trash barrel over in the corner.

He looked so down and out. "I spent thirty-five dollars on that there tie," he fussed. Then he looked at her. "Your hair's all a rat's nest, in case you didn't know."

They shared a good laugh. "We're both in a bad way, I daresay. That fancy tie nearly got you strangled."

He agreed. "Life's got a stranglehold on me, that's for sure."

Something about the way he said it gave her pause, and her mind went back to her own present dilemma. "What do you know about the casting of lots?" she asked her brother.

"Nothin' much."

"Ach, surely you do."

"Well, I have something of a problem with it."

"How so?"

"It doesn't work unless you fast and pray beforehand, I'm told."

Just what Julia might say!

He stared down at his shirt, now wet and dirty from his struggle with the cow. "But don't listen to me, sister. Daed says I'm a Dummkopp. Sure looks like he's right."

She smiled at her favorite brother. "Aw, you're not dumb, Yonie. Just ferhoodled . . . like me."

He nodded, wiping at a streak of dirt on his shirt.

"Well, I best be headin' back," she said. "I needed to see you fighting for your own way I guess—you and the cow." Somehow she leaped ahead in her mind, suddenly grasping the stupidity of demanding one's way at any cost.

She waved to him, eager to get back to Essie . . . and as soon as possible, to Ben.

Chapter 34

After breakfast the next morning, and following her outdoor chores, Annie ran to the neighbors' barn and used their phone. Ben sounded pleased to hear from her and said he'd be happy to bring her art stored in Julia's attic. Annie scurried back to Essie's.

Ben's been wanting to see all my work, so today's the day!

When he arrived, Annie was giddy with joy—and nervous, too. She helped him carry the boxes into the front room and then waved him out into the kitchen to wait, saying, "Give me ten minutes."

He smiled, clearly curious, and left the room.

Gingerly Annie opened the boxes and removed the paintings, propping them one by one against the walls, creating something of a gallery around the room.

Essie peeked in to see what she was doing. "My, oh my, what's all this?" she asked, a smile of wonder on her pretty face.

"Ben's been asking 'bout these," Annie told her. "And I've been puttin' him off." *In more than one way. . . .*

After making over the paintings, saying she'd never seen the likes of so many "perty pictures," Esther offered to keep the children occupied. "You know, so the two of you can have some time to yourselves."

But before calling for Ben, Annie looked around the room alone, whispering a prayer for strength. Slowly, her eyes took in each drawing, each painting, recalling the precious time and joy of creating them in the privacy of Julia's attic.

Finally, Annie ushered Ben back into the front room. He seemed genuinely pleased to study and admire her work, beginning with the very first drawing she'd kept, then moving on to her paintings.

When she'd answered his questions about various ones, the two of them settled down on the settee to talk.

"Annie, I'm so glad you called." Ben reached for her hand, scanning the room, taking in all of her art. "Every piece you've shown me here is excellent—amazing. How can I possibly ask you to walk away from this?"

She fought back tears, wanting so much to see his dear face, his eyes . . . the way he looked at her with such affection. "I couldn't decide this before, but now I can." She sighed, leaning her head on his shoulder. "Oh, Ben, I want to join church. I'm willing to give up my art for you."

"Annie?" He touched her face, his eyes searching hers. "Are you sure?"

She looked at him, so near. "And I want something else." She leaned close to whisper. "Is your proposal of marriage still good?"

"Of course it is."

"Oh, Ben . . . I do love you," she professed, her breath coming quickly. "I want to be your bride."

It was all she could do not to cry as his lips found hers in a tender kiss. "We must go and talk to my father right away." Overwhelmed with a mixture of joy and love, she was anxious to do the will of her heavenly Father . . . obeying this sacred ordinance she had so long put off. "I just hope it's not too late to get into baptismal instruction," she said.

"Well, what're we waiting for? My car's outside!" He took her hand and lifted it to his lips. "Oh, and I'll need some lessons on hitching up a horse, by the way."

She laughed. "This is going to be so much fun," she said, following him through the kitchen and outside.

"An adventure," Ben said.

"That's puttin' it mildly," she said, her heart so full she felt she would surely burst.

Jesse was worried when Ben and Annie came rushing out to the barn, nearly breathless, asking if they might talk with him privately. He feared Annie had come to say she was "jumpin' the fence"—planning to go fancy with her beau.

Annie got things started. "We'd like to ask you a favor, Daed."

Glancing at Annie first, Ben explained, "I don't know if you would consider special treatment, but we'd like to have baptismal instruction to join church this fall. I understand we've missed some weeks."

"You and Annie both, ya say?" The joyful words nearly caught in his throat.

"Yes, sir," Ben said.

If ever there was a blessed day, it was this one. Jesse shook Ben's hand, glad for the strong grip—a sure sign of a good man. "I'll see to it that you get caught up, jah. No question on that."

"Thanks, Preacher," Ben said, looking fondly at Annie.

"Don't thank me. . . ." He paused, gathering his wits. Such a fine surprise this was! "I'll teach you all you need to know for that most holy day myself. And we'll talk with the bishop, if need be, and all the brethren, since you've got yourself a lot of catchin' up to do . . . Isaac." He couldn't help but grin now, looking at this fine young man. A man of the People, for sure and for certain.

He turned to his daughter, this girl who'd given him fits a-plenty. "Annie, I'm mighty pleased at this important step you're makin'. You and Ben both." He assumed the next step forward would be marriage, but he would pretend he didn't suspect as much. Let the young folk have their secret romance, as his parents and grandparents and all the great-grandparents before him had done. It was their way. . . .

———

Zeke agreed to stay put at Preacher Zook's place, at least for a week or so— sharing a room in the Dawdi Haus with his own father. His head was still swimming with all that had happened since Dat's return and the confirmation that Ben was his brother. *God knew the end from the beginning*, he thought.

Several days after Zeke moved into the Zooks' Dawdi Haus, Irvin offered to drive him home for his first visit, and Preacher Jesse rode along in the back seat.

"Miracles do happen," Zeke said, grinning.

As they drove on Frogtown Road, Zeke kept seeing young Amish boys on in-line skates or scooters, and he began to laugh. Not the cackling, irrational laughter he was known for when folk looked at him half cockeyed. It was a hearty, satisfied, even gleeful laughter, born out of overcoming much sorrow and defeat. For the first time in years, he was experiencing hope.

"The lost is found," Zeke said, sitting up front with Irvin. "And don't mistake my meanin', Preacher." He turned around to glance at Jesse. "You've heard of the ninety and nine . . . the lost sheep. Well, that's me. The Good Lord's reached down from on high and found me, I have to say." He hoped Irvin, of all people, understood.

But Jesse Zook's swift words took some of the joy out of the return home when he stated, "The brethren will be wantin' a word with you, when you're able."

Zeke froze, the mirth of the moment fading.

I've been found out.

Once Zeke had greeted Esther and was settled in at the kitchen table, the preacher and Irvin left him to visit with her. He sat drinking his wife's tasty brewed coffee while the children napped upstairs. They were alone together for the time being, as Annie had kindly gone home to spend the afternoon with her Mamm. Even though Zeke was enjoying sharing a room over yonder with Dat, he was mighty glad to spend time with Esther now.

He could see in Esther's eyes that she was struggling to recognize him, here in her kitchen where they'd fought and he'd caused her such heartache again and again. No doubt she was confused as to what had transpired in him, but in all truth, the change had come in stages—through Irvin's talks and prayer, his father asking for forgiveness, and most of all his father recognizing Ben for who he was. *Ben was always my brother, and I never saw it! But the Good Lord opened my blinded eyes . . . in more ways than one.*

He had been fortunate enough to see quite a lot of Ben recently—he and Dat both had. Dat planned to sell his home in Canada and move back to Paradise permanently—a bittersweet prospect considering Zeke's impending shun to come. In time, neither his brother nor Dat would be allowed free association with him. Yet even this could not dishearten Zeke. No matter how anyone looked on it, God had worked a wonder in their lives. And Zeke had no doubt they had not seen the end of God's compassion and power. Zeke, after all, considered himself living proof of that.

"We'll trust God to see us through the storm to come," Zeke told his wife, words that still seemed out of place coming from his lips, though ever so true.

Esther nodded, eyes brimming with tears. "It's wonderful-good the way our Lord works, jah?"

He led her upstairs to their room, mindful of the sleeping baby in the corner. Zeke kissed her yet again, vowing never to lay a hand of rebuke on this lovely woman the Good Lord had given to him. "My wife . . . my bride," he whispered, reaching for her hand and pressing it against his heart. "Will ya ever find it in your heart to forgive me? My awful harsh ways?"

Esther leaned up and kissed his face,

touching his soft beard. "Ach, how I love you."

He was moved to tears himself and caressed her face. "Dear lady of mine."

They stood together quietly. Oh, how he loved her . . . too much to fall back into his old ways. Still, he planned to talk and pray with Irvin twice each week to keep himself accountable. *For as long as necessary*, the kind man had suggested.

Esther sighed, tucked in his arms. "I prayed for this day to come, Zeke. I prayed earnestly."

"And God heard, didn't He?"

Zeke stroked her face, then was surprised when she took his hand and led him down the narrow hallway to Annie's room, where they could talk without worrying about waking Essie Ann. They sat on the edge of the bed, and Esther's eyes shone with great compassion.

He'd hated mentioning it, as fondly as she was looking at him just now. "We may end up bein' shunned together, and what would you think of that, Esther?"

She nodded. "I presumed as much. Irvin's church will take us in. I know that for sure. If that's what you want."

He leaned his cheek against her head. Repentance wasn't the issue this time. "I want to tell you something. I've become a follower of the Lord Jesus, just as you are, Essie. Through reading Scripture and my talks with Irvin . . . well, it seems so simple. Life really is quite that—you choose to follow God or you don't."

She listened, eyes blinking as the tears fell.

"No amount of talk from the brethren or anyone else is goin' to change what I know in my heart . . . in my knower. God brought Isaac back to me—to us—for a reason. I never was at fault, the way I made myself out to be all those years. I should've obeyed my father that night, jah, but I didn't cause my brother's disappearance." He stopped to kiss her cheek. "I'm on the path to healing. And I want to show my gratitude by givin' all the rest of my days to God's dear son, Jesus."

"I know exactly how you feel," Esther said.

Zeke's heart was full, and he took Esther's hands in both of his and offered a prayer of thanksgiving before he kissed her a dozen times more.

After visiting with her Mamm and brothers for much of the afternoon, Annie walked upstairs to her old bedroom and sat

herself down at her writing desk—a gift
from her father when she was a girl. Somehow it seemed right that this was where she
would pen this particular letter to Lou, as
she had so many others over the years.
Finding a few stray sheets of paper and a
stubby pencil in the drawer, Annie told her
friend the good news.

> *I've decided to remain Amish. Are*
> *you surprised? Probably not. You said all*
> *along this was where I belonged. And you*
> *were right! Come this September, Ben*
> *and I will be baptized together.*
>
> *I am also going to get married, and*
> *not to just anyone, mind you. (I promised*
> *you I'd only marry for love, didn't I?)*
> *He's my dearest love, Ben Martin, also*
> *known as Isaac Hochstetler by a few old*
> *codgers here, stuck in their ways. Ain't*
> *that a funny one—a fine beau with two*
> *full names?*
>
> *You're more than welcome to attend,*
> *Lou, if you can get away, though I'll*
> *surely understand if you can't. The wed-*
> *ding will be sometime in November. I'll*
> *let you know the date and time when it*
> *gets closer, just in case you can come.*

———

The golden, hot summer months passed
quickly, and the soft autumnal glow of

harvest and of silo-filling days would soon follow.

Ben worked as hard as any of the men in the church district, if not harder, or so Daed liked to say each night at supper. Annie found this ever so satisfying, glad her decision was settled and secure. There was a wondrous peace and a new fulfillment in walking God's path—the way of the People. More than that, she'd secretly embraced Essie's and Julia's love of the Lord Jesus. Ben had, too. She and her soon-to-be husband had talked at length, agreeing to walk the way of the "silent believers," as many amongst the People fittingly did so as not to lose their family connection nor encounter the shun. It was a choice made not out of cowardice but out of respect.

Annie, of course, was eager to move home to spend her last weeks and months as a single woman with her family. So when Irvin, as well as the brethren, agreed that Zeke was ready, he had returned to Essie and the children, and Annie asked for Yonie's help moving her belongings back home. This in spite of his joking that she needed to decide where she wanted to be and stay put for once.

In addition to baptismal classes, Sam and Annie gave Ben a crash course in speaking their language, but every now and then he tripped up and said something funny about a coffin when he meant to say a window shutter, or a skull when he meant a handsaw. Slips like that were amusing and fun for everyone he encountered.

Ben had never been one to exclude his family. He wished he could fly home and see their expressions, because he was fairly sure they'd be thrilled for him—once they recovered from yet another shock. His mother especially would be excited, even though she would no doubt cry if she and Dad were brave enough to come to an Amish wedding.

When the phone rang and rang, he assumed no one was at home. But on the seventh ring, his father finally answered. "Hello, Ben . . . saw your name on the ID. I see you're still using your cell phone. How *are* you?"

"Great, Dad. How're you doing?"

"Oh, just fine." He chuckled. "I've been reading up some on the Amish, trying to picture exactly what you're up to these days."

Ben laughed, too, then asked, "Is Mom around? I've got something important to tell you both."

"Not a problem. I'll switch you onto the speaker phone."

Ben waited until he heard his mom in the background.

"Don't know if you're ready for another surprise, but . . ." He paused, wanting to phrase this just right.

"Go ahead, Ben," his father spoke up. "We're listening."

Taking a deep breath, Ben pressed ahead. "I'm getting married . . . and I'd like you to meet my bride-to-be as soon as possible."

He heard a loud gasp on the other end of the line and assumed it was his mother. "My word, this is good news," she said. "Wait till your sisters hear."

"Why don't you bring her on down?" Dad offered. "We'll make room for her in the guest room. Stay as long as you like."

"Thanks, Dad. You'll all love her," he added.

"We love *you*, Ben, so we know we'll love her, too," Mom said. "She's Amish, I'm guessing?"

"Yes. I've talked a little about her before. She's an Amish preacher's daughter named Annie Zook," he said. "The prettiest, sweetest young woman I've ever known."

"Your sisters will want to show her the

town, no doubt," Dad said.

"They might even try to modernize her for you," Mom teased.

"Oh, Annie's been there and back already, trust me." He wouldn't divulge the details of their struggle to come to this point—at least not now. Thankfully, that part of their relationship was past. "I'm getting my girl," he declared. *At last.*

Chapter 35

A few weeks prior to baptism, Ben happily took Annie home to meet his Kentucky family. They wore their Plain attire, which Ben had been doing for some time. His parents seemed taken aback by this, but his sisters said it was "very cool," with something of a wink and a nod. As he had guessed, his sisters took to Annie like she was their own sibling, welcoming her into their home and their hearts. His parents, too, were quickly won over by her kind, endearing ways.

Even though he'd driven his car, he made a point of telling Annie that this trip was it for him. When they returned to Pennsylvania, he intended to sell the car and purchase a family carriage for his first driving horse. The bishop himself had told Ben that, other than the Lord's Day, he was at liberty to call on a paid driver—as were any of the People—whenever it was unsafe or too far to take the team.

While Ben and Annie were gone, Daniel Hochstetler traveled back to Canada to pack up his life there. He then moved his belongings into Jesse Zook's Dawdi Haus, planning to live there permanently, especially as Daniel was not permitted by the brethren to openly fellowship—or reside—with his shunned son and daughter-in-law. Still, there were rumors he was seeing Zeke and Esther quietly, holding family near while attempting to satisfy the Ordnung. Ben and Annie were in a similar pickle—trying to keep a relationship with Zeke and Essie without violating the rules of the shun. It was a constant juggling of both love and dedication.

———

The rows of benches set up in the barn were conspicuously empty the morning of baptism as Jesse paced along the center aisle. The People would soon file in, the women siting on the left and the men on the right. The barn would get mighty hot if the weather forecast was correct—downright warm for mid-September—much better than meeting in a too-crowded house on this Lord's Day. *At last my daughter will make her kneeling vow to the Lord God and the People.*

Truly Jesse believed Annie had already begun to walk the straight and narrow, and for that reason he had moved heaven and earth, so to speak, to do all he could for both Annie and Ben. Carefully he'd instructed them in the ways of Jehovah God, though he suspected they were doing quite a lot of digging into the Scriptures on their own. Ben, especially, had asked a good many questions, some out of the ordinary, and Jesse hadn't known all the answers. He had felt ashamed, being the man of God and all. But he did what he could, asking the bishop and Preacher Moses, although Ben's questions stirred things up amongst the brethren more than once during the short weeks of baptismal training.

Sighing now, he hoped for the best for his Annie and her beau. He prayed, too, that the Holy One of Israel might cover them with His loving watch-care over their lives and the lives of their offspring, for surely they would marry first opportunity following baptism. Most of the young people did exactly that after making their life-long promise to the church and to God.

Jah, Annie's as good as hitched.

Annie noticed the man formerly called Ichabod sitting with some of Preacher Moses' married sons and grandsons. She wondered what he must be thinking on the day that his own Isaac was being baptized by the very church that had nominated him for preacher so long ago.

When the time came for Annie to bow her head, she did so along with Ben and the other baptismal candidates, more aware of the sweet smells of the haymow during this hushed time of reverence. She felt warm as she sat quietly, contemplating the vow soon to be made. This day represented all the years of her parents' hopes and dreams for her and her brothers yet to join church. She knew she mustn't open her eyes to glance at the People gathered there, nor look at Ben, even though she wished to. Ben had become more to her in the past months than merely a beau. He was her dearest friend, too, and a student of the Word, as he liked to say. *I'm learning all I can about the God who made me,* he would tell her. And she listened with rapt attention when he shared the many verses that had changed his thinking . . . and his heart.

They'd made a secret pact, vowing to live out their days with their eyes fixed on the Lord Jesus. Ben had led the way to her

receiving the Savior; Cousin Julia had plant-
ed the seed. And dear Essie had watered.
Even Lou had played a part.

Several hymns were sung, signaling her
to file up to take her place in the center section with all the others, near the ministers'
bench. There they sat, waiting for the bishop, the two preachers, and the deacon to
enter the barn.

At one point, Annie caught the reverence and wonder in Ben's eyes as the final
stanza was sung in unison. *A day of
dedication . . .*

She observed the sincerity on the part of
her darling, and her heart rose up with glad-
ness for God's guiding hand on her life. Not
only for bringing Isaac home but for bringing her, as well, to this most holy ordinance.

Later, during her father's offering of the
second sermon, he made a slight departure,
repeating much of what had been said at the
time of Daniel's recent kneeling repentance.
Annie wondered at first where her father
was going with his remarks, but she understood more fully when he admonished them
that Isaac of old had been given back to
Abraham due to his inherent trust that God
would provide a lamb. "Jehovah was and is
faithful. At times this is demonstrated by
the quiet entreaty of others."

Daed paused, looking now at Ichabod. *"You are no longer in exile,"* he had declared on the day of Daniel's atonement. *"From this day forth you are to be called a brother."*

Annie paid close attention as her father made known to them yet again, "You are one of us . . . Daniel."

On her wedding day in November, Annie was quite frustrated with herself for having impulsively chopped off her long locks. Yes, her hair had grown out a few inches in the months since she'd cut it, but even with Mamm's help, twisting her too-short hair into a bun was nearly an impossible chore. When Mamm was finally securing the last pin, a knock came at the door.

Annie was amazed as well as delighted to see Lou standing in the hallway outside her bedroom. "Ach, Lou, you came! I can hardly believe it!"

"Well, you said I was welcome, didn't you? So here I am."

The two hugged carefully, so as not to muss Annie's freshly ironed blue cape dress and long white apron. Mamm slipped out of the room to give them some time alone.

"Bless your heart," Annie said. "I tried

not to get my hopes up, but I'm ever so happy you're here."

"Well, just so you know . . . I'll be sharing the wedding feast with another English-er." Lou's smile burst across her face.

"And who would that be?"

"Oh, you . . ."

Annie giggled. "Sam?"

Lou nodded. "Don't be too excited. I'm not getting serious with him, if that's what you think. For now anyway, I'm focusing on my relationship with the Lord, thanks to your cousin Julia."

"My cousin's quite a zealous witness, jah?" Annie reached for Lou's hand, whispering, "And I know exactly how you feel—ever so free inside."

Lou's eyes filled with tears.

"Oh, Lou . . ." Annie said, squeezing her dear friend's hand. "We've had quite an interesting journey together, ain't so?"

Annie struggled not to cry but sensed Ben's own emotion as he sat next to her, waiting for their time to stand before the gathering of more than two hundred people who were jam-packed into her father's house.

She looked across the faces to see Mamm's, her eyes shining with truest joy.

And there were Luke and Omar, solemn-faced, and Yonie, who'd let his hair grow out again, much to Daed's delight. And Essie and Zeke together at last, Essie great with child, sitting in the back with the Englischers, including the Martin family, Lou and Sam, and cousins Irvin and Julia Ranck. *All the People . . . and then some, here for Ben and me.*

Annie's heart swelled with love for her God and her soon-to-be husband. Paradise had never seemed so sweet on any other day, and Annie counted her blessings, glad she had stayed the course. She looked past this most happy moment toward all the years ahead, Lord willing, and realized that on the final day of her life, she could breathe her last knowing she had chosen wisely and well.

Epilogue

Prior to my marriage to Ben Martin, I donated my worldly English clothes to a women's shelter and put away my art for good. After our wedding day, I was content to cook and bake and tend to my husband, as well as my flower gardens, which bring me such joy and a few raised eyebrows. Such pleasure I find in mixing colors ... and that's putting it mildly!

Ben and I have joked between ourselves about which name he should use. But since he is more accustomed to one over the other, and since Benjamin is also a good, solid Amish name, Ben it is.

For the first few weeks and months after our all-day wedding service and feast, we made our traditional visits to relatives and close friends as newlyweds, staying overnight on weekends and returning here to my father's house on Monday mornings in time to help Mamm wash clothes. Sam was so kind to help Ben draw up blueprints for our very own home, which we built on some of Daed's land. With Ben's good Kentucky contacts, he's been helping Irvin with the horse business, as well. So this past year since our wedding day, the Lord has opened plenty of wonderful-good doors of employment for Ben.

When I can, I still write to Lou. Her thoughtful wedding gift—the framed painting of her cat, Muffin—is a reminder of the months she spent here in Paradise. She and Sam still correspond by letter, Lou tells me, and talk quite often by cell phone, too, but there is no word of a pending courtship between them. I can still hope, can't I?

After all, my brother Yonie surprised us all by starting to court Susie Esh's little sister, with some convincing talk of joining church next year. Daed and Mamm are so pleased.

Often Ben and I walk down the road to what we refer to as "our bridge," but it's simply boards and stone, the best part of it being the swiftly moving creek beneath. It keeps us ever mindful of life, how it streams by in an awful rush if one is not careful to stop and listen . . . and honestly see.

Right following our first wedding anniversary, Daed surprised me but good, saying he'd been thinking about something for quite a while, insisting I go with him to visit Bishop Andy. So there I sat sheepishly in the man of God's front room while Daed talked the bishop's ears off, trying to convince him that since it was my painting that drew Isaac back home to the People, I should be permitted to use my artistic talents for the Lord God.

Well, I was beyond speechless. The two of them got up and headed out to the barn, leaving me alone, while the bishop's wife busied herself in the kitchen.

Finally, when I felt my head might burst from holding my breath, hoping against hope—and all this after I'd put my longing for art out of my mind—Daed came back in and told me what they'd decided.

"There are certain conditions," he began, and the thought of limitations had never sounded sweeter to me. On the ride back home, he described them precisely.

I was going to be allowed to express myself artistically, but I could never paint a portrait of a person. Not surprising! But horses grazing, peacocks strutting, and landscapes are all just fine to paint, provided I'm completely caught up on my domestic chores, as related to being a wife . . . and someday a mother. Only in the quiet at the end of the day, when all that needs doin' is done, am I free to draw or paint.

So Ben has helped me set up a little studio in our house, and he is always welcome there, watching me stroke the page with a brush or smudge my finger against the canvas for that "just so" effect. Sometimes he even comes in and leans over to kiss me.

Oh, what I would have missed . . .

It is still a surprise to think of Daed sticking his neck out like that. I often recall Essie's prudent words about letting go of something you love—and what a joy there is in having it returned. In my case, it has come in a fuller measure than I'd ever dreamed possible.

So Ben was right all along; God does work all things together for good to those who love Him. I am so grateful to the Almighty for leading me to make the right choice.

For some it's ever so hard to choose wisely. I know this from experience . . . and to my own shame. The memory of my willful ways, of learning to let go and watching what happens when I do, has been a journey to be reckoned with. I have gained the devotion of a kind and loving man, and the respect of my father and the People. I am happy to say the preacher's daughter is truly home.

Acknowledgments

Typically novelists do not talk about their characters—at least not while creating them. Now that the story is completely told and you are reading this final book in the ANNIE'S PEOPLE series, I'd like to say something about its characters, who continue to live on in my mind and heart. Just as Annie and Isaac became aware of their special friendship as young children, I, too, have been blessed with the dearest of lifelong friends, who, in some cases, are also my relatives. I wish to thank each one for this precious gift. Some of these dear ones have also offered countless hours of research and fact checking on my novels, and although they have asked to remain unnamed, I am most grateful.

My editors are my joy and delight. Talk about friends! A tremendous amount of thanks goes to: Julie Klassen, David

Horton, Carol Johnson, Rochelle Glöege, Ann Parrish, and Jolene Steffer.

Also, my first readers help me keep up this writing pace: Dave, my husband, and Julie, our daughter. Thanks not only for your keen eyes but for the delicious snacks, too!

Kudos to Dana Silva, who offered invaluable help with foster care research, as did Kentucky state adoption specialist Martha Vozos. Blessings and appreciation to Hank and Ruth Hershberger, who carefully explained the process of Amish ordination, and Dawn Beasley, who helped research the setting. Many thanks to Rev. James Hagan, who, as a former policeman, answered forensics questions and contacted the Colorado Bureau of Investigation. Hugs to my teacher-sis, Barbara Birch, who meticulously proofread the final galleys, and to my uncle, Bob Hirschberg, photographer extraordinaire, who helped me "live" in the Maple Lane Farm B&B on Paradise Lane, featured in book two, *The Englisher*.

Heartfelt appreciation to my wonderful parents, Herb and Jane Jones, who faithfully pray as I walk the sometimes thorny path of my stories.

All my love and devotion to the dear Lord Jesus, who guides me in all things, heavenly and otherwise.